BURN FOR BURN

Also by Jenny Han

The Summer I Turned Pretty
It's Not Summer Without You
We'll Always Have Summer
Shug

Also by Siobhan Vivian

A Little Friendly Advice
Not That Kind of Girl
Same Difference
The List

BURN
FOR
BURN

JENNY HAN &
SIOBHAN VIVIAN

SIMON & SCHUSTER BFYR

NEW YORK LONDON TORONTO SYDNEY NEW DELHI

SIMON & SCHUSTER BFYR

An imprint of Simon & Schuster Children's Publishing Division
1230 Avenue of the Americas, New York, New York 10020
SIMON & SCHUSTER BFYR is a trademark of Simon & Schuster, Inc.
For information about special discounts for bulk purchases, please contact
Simon & Schuster Special Sales at 1-866-506-1949
or business@simonandschuster.com.
The Simon & Schuster Speakers Bureau can bring authors
to your live event. For more information or to book an event, contact
the Simon & Schuster Speakers Bureau at 1-866-248-3049 or visit
our website at www.simonspeakers.com.
Book design by Lucy Ruth Cummins
The text for this book is set in Stempel Garamond.
Manufactured in the United States of America
2 4 6 8 10 9 7 5 3 1
Library of Congress Cataloging-in-Publication Data
Han, Jenny.
Burn for burn / Jenny Han and Siobhan Vivian.—1st ed,
p. cm.
Summary: Three teenaged girls living on Jar Island band together to enact
revenge on the people who have hurt them.
ISBN 978-1-4424-4075-3 (hardback)
ISBN 978-1-4424-4077-7 (eBook)
[1. Revenge—Fiction. 2. Friendship—Fiction. 3. High schools—Fiction. 4.
Schools—Fiction. 5. Islands—Fiction.] I. Vivian, Siobhan. II. Title.
PZ7.H18944Bu 2012
[Fic]—dc23
2011050036

For our grandmothers,
Kyong Hui Han and Barbara Vivian

BURN
FOR
BURN

MARY

THE MORNING FOG HAS PAINTED EVERYTHING WHITE. It's exactly like one of my rabbit-hole dreams, where I get trapped, suspended in a cloud, and I can't seem to wake myself up.

Then the foghorn blares, the mist breaks into lace, and I see Jar Island, spread out along the horizon just like in one of Aunt Bette's paintings.

That's when I know for sure that I've done it. I've actually come back.

One of the workers ties the ferry to the dock with a thick

rope. Another lowers the bridge. The captain's voice comes over the loudspeaker. "Good morning, passengers. Welcome to Jar Island. Please make sure to collect all your belongings."

I'd almost forgotten how beautiful it is here. The sun has lifted above the water, and it lights everything up yellowy and bright. A hint of my reflection in the window stares back at me—pale eyes, lips parted, windblown blond hair. I'm not the same person I was when I left here, in seventh grade. I'm older, obviously, but it's not just that. I've changed. When I see myself now, I see someone strong. Maybe even pretty.

Will he recognize me, I wonder? Part of me hopes he doesn't. But the other part, the part that left my family to come back, hopes he does. He has to. Otherwise, what's the point?

I hear the rumble of cars parked on the freight deck as they get ready to drive off. There's a bunch more on shore, in a long line that reaches the entrance to the parking lot, waiting to pull aboard for the return trip back to the mainland. One more week of summer vacation left. I step away from the window, smooth my seersucker sundress, and go back to my seat to get my things. The seat next to mine is empty. I stick my hand underneath, feeling around for what I know is there. His initials. RT. I remember the day he carved them with his

Swiss Army knife, just because he felt like it.

I wonder if things have changed on the island. Does Milky Morning still have the best blueberry muffins? Will the Main Street movie theater have the same lumpy green velvet seats? How big has the lilac bush in our yard grown?

It's strange to feel like a tourist, because the Zanes have lived on Jar Island practically forever. My great-great-great-grandfather designed and built the library. One of my mom's aunts was the very first woman to be elected alderman of Middlebury. Our family plot is right in the center of the cemetery in the middle of the island, and some of the headstones are so old and moss covered, you can't even see who's buried there.

Jar Island is made up of four small towns. Thomastown, Middlebury, which is where I'm from, White Haven, and Canobie Bluffs. Each town has its own middle school, and they all feed into Jar Island High. During the summer the population swells to several thousand vacationers. But only about a thousand or so people live here year round.

My mom always says Jar Island never changes. It's its own little universe. There's something about Jar Island that lets people pretend the world has stopped spinning. I think that's part of the charm, why people want to spend summers here. Or why the diehards put up with the hassles that come with living here year round, the way my family used to.

People appreciate that there isn't a single chain store, shopping mall, or fast-food restaurant on Jar Island. Dad says there's something like two hundred separate laws and ordinances that make building them illegal. Instead people buy their groceries at local markets, get prescriptions filled at soda-shop pharmacies, pick out beach reads at independent bookstores.

Another thing that makes Jar Island special is that it's a *true* island. There are no bridges or tunnels connecting it to the mainland. Aside from the one-strip airfield that only rich people with private planes use, everyone and everything comes in and goes out on this ferry.

I pick up my suitcases and follow the rest of the passengers off. The dock runs straight into the welcome center. An old 1940s school bus painted with the words "JAR ISLAND TOURS" is parked in front and getting washed. A block behind that is Main Street—a quaint strip of souvenir shops and lunch counters. Above it rises Middlebury's big hill. It takes a second for me to find it, and I have to shade my eyes from the sun, but I pick out the pitched red roof of my old house at the tippy top.

My mom grew up in that house, along with Aunt Bette. My

bedroom used to be Aunt Bette's bedroom, and it looks out at the sea. I wonder if that's where Aunt Bette sleeps, now that she lives there again.

I'm Aunt Bette's only niece; she doesn't have any children of her own. She never knew how to act around kids, so she treated me like an adult. I liked it, getting to feel grown-up. When she'd ask me questions about her paintings, what I felt about them, she actually listened to what I had to say. But she was never the kind of aunt who'd get on the floor and help me do a puzzle, or who'd want to bake cookies together. I didn't need her to be. I already had a mom and dad who'd do those things.

I think it'll be great, living with Aunt Bette now that I'm older. My parents both baby me. Perfect example—my curfew is still ten o'clock, even though I'm seventeen. I guess after everything that happened, it makes sense that they're extra protective.

The walk home takes longer than I remember, maybe because my suitcases are slowing me down. A few times I stick out my thumb to the cars chugging up the hill. Some of the locals hitchhike on Jar Island. It's an accepted thing, a way to help out your neighbors. I was never allowed to, but for the first time I don't have my mom or dad looking over my shoulder. No one picks me up, which is a bummer, but there's always tomorrow or the next day. I have all the time in the world to hitchhike or do whatever I want.

I walk right past my driveway without realizing it and have to double back. The bushes have grown big and bristly, and they hide the house from the road. I'm not surprised. Gardening was Mom's thing, not Aunt Bette's.

I drag my bags the last few feet and stare at the house. It's a three-story colonial covered in gray cedar shingles, white shutters bolted to each of the windows, with a cobblestone wall edging the yard. Aunt Bette's old tan Volvo is parked in the driveway, and it's covered in a blanket of tiny purple flowers.

The lilac bush. It's grown taller than I thought possible. And even though plenty of flowers have fallen, the branches still sag with the weight of millions more. I take as deep a breath as I can.

It's good to be home.

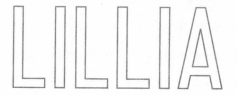

LILLIA

IT'S THAT TIME OF YEAR AGAIN, THE END OF AUGUST, only one more week till school starts. The beach is crowded, but not July Fourth–crowded. I'm lying on a big blanket with Rennie and Alex. Reeve and PJ are throwing a Frisbee around, and Ashlin and Derek are swimming in the ocean. This is our crew. It's been this way this since the ninth grade. It's hard to believe we're finally seniors.

The sun is so bright, I can feel my tan getting even more golden. I wriggle my body deeper into the sand. I love the sun. Next to me Alex is putting more sunscreen on his shoulders.

"God, Alex," Rennie says, looking up from her magazine. "You need to bring your own sunscreen. You used up half my bottle. Next time, I'm just going to let you get cancer."

"Are you kidding me?" Alex says. "You stole this out of my cabana. Back me up, Lil."

I push myself up on to my elbows and sit up. "You missed a spot on your shoulder. Here, turn around."

I squat behind him and rub a dollop of sunscreen onto his shoulder. Alex turns around and asks, "Lillia, what kind of perfume do you wear?"

I laugh. "Why? Do you want to borrow it?" I love to tease Alex Lind. He's so easy.

He laughs too. "No. I'm just curious."

"It's a secret," I say, patting him on the back.

It's so important for a girl to have a signature scent. A scent everyone knows you by, so that when you walk down the hallway at school, people turn and look, like a Pavlovian response or something. Every time they smell that perfume, they'll think of you. Burnt sugar and bluebell, that's the Lillia scent.

I lie back down on the blanket and flip onto my stomach.

"I'm thirsty," I announce. "Will you pass me my Coke, Lindy?"

Alex leans over and rummages through the cooler. "All that's left is water and beer."

I frown, and look over at Reeve. He's got a Frisbee in one hand, my Coke in the other. "Ree-ve!" I yell out. "That was mine!"

"Sorry," he calls back, not sounding sorry at all. He throws the Frisbee in a perfect arc, and it lands over by some cute girls sitting in beach chairs. Exactly where he wanted it to land, I'm sure.

I look over at Rennie, whose eyes are narrow.

Alex stands up and brushes sand off his shorts. "I'll get you another soda."

"You don't have to," I say. But of course I don't mean it. I really am thirsty.

"You're going to miss me when I'm not here to get your drinks," he says, grinning at me. Alex, Reeve, and PJ are going on a deep-sea fishing trip tomorrow. They'll be gone for a whole week. The boys are always around; we see them nearly every day. It will be strange to finish out the summer without them.

I stick my tongue out at him. "I won't miss you one bit!"

Alex jogs over to Reeve, and then they head off to the hot dog stand down the beach.

"Thanks, Lindy!" I call out. He is so good to me.

I look back over at Rennie, who's smirking. "That boy would do anything for you, Lil."

"Stop it."

"Yes or no. Do you think Lindy's cute? Be honest."

I don't even have to think about it. "Yeah, he's obviously cute. Just not to me." Rennie has gotten it into her head that Alex and I should become a couple, and then she and Reeve can become a couple, and we can go on double dates and weekend trips together. As if my parents would ever let me go away with guys! Rennie can go ahead and get an S.T.D. from Reeve if she wants, but Alex and I are not happening. I don't see him that way, and he doesn't see me that way. We're friends. That's it. Rennie gives me a look, but thankfully she doesn't push it any further. Holding up her magazine, she asks, "What do you think about me doing my hair like this for homecoming?" It's a picture of a girl in a sparkly silver dress, her blond hair flowing behind her like a cape.

Laughing, I say, "Ren, homecoming is in October!"

"Exactly! Only a month and a half away." She waves the magazine at me. "So what do you think?"

I guess she's right. We probably should start thinking

about dresses. There's no way I'm buying mine from one of the boutiques on the island, not when there's a 90% chance some other girl will show up wearing it too. I take a closer look at the picture. "It's cute! But I doubt there'll be a wind machine."

Rennie snaps her fingers. "Yes! A wind machine. Amazing idea, Lil."

I laugh. If that's what she wants, that's what she'll get. Nobody ever says no to Rennie Holtz.

We're discussing possible homecoming looks when two guys come over by our blanket. One is tall with a crew cut and the other is stockier, with thick biceps. They're both cute, although the shorter one is cuter. They're definitely older than us, definitely not in high school.

Suddenly I'm glad I'm wearing my new black bikini and not my pink and white polka-dot one.

"Do you girls have a bottle opener?" the tall one asks.

I shake my head. "You can probably borrow one from the concessions stand, though."

"How old are you girls?" the built one asks me.

I can tell Rennie is into him, the way she tosses her hair over to one side and says, "Why do you want to know?"

"I want to make sure it's okay to talk to you," he says, grinning. He's looking at her now. "Legally."

She giggles, but in a way that makes her sound older, not like a kid. "We're legal. Barely. How old are you guys?"

"Twenty-one," the taller one says, looking down at me. "We're seniors at UMass, here for the week."

I adjust my bikini top so it doesn't show so much. Rennie just turned eighteen, but I'm still seventeen.

"We're renting a house down Shore Road in Canobie Bluffs. You should come over some time." The built one sits down next to Rennie. "Give me your number."

"Ask nicely," Rennie says, all sugar and spice. "And then maybe I'll think about it."

The tall guy sits down next to me, at the edge of the blanket. "I'm Mike."

"Lillia," I say. Over his shoulder I see the boys coming back. Alex has a Coke in his hand for me. They're looking at us, probably wondering who these guys are. Our guy friends can be super-protective when it comes to non-islanders.

Alex frowns and says something to Reeve. Rennie sees

them too; she starts giggling extra-loud and tossing her hair around again.

The tall guy, Mike, asks me, "Are those guys your boyfriends?"

"No," I say. He's looking at me so intently, I blush.

"Good," he says, and smiles at me.

He has really nice teeth.

KAT

IT'S THE BEGINNING OF A PERFECT SUMMER NIGHT, THE KIND where all the stars are out and you don't need a sweatshirt, even down by the water. Which is a good thing, because I left mine at home. I passed out after I got home from work, slept right though dinner. When I woke up, I had, like, five seconds to catch the next ferry to the mainland, so I threw whatever clothes were on my floor into my bag, high-fived my dad good-bye, and ran the whole way from T-Town to the Middlebury harbor. I know I forgot something, but Kim will let me pick through her closet, so whatever.

Main Street is packed. Hardly any of the stores are open at this hour, but it doesn't matter. Tourists just aimlessly mosey along, stopping at the windows to peer inside at the crappy Jar Island–branded sweatshirts and visors.

I hate August.

I groan as I push past them and make my way to Java Jones. If I want to be awake for the Puppy Ciao encore set, I'm going to need caffeine.

Puppy Ciao is playing at the music store where Kim works, a place called Paul's Boutique on the mainland. Paul's Boutique has an attached garage space where they have shows, and if it's a band I want to see, Kim lets me stay the night at her apartment. She lives right above the store. The bands usually crash there too, which is cool. The singer in Puppy Ciao looked pretty hot on their album cover. Not as hot as the drummer, but Kim says that drummers are always trouble.

I take the stairs up to Java Jones two at a time. But as I'm about to push the door open, one of the workers twists the lock.

I knock on the glass. "I know you're closing, but could you hook me up with a quick triple shot to go?"

Ignoring me, the worker unties his apron and unplugs the neon sign. The front window goes dark. I realize that I probably sound like one of the rich a-hole Jar Island tourists who think store hours don't apply to them, the kinds of entitled snobs I'm forced to deal with all day at the marina. So I flick my half-smoked cigarette to the curb, push my hands deep into my pockets so my cutoffs sink low on my hips, and throw in a desperate, "Please! I'm local!"

He turns and stares at me like I'm a huge pain in the ass, but then his face softens. "Kat DeBrassio?"

"Yeah?" I squint at him. He looks familiar, but I can't place him.

The guy unlocks the door and opens it. "I used to race dirt bikes with your brother." He holds the door open for me. "Careful. Floor's wet. And tell Pat I say 'what up.'"

I nod and walk on tiptoes in my motorcycle boots past another employee pushing a knotted mop back and forth. Then I heave my bag up onto the counter while the guy makes my drink. That's when I notice that Java Jones isn't completely empty. There's one last customer left.

Alex Lind is sitting alone at one of the back tables, hunched over a small notebook. I think it's his diary or something. I've caught him secretly scribbling things down in it a couple of times, when he thought he was being stealth. He's never showed it to me before. Probably because he thinks I'd make fun of whatever is inside it.

The truth is, I probably would. It's not like hanging out for a few weeks makes us *actual* friends.

I'm not going to interrupt him. I'll just get my drink and go. But then his pencil grinds to a halt in the middle of a page. Alex bites down on his lower lip, closes his eyes, and thinks for a second. He looks like a little kid concentrating on his nightly prayers, vulnerable and sweet.

I'm going to miss the dude.

I quick rake my fingers through my bangs and call out, "Yo, Lind."

He opens his eyes, startled. Alex quickly slides his notebook into his back pocket and shuffles over so he's next to me. "Hey, Kat. What are you up to?"

I roll my eyes. "I'm going to Kim's to see a band. Remember?" I told him not five freaking hours ago, when he stopped by the marina on my lunch hour. That's how we started hanging out. We met at the yacht club in June. I knew who Alex was before then, obviously. It's not like our high school is huge. We'd never actually talked to each other. Maybe once or twice in art last year. We roll with very different crews.

Alex came by one day with a new speedboat. As he tried to drive away, he stalled out.

I threw him out of the driver's seat and gave him a quick lesson. Alex was impressed with how I handled his boat. A few times, when I really gunned it, I saw him grip the sides, white-knuckled. It was kind of cute.

I was hoping he'd hang out with me today for the rest of my shift so work would be less boring. And because I knew he was heading out tomorrow for his fishing trip. But Alex left me to meet his friends at the beach. His real friends.

"Yeah," Alex says, nodding. "That's right." Then he leans forward and rests his elbows on the counter. "Hey, tell Kim I said thanks again for letting me stay over, okay?"

I took Alex to see Army of None play at the record store in July. He'd never heard of them before we started hanging out, but now they're his favorite band. I was embarrassed, because Alex wore a Jar Island country club polo shirt, cargo shorts, and flip-flops to the show. Kim gave me a look as soon as we walked in, because he was dressed so corny. Alex bought one of the band T-shirts and put it on right away. People who wear the shirt of the band they're going to see play are lame, but it was better than his polo shirt for sure. Once the show started, Alex blended in just fine, bobbing his head along to the music in time with everyone else. And he was super polite at Kim's apartment. Before he got into his sleeping bag, he grabbed the empty beer bottles and put them out in the alley for recycling.

"Do you want to come with me? The show's sold out, but I can get you in."

"I can't," he says with a heavy sigh. "Uncle Tim wants to set sail at dawn." Alex's uncle Tim is a balding perma-bachelor. He doesn't have a family or any real responsibilities, so his money goes to toys—like the new yacht he and Alex and his friends are taking out on a bros only deep-sea fishing trip.

I shrug. "Well, then, I guess this is good-bye for real." I salute him like a navy officer. "Have a good trip," I say, sarcastic, because I don't mean it. I wish he wasn't going. Without Alex coming to visit me at work, this week is going to completely suck.

He straightens up. "I can give you a ride to the ferry."

"Don't worry about it."

I start to walk away, but he grabs the strap of my bag and pulls it off my shoulder. "I want to, Kat."

"Fine. Whatever."

As he drives down toward the ferry landing, Alex keeps staring at me out of the corner of his eye. I don't know why it makes me feel weird, but it does. I turn to the the window, so he can't see me, and I say, "What's with you?"

He lets out a big sigh. "I can't believe summer's already over. I don't know. I feel like I wasted it."

Before I can stop myself, I say, "You wasted it with your loser friends, maybe. Not hanging out with me." And I hate myself for sounding like I care.

Usually, Alex defends his friends when I make fun of them, but this time, he doesn't say anything.

For the rest of the ride, I think about what's going to happen when school starts, if Alex and I will still be friends. Sure, we've hung out a bunch this summer, but I don't know if I want to associate with the kid at school. In public.

Alex and I . . . we work best like this. When it's just us.

Alex pulls into the ferry parking lot. Before he has a chance to park, I make a split-second decision and say, "I can bail on the show, if you want to hang out tonight." It's not like I'm some Puppy Ciao groupie. Plus, they'll probably come around again. But me and Alex? This might be it for us. Our last night. And I think, on some level, we both know it.

Alex grins. "Seriously? You'll stay with me?"

I open my window and light up a cigarette to hide the fact that I'm smiling too. "Yeah, why not? I want to see this Richie Rich yacht for myself."

So that's where Alex takes us. We pull up to his uncle Tim's mansion, where the thing is docked. As we walk toward it, I immediately start making fun of how gaudy it is, but what I'm thinking is, *Holy crap. This yacht is bigger than my freaking house.* It's definitely the nicest boat I've ever seen. Better than any of the other yachts in the marina.

Alex climbs aboard first, and I'm right behind him. He gives me a quick tour, and it's even more posh on the inside. Italian marble and about a hundred flat-screen televisions, and a wine cellar filled with bottles from Italy, France, South Africa.

I think of Rennie. She'd die over this place.

Just as quick, I push her out of my head. It hardly happens anymore, but I hate that it happens at all.

I'm trying to figure out the stereo when Alex comes up beside me. Really close beside me. He pushes my hair off to one side. "Kat?"

I freeze. Alex's lips brush against my neck. He grabs my hips and pulls me toward him.

He's not my type. Not even close.

That's why it's so crazy. Because as soon as I turn my head, we're kissing. And I suddenly feel like I've been waiting the whole summer for it to happen.

ONE WEEK LATER

I'M SITTING ON MY BATHROOM COUNTER, TRYING TO remember what the makeup lady at Saks told me about how to do eyeliner on Asian eyes. Only . . . I can't think straight.

I think she said to wing it just the tiniest bit. I do my right eye first, and it looks okay. I'm finishing up my left eye when my little sister, Nadia, bangs on the door so loudly that I jump.

"Lil! I need to take a shower!" she yells. "Lilli-uhh!"

I pick up my hairbrush and then reach over and unlock the door. Nadia rushes in and turns on the water. She sits on the edge of the tub, in her big soccer T-shirt with her shiny black hair mussed up in the back and watches me brush my hair. "You look pretty," she says, her voice scratchy with sleep.

Do I? At least the outside is still the same.

I keep brushing. Twenty-three, twenty-four, twenty-five, done. I brush my hair twenty-five strokes every morning. I've done it that way since I was little.

Today will be like any other day.

"But I thought you weren't supposed to wear white after Labor Day," Nadia adds.

I look down at my sweater. It's new—white cashmere, soft and snug. I'm wearing it with my white short shorts. "Nobody follows that rule anymore," I tell her, hopping down from the counter. "Besides, this is winter white." I swat at her butt with my hairbrush. "Hurry up and get in the shower."

"Do I have time to curl my hair before Rennie gets here?" she asks me.

"No," I say, closing the door behind me. "Five minutes."

Back in my room I start filling my brown saddlebag with my school things, like I'm on autopilot. My new pen and the leather planner my mom got me as a back-to-school gift. Lollies. Cherry ChapStick. I try to think if I'm forgetting something, but nothing comes to mind, so I grab my white espadrilles and head down the stairs.

My mom is in the kitchen, wearing her robe and drinking an espresso. My dad bought her one of those fancy espresso machines for Christmas, and she makes a point of using it at least once a week, even though she prefers tea, and even though my dad is hardly ever at home to see her use it. He's a doctor, the kind who does research. For as long as I can remember, he's been working on some new drug to cure cancer. He spends part of the month working at a lab in Boston, and he gets sent all over the world to present his findings. He was on the cover of some science journal this summer. I forget the name of it.

Gesturing to the plate of muffins, my mom says, "Sit down and eat before you go, Lilli. I got those sugary ones you love."

"Rennie will be here any minute," I say. When I see the disappointed look on my mom's face, I take a muffin and wrap it in a napkin. "I'll eat it in the car."

Touching my hair, she says, "I can't believe you're a senior in high school. One more year and you'll be away at college. My pretty girl is grown-up."

I look away. I guess I am grown-up now.

"At least I still have my baby. Is Nadi getting ready?"

I nod.

"You have to look out for Nadi now that you're at the same school. You know how she looks up to you, Lilli." My mom squeezes my arm, and I swallow hard. I do have to look out for Nadia better. Not like how I did on Saturday night, when I left her at Alex's party. She was with her friends, but still.

I should have stayed.

Rennie's horn honks outside, and I stand up. "Nadia!" I yell. "Rennie's here!"

"Just one more minute!" Nadia shrieks back.

I hug my mom and head for the garage door.

"Take a muffin for Rennie," she calls out as I close the door behind me. Rennie wouldn't eat it anyway. She goes off carbs at the start of every cheerleading season. She only lasts about a month before she gives in, though.

In the garage I slip on my espadrilles, and then I walk down the driveway to Rennie's Jeep.

"Nadia's right behind me," I say, climbing inside.

Rennie leans over and hugs me good morning. *Hug her back,* I tell myself. And I do.

"Your skin looks awesome against the white," she says, eyeing me up and down. "I wish I could get as tan as you."

Rennie's wearing tight jeans and an even tighter lacy scoop neck top, with a nude cami underneath. She's so tiny, I can see her rib cage. I don't think she's wearing a bra. She doesn't have to. She's got a gymnast's body.

"You're pretty tan too," I say, clicking my seat belt.

"Bronzer, baby." She puts on her sunglasses and starts talking a mile a minute. "So here's what I'm thinking for the next party. It came to me in a dream last night. The theme will be . . . Are you ready for this? The roaring twenties! The girls could wear flapper costumes with, like, a feather headpiece, and long beaded necklaces, and then the boys could wear zoot suits and fedoras. Hot, right?"

"I don't know," I say, looking out the window. Rennie's talking so fast and so much, it's making my head pound. "The guys might not be into it. Where are they supposed to find that stuff on the island?"

"Hello, it's called the Internet!" Rennie taps her fingers on the steering wheel. "What's taking Nadia so long? I want to get there before everybody else does so I can claim my parking spot for the year." She presses her hand down on the horn—once, then twice.

"Stop," I say. "You're going to wake up my neighbors."

"Oh, please. The closest house is, like, half a mile down the street."

Our front door flies open, and Nadia comes running down the steps. She looks tiny against our massive white house. It's different from most of the other houses on the island—modern lines and lots of glass. My mom helped design it. It was originally our summer home, and then we moved to Jar Island for good before my freshman year. I was the one who begged to move here, to be with Rennie and my summer friends.

My mom waves at us from the front door. I wave back.

"So are you yay or nay on the twenties party?" Rennie asks me.

I honestly don't care, but I know my answer matters to her—which is why I feel like saying nay.

But before I can, Nadia is at the car, her hair sopping wet. She's got on her new jeans and the black top the three of us bought together when we went shopping back in July. That feels like forever ago.

She climbs into the backseat. I twist around and say, "You should have dried your hair, Nadi. You know you always get colds when you go around with wet hair."

Breathlessly she says, "I was scared you guys would leave without me."

"We wouldn't leave you!" Rennie cries, turning the wheel. "We're your big sisters. We'll always look out for you, honey bun."

Something nasty is on the tip of my tongue, and I swallow hard to keep from saying it. If I say it, we'll never be the same again. Even worse than now.

We pull around our circular driveway and down the road.

"Cheerleading practice is at four," Rennie reminds me, bouncing in her seat to the music. "Don't be late. We need to evaluate the fresh meat. See what we've got to work with. Did you remember to bring your mini camcorder so we can tape them?"

I open my bag and look, even though I know it's not there. "I forgot."

"Lil! I wanted to evaluate them later tonight in HD." Rennie lets out a grumbly sigh, like she's disappointed in me.

I shrug my shoulders. "We'll deal." That's what we're doing right now, isn't it? Dealing? But Rennie's clearly better at it than me.

"Nadi, who's the prettiest of all your friends?" Rennie asks.

"Patrice," Nadia says.

Rennie makes a left, and we pass the small rental cottages that populate Canobie Bluffs. I focus on one in particular. There's a caretaker outside closing it up for the season, now that it's empty. I think it's Reeve's dad. He's bolting the shutters on the first floor windows. He hasn't gotten to the master bedroom yet. Those ones are still wide open.

I turn my head away, and out of the corner of my eye, I look at Rennie. Just to see if she has noticed it too. But there's nothing there—no recognition, no alarm, nothing.

"Nadi, you're so much prettier than Patrice. FYI, I'm only taking the cream of the crop for the varsity squad," Rennie says. "Let me know if there's anyone you want to cheer for, and I'll hook it up."

Immediately Nadia says, "Alex. Can I cheer for Alex?"

Rennie gasps. "Ooh! You better ask your sister. He's her boy toy."

"Rennie, be quiet." I say it more snappishly than I intended, and she makes a face to Nadia in her rearview mirror. I take a breath. "Nadia, there's a whole line of junior and senior girls ahead of you for Alex. We can't show favoritism like that. I mean, how would it look, us giving a senior starter to a freshman? Besides, you still have to try out. You haven't made the squad yet."

At this, Rennie nods. "Lil's right. I mean, you're basically in but we have to treat you the same as everybody else. Even though you're clearly special." Nadia wriggles in her seat like a puppy. "Oh, and make sure to tell your friends that if they're even one minute late, they're going to be sent home. Period. As captain I need to set the tone for this season."

"Got it," Nadia says.

"Good girl. You're going to be our freshman star."

I feel like I am floating above myself as I say, "She needs to work on her back handspring. It's weak."

It gets really quiet.

I flip down my visor to look at Nadia. The corners of her mouth are turned down, her dark eyes hurt.

Why did I say that?

I know how badly she wants to make the squad. We practiced all summer, back handsprings and tumbling and stunts and our routines. I told Nadia that when Rennie graduates, it will be her on the top of that pyramid. I told her she'll be set at Jar High. Just like her big sis.

But now I'm not so sure I want her to be anything like me or Rennie. Not anymore.

CHAPTER TWO

KAT

I CLIMB OVER THE CHAIN-LINK FENCE THAT SURROUNDS the Jar Island High parking lot. Alex's SUV is parked near the football field, shiny and freshly washed for the first day of school. I try to ignore that my heart is pumping triple time, filling my chest, my throat, my ears with heat.

Saturday was my eighteenth birthday. I spent the night at my kitchen table, doing whiskey shots with my brother, Pat, and eating the frozen chocolate cake Dad had picked up from the supermarket.

"Oh, Judy." My dad said it after every shot, as if she were sitting at the table, knocking them back with us. "Look at our baby girl."

"I'm a woman now," I corrected.

"One hell of a woman," he added, and nudged his shot glass forward for a refill.

"Eww, Dad. That's gross," Pat said, and poured us another round.

Alex was supposed to come home that day, but I wasn't sure when. Or if he'd call. I wouldn't let myself think about it. I'd wasted too much brain power on him already.

I spent most of the week Alex was gone going over and over what happened on our last night together. Unlike the band guys I meet at Kim's place, I didn't have to worry about how far things with Alex would go, but it was still really hot, the way he took charge. And it was so taboo, him and me together. We were never supposed to become friends, never mind make out all over his uncle's multimillion-dollar yacht.

I knew for a fact that Rennie would give Alex so much shit if she knew we hooked up. I was sure I'd get it too, from Rennie, from Reeve, from everyone. Not that either of us thought about that when we were going at it. But it had to have occurred to him afterward, the same way it had for me.

And then he texted me.

Welcome home party at my place. Stop by if you're not doing anything.

I pushed back my chair. Pat said, "What are you smiling about?"

I barely heard him. I was thinking about my black lace top with my cut-offs, but then I was like, what if his parents are there? I should probably wear something classy.

I sat back down. What was I getting so crazy over? It was one night. I needed to pump my breaks.

I shut off my phone and told my brother to pour me another whiskey shot.

Around one in the morning I was officially drunk. My dad had gone to bed and Pat was passed out on the living room floor. Our dog Shep was scratching at the back door with his paw, so I grabbed his leash and took him for a walk.

Of course I ended up at Alex's house. Even though White Haven was a good six miles from T-Town.

There had definitely been a party, but it was long over. Plastic cups and trash were scattered around the path leading to the backyard. There was music on, the bad dance-y crap that's always on the radio, but the volume was turned way down. The lights around the pool were off. There was food sitting out, bowls of chips and a plate of uneaten hamburgers, guacamole turning brown, cups filled with melted pink drinks and paper umbrellas. There were other decorations too. Fishing nets, tiki torches, conch shells. A rumpled-looking captain's hat hung on a fence post. I heard Shep chewing on something he'd found on the ground. I had to wrestle it out of his mouth. A plastic pirate eye patch.

I walked over to the pool house where Alex stays and peered in through a window to see if he was awake.

He was asleep in his bed, lying on his side, on top of the sheets. Some of the copper in his hair had turned lighter, like the color of sand. And he was tan. Tan with freckles.

He looked so cute, it took me a second to notice the small body curled up in the sheets next to him.

I pass the fountain on my way into school. Alex is there, standing with his friends. Rennie and Lillia are both dressed for the first day of school in some stupid movie. Lillia's got a lollipop in her mouth. That GoodyTwo-shoes has a serious oral fixation. And Rennie. Just the way she stands in her heels, one hip out to the side, hand on her back, pushing her pathetically small chest out as far as it can go, I can tell she's ready to own the school, now that she's a senior. She's been waiting for this moment her whole freaking life.

Alex turns his head, and our eyes meet. I wonder for a second if he'll pretend not to see me. Which would be fine. But he doesn't. He comes right over, all smiles.

"Kat," he says. "Hey, happy birthday."

It catches me off guard, that he remembered. And that he celebrated it with another girl in his bed. I have no clue who it was. Not that it matters. "Sorry I couldn't make your party. Did you have a good time?" I ask, trying not to sound jealous of the girl that he hooked up with instead of me.

"Not really." Alex shrugs. "I didn't even know there was going to be a party. It was all Rennie. She was just looking for a reason to have a party."

Rennie? So Rennie was behind his party? It made sense. Those tacky ass decorations and crap. And it's not like she could invite the whole school over to her mom's two-bedroom condo.

Alex keeps going. "Apparently she got Lillia to ask my mom if they could have the party at our house. She had my dad at the grill, cooking steaks. There were a ton of people there, and everyone was in costume. My dad was in a freaking scuba suit. You know how good Rennie is with parents." Alex shakes his head, rueful. "She got pissed at me when I wouldn't wear a sailor hat."

"Wait," I say. "There were costumes?"

"Yeah. Rennie was a mermaid."

I grit my teeth. Of course she was. *The Little Mermaid* was the only game Rennie wanted to play in Lillia's pool when we were kids. "Sounds fun," I say, really sarcastic, and then try to step around him.

"Like I said before, *not really*." He steps in my way and lowers his voice. "Wait. Are you mad at me? You did get my text, right?"

I look him hard in the eyes and say, "Why would you invite me to one of Rennie's parties?" He knows our history. Everyone does. And I'd like to ask a follow-up question, about the girl in his bed, but I get distracted by what I see over his shoulder.

Rennie is watching us.

"Al-ex!" she calls out in a singsong voice. "Can you come here for a sec?"

"Alex is busy," I say. "And you shouldn't interrupt people who are *tal-king*!" I singsong back.

Rennie sighs. She grabs Lillia's hand and pulls her up from

where she's sitting on the fountain edge. "Come on, Alex. We need to talk to you." But Lillia shakes herself free.

Alex glances over his shoulder. Annoyed, he says, "How about I just call you later."

I wave him off. "Whatever." Because I don't want to get into this now, with everyone watching us.

"I'll hit you up after football practice," he says as he walks backward away from me.

I hear Rennie say to him, "What were you even talking to her about? Are you trying to hire her to clean your uncle's yacht?"

Alex starts to say no, but Rennie cuts him off. "You have to be careful, Lindy. I mean, you can't just let whoever on his boat. What would happen if she took something?"

I feel my whole body go stiff. Rennie's the one who liked to shoplift. Mostly makeup from the drugstore, but sometimes a shirt or a bracelet from one of the Main Street shops. I used to be her lookout.

Rennie has spread a hundred rumors about me over the years— how my dad is a meth dealer and he's grooming my brother, Pat, for the family business; how I once tried to French kiss her at a sleepover; and how she looked into getting a restraining order because I stalked her when she stopped being friends with me.

All kinds of lies, just so she could have something interesting to say. I didn't even care enough to set the record straight. It was hilarious, what a huge liar she was. She actually believed her own bullshit. Anyway, it wouldn't have mattered what I said. People were going to believe what they wanted to believe.

Only now, for whatever reason, I don't want Alex thinking I'm some low-life dirtbag.

Over his shoulder Rennie gives me a pleased buh-bye wave.

Before I can even think about what I'm doing, I'm running to catch up to them. Once I do, I lower my shoulder and bump into Rennie as hard as I possibly can.

CHAPTER THREE

MARY

WHEN I WOKE UP THIS MORNING, I HAD BUTTERFLIES IN my stomach. Lots of them. This is the day I've been waiting for.

I coast through Middlebury and pick up the bike path along the edge of the water where the shore turns rocky at the start of Canobie Bluffs. At the sharpest cliff the path curls into the woods. It's cool here, under the pine trees, and I like the quiet sound my tires make slipping against the sandy trail.

Aunt Bette was still asleep when it was time for me to leave, but luckily my old yellow Schwinn was in the garage and in pretty much perfect condition. Not even dusty.

I wonder what will happen. When everyone else fades away and it's just the two of us standing toe to toe.

I could say, *Hello, Reeve,* calm and even.

I could say, *Didn't think you'd see me again, did you?*

The possibilities spin around in my head faster than my pedals. I don't even think about what he'll say to me. It doesn't matter. I'm gonna get my moment, and that's that.

The bike path lets out at the back of Jar Island High School. I skid to a stop. The high school stretches out just beyond the football field. I'm struck by how huge it is.

I came here once, as a kid with Mom and Dad, to see a theater company put on a musical version of *The Secret Garden* in the performing arts auditorium. I guess at the time I thought that was all there was, but now I see that the auditorium is a whole separate building from the school. There's also one for the gym, and one for the pool. Kids are everywhere, hundreds of faces, swarming the place like ants. I keep thinking I'll see someone I know, but I don't. Everyone's a stranger.

I follow the flow of students down a concrete path until it opens up to a big central courtyard. A bunch of guys are playing Ultimate Frisbee on the lawn. There are a few benches, a couple of trees, and in the center, a big bubbling fountain that sends sprays of mist into the blue sky.

Reeve is here somewhere. I know it. I can feel it.

I smooth my hair and take a slow spin.

A girl in cutoff shorts, a black tank, and a cropped black hoodie, dark hair blowing behind her, charges toward another girl, a smaller one with wavy brown hair, and slams into her hard. So hard I hear the smack from where I'm standing.

The smaller girl stumbles on her high heels, and she almost falls into the fountain. She lets out a bloodcurdling scream. I recognize her now. I think maybe I met her once, a long time ago. Maybe at Sunday school or day camp or something.

The one in the cutoffs says, "You were the klepto, Rennie! I've never stolen anything in my life!" Rennie. That's right. That's the small girl's name. She was in my swim class at the Y in the third grade. The other girl gets up in Rennie's face. A boy with auburn hair tries to hold her back, but she pushes him away. "And if I hear you spreading any more lies about me, I'll kill you." The way the girl says it, dead serious, gives me goose bumps.

People all over the courtyard slow down to watch, like seagulls circling beach trash. I have this helpless feeling, this sick feeling. But everyone else looks entertained. Everyone except the auburn-headed boy.

Rennie stands up straight. "Umm . . . you'll *kill* me? Really?" She laughs. "Okay, no more lies, Kat. I'll get real with you right now. Remember that time you came over in ninth grade, begging me to be your friend again?" The smile on the other girl's face—Kat—disappears. "You were crying, and you kept trying to hug me? Just so you know, the whole time I was thinking how your breath smelled like shit. How it kind of always smelled like shit, even right after you'd brushed your teeth. And I was so relieved when you left that I'd never have to smell your shitty-ass breath again."

Kat's mouth wrinkles up. She wants to say something but can't. I see it in her face, in her eyes. She starts to cough, and at first I think she's holding back tears. But then Kat's head tips back slightly and she spits a huge loogey in Rennie's face.

Everyone watching cries out, "Eww!"

The boy says, "Jeez, Kat!"

"OH MY GOD!" Rennie screams, wiping at her face furiously. "You are *such* trash, Kat!" She looks around at everyone watching her, and her cheeks turn bright pink. "Oh my God," she says again, this time a whisper to herself.

Kat walks away. She makes eye contact with me as she passes. Her eyes are flashing, and I can barely breathe.

I feel turned around, not sure which way is up or down, or where to go. Is this what life at Jar Island High is like? 'Cause if it is, I'm not sure I'll survive the day.

A pretty Asian girl comes to Rennie's side and holds out a tissue, but Rennie doesn't take it. Instead she wilts as a tall brown-haired guy scoops her up and offers her his T-shirt sleeve to wipe her face on. "Come here, girl," I hear him say. "Fighting on the first day of school! Ren, you know you're better than that. Don't let DeBrassio drag you down in the gutter with her . . . But I have to say, watching you two throw down was kinda hot." He tips his head back and lets out a laugh he must have been holding in.

I don't hear it. I don't hear anything. Just the pounding in my ears. Everything else is on mute. Because it's him. Right there in front of me, after all these years. It's Reeve Tabatsky.

I'd know him anywhere. He has the same brown hair, same Roman nose. And those eyes. Green like sea glass. He's taller now, much taller. Broad shoulders, muscular arms. He's wearing a white T-shirt and a worn-looking pair of khakis, and he has a pair of mirrored aviator sunglasses perched at the top of his forehead.

When we were young, he was a good-looking kid. But now . . . he's beautiful. He's so beautiful.

My legs start to quiver. I can't do this. I want to run away, to hide, but I can't move. I just stand there, rooted to the spot.

The two of them walk in my direction, Reeve's arm slung around Rennie's shoulder. I hold my breath and wait for a flash of recognition, something, anything, as Reeve gets closer. But there's nothing. He walks right past me, so close we nearly touch. He doesn't notice me.

I spin around and stare at his back. Did he not see me? Or could it be that he was too distracted by Rennie hanging all over him. Or maybe he did see me but I've changed so much, and that's why he didn't recognize me. I'm probably the last person he'd expect to see again.

Dazed, I follow them inside the building. Reeve and Rennie disappear down a hallway together, swallowed up by a crowd of other students. I don't know where to go. I wander around and end up ducking into the girls' room as someone exits. I slip into the dwindling space of the closing door.

My stomach seizes up. I hurry to the last stall and collapse at the bowl, the ends of my hair skimming the water.

I take a couple of deep breaths. In and out. Maybe it wasn't any of those things.

Maybe I wasn't worth remembering.

CHAPTER FOUR

LILLIA

WE'RE SITTING AT OUR NEW LUNCH TABLE WITH THE regulars—me and Rennie, Ashlin, Alex, Reeve, PJ, Derek, plus a couple other guys from the football team. We inherited this table from last year's seniors. It's a tradition. Star table, center of the so-called action. The last day of school junior year, the coolest seniors call the coolest juniors over and invite you to have lunch with them. It's like the passing of the popularity torch. Too bad it's just the same as any other gross table in this cafeteria.

Ashlin is being annoying, going on and on about the sauna

her parents had installed. I finally say, "Ashlin, nobody cares," and her mouth snaps shut, her brown eyes hurt. I feel kind of bad, so I add, "Just kidding."

Rennie snags a powdered sugar doughnut off my tray and pops it into her mouth.

"I thought you weren't eating carbs during cheer season," I say, and I pull my lunch tray closer. I only have three left.

Rennie makes a face at me. "I deserve some comfort after this morning. I should probably get an AIDS test or something. Who knows what kind of germs that skank is harboring." She gags, and her tongue is white from powdered sugar.

I can't believe Kat DeBrassio spit in Rennie's face. I mean, that was totally gross. But it's not like Rennie didn't have it coming. I just can't believe someone called her out on it.

Reeve pulls his chair up closer to us. I scoot away a little. He must have used half a bottle of cologne this morning. It's giving me a headache. He drawls, "Rennie, honey?"

"Yes, Reevie baby?" Rennie flips her hair around.

"You know you're my wifey, right?"

Eww.

"Of course."

"And a wifey has to make sure her man is taken care of," he

continues. I make a *Gag me* face at Ashlin, who giggles. Reeve sees me do it, and he waves his hand at me dismissively before turning back to Rennie. "Anyway . . . will you *please* make sure that I get a cheerleader who knows what she's doing this year? I'm serious. I can't have a girl up there representing number sixty-three if she's just a pretty face. Whoever gets the job, she's gonna have a lot of airtime, and she's got to have the entire package."

"What's the entire package?" Rennie purrs.

Reeve ticks off his fingers. "Rhythm, good hand-eye coordination, flexible enough to do some of the more complicated moves. No cartwheel bullshit. I want back handsprings, pop and lock. Good variety. You know what I'm saying."

"I know exactly what you're saying, Reevie," Rennie says, her eyes bright. "Consider it taken care of." Reeve reaches across the table and pinches her cheek.

Rennie slaps his hand away, laughing. "What about you, Alex? Who do you want?"

"I don't care," he says, and he goes back to talking to Derek.

Rennie mouths to me, *What's his problem?* I shrug back. *PMS,* she mouths.

She leans forward and takes another doughnut off my tray. "What do you think about me giving Alex to Nadia? . . . I mean, it's definitely true that if she nabbed a senior player, she'd be hot shit with her little freshman piggies."

I snatch the doughnut right back. "Yeah, whatever." I still feel bad about what I said to Nadia this morning. Maybe this will make her feel better.

"So you're cool with that?"

"Why wouldn't I be?" I know what she's getting at, but I refuse to play along. Like I've told her a thousand times, I don't see him that way.

"O-kay."

I get up from the table and walk over to the soda machine before she can say anything else.

I'm trying to decide between grape soda and Coke when Alex comes up behind me. "Hey, Lindy," I say, pressing Coke. It occurs to me that Rennie is probably leaning on Alex just as hard as she's been leaning on me. I bet she's telling him the same lies too. That I've been dreaming of him. That we're supposed to be together.

Flatly, he says, "That's all you have to say to me? 'Hey, Lindy?' Have you not noticed that I've been giving you the cold shoulder since Saturday?"

I stare at him, my mouth an *O*. What's the matter with him?

"I can't believe you, Lillia," he says, seething. "You and Rennie ambush my house for a freaking party and you make a huge mess with glitter everywhere, and then you dip out after half an hour to go to another party! What the hell!"

I've never seen Alex like this before, so pissed. But he's right to be upset. We never should have left like that. "I'm sorry," I whisper. He has no idea how sorry I really and truly am.

He shakes his head at me and turns to go, but I reach out and grab his shirtsleeve. Tugging on it, I say, "Don't be mad."

He's glaring at me, but he doesn't shrug me off. "When are you going to come and get your decorations and crap?"

Quickly I say, "Rennie and I will come over after cheerleading tryouts today and pick everything up."

Alex doesn't say anything. He just walks away. Not back to the table but straight out of the cafeteria.

Rennie got it into her head that we should have a welcome home party for the boys. She decided that the theme would be "Under the Sea," and she would be a mermaid. The other senior girls were allowed to wear bikinis and grass skirts and leis. The juniors and sophomores were sexy fishermen. We let Nadia invite three of her freshman friends, but they had to dress as minnows, and they had to wear flippers on their feet the whole time or else they'd have to leave.

There was one more condition—I told Nadia she wasn't allowed to drink. She agreed right away. When she showed up with her friends, all dressed in green tanks and green shorts, and waddling in their flipper feet, I gave her a virgin piña colada. I had one too, even though Rennie kept trying to top mine off with one of the bottles of rum she had hidden around the backyard.

The party was a hit. Music was blasting out of the speakers, we had tiki torches lit over the lawn, people were dancing, and swimming in the pool. Even the guys got into the spirit of things. Reeve took a sheet off Alex's bed and made himself a toga and called himself Poseidon. He was walking around with a rake, calling it his trident. I was pretty sure he just wanted an excuse to take his shirt off. Alex was wearing his fishing hat, and the other guys at least had on swimming trunks and zinc oxide.

Rennie was wearing a tight blue skirt, a shell bikini top, and fishnet stockings. She spent a week's worth of her hostessing money on the wig and the rhinestone starfish barrette she found online. I was a *Baywatch* lifeguard in my red one-piece bathing suit, short white shorts, and flip-flops. I had a whistle around my neck and a lifeguard float strapped to my back. Ashlin was a jellyfish. She had on a sheer white beach cover-up over her white bikini, and she braided long strips of white crepe paper into her blond hair.

Rennie and I were by the grill sipping our drinks and surveying the scene when Mrs. Lind came up to me and gave me a big hug.

"Lillia, this was *such* a good idea," she said, kissing me on the cheek. She was wearing a Hawaiian muumuu, and she had a flower in her hair. "Alex was so surprised!"

She went off to bring out more seafood kebobs, and Rennie elbowed me. "See? I told you it would be fine. What were you so worried about?"

"I wasn't *worried*," I said, adjusting my lifeguard float. "I just think it's a little weird to ask someone's mom if you can have a party at their house."

"Lil," she said airily, "Alex's mom loves you. You're the daughter she never had. She gave you that pink Dior wristlet for your birthday! I looked it up on the website, and I'm telling you, it did not come cheap. It was, like, six hundred dollars!"

Rennie borrowed that wristlet months ago and hasn't given it back. It's more her style than mine anyway.

She was already bored of the conversation, so she was scanning the yard, running her hand through her long blond wig. "What the eff is Teresa Cruz doing here? I distinctly remember not inviting her. Look at her. She's wearing a lei and a grass skirt. This isn't a luau," she fumed. "She's so remedial. And I don't know what's up Reeve's butt. He barely said hi to us, and hello, this party is for him."

I was looking for Teresa in her dumb getup when Alex caught my eye and waved at me. He was standing around with Reeve and Derek and his uncle. They were all smoking cigars except Alex. I started to head over to them, when Rennie grabbed my arm. "Ohmygod," she said. She had her phone in her hand, and she waved it at me, her eyes bright. "He texted me."

"Who? Reeve?"

"Ian!" Ian was one of the UMass guys we met at the beach. He and Rennie had hung out earlier in the week. He'd taken her out to dinner, but then she hadn't heard from him again. "They're having a party! It's the last night of their rental. We have to go."

"Right now?"

"Yes!"

Laughing, I said, "Ren, we can't leave. This is our party,

remember? We have to bring out the cupcakes and fireworks and stuff." Nadia and I spent the afternoon decorating those cupcakes. We put blue food coloring in the frosting and crushed up graham crackers to look like sand.

Rennie pouted at me, pushing her lower lip out. "Please, Lil! He's really cool. He's premed! And I told you how his friend Mike kept asking about you. Can't we just go and hang out for a little bit? We can come right back. No one will even notice we're gone!"

I looked around the yard. Ashlin was over by the pool house, playing poker with some of the guys. Derek was trying to peek at her cards, and she kept laughing and pushing him away. She definitely wouldn't have noticed if we left, not with the attention Derek was giving her.

I asked, "What about Nadia?"

"She's fine! Look, she's having fun."

I spotted Nadia, sitting by the pool with her friends, her legs in the water, kicking with her flippers. They were giggling and splashing. Rennie pulled on my arm and swung it from side to side. Pleadingly she said, "Puh-leaaase, Lil. This is my last chance to see him. They're leaving tomorrow. It's now or never!"

I sighed. "An hour, and then we come right back. Promise?"

Rennie squealed and hugged me. "Yay!" Then she looked down at her mermaid costume and frowned. "We can't show up like this. We're going to look so high school."

"We can change in the car," I said quickly. If we went to Rennie's house to get ready, it would take forever. I just wanted to go and come back so people could hurry up and enjoy our cupcakes, even if they were a box mix. I didn't set them out with the other food because I wanted to pass them around special.

Rennie shrugged. "Okay, then. I'm gonna go check my makeup. I'll meet you at the car in two secs."

She ran toward the house, and I headed for her Jeep. I was rummaging in my overnight bag for the tank top I'd been wearing earlier, when I felt someone tug on my hair. I whirled around.

Reeve.

He reached over my shoulder and pushed his arm against the door, closing it. "Where are you sneaking off to?" he demanded, leaning in close.

"None of your business."

"Come on. Tell me."

I tried to push him away from the Jeep, but he wouldn't budge. "Reeve, move!"

"So you throw the kid a welcome home party and then bail on it?" Reeve wagged his finger at me. "You're not a nice girl, Cho." Then he strutted off.

"I never said I was," I called after him.

I open up my soda and sip on it as I walk back to our lunch table. I sit down where Alex had been sitting, next to PJ and Reeve. Reeve's looking at me just like he did that night, eyes narrow and suspicious. He says, "What are you pouting about now, Cho? Having to buy your own soda?"

"Shut up."

"Girls like you—," he starts to say, and then he gestures at me, and his arm accidentally knocks over my Coke. It splashes over the front of my sweater. Yelping, I jump up. PJ and Reeve push back their chairs to avoid the spill. I feel the Coke seeping through the cashmere onto my bra. The big brown spot spreads across my front. "You . . . you ruined it."

"Chillax, Lillia. It was an accident." Reeve comes at me with a napkin, trying to dab at the stain.

I recoil. "Don't touch me!"

Sneering, Reeve says, "Oh, I forgot. Princess Lillia doesn't like to be touched. Isn't that right?" He winks at me.

"Reeve, leave her alone," Rennie says.

My eyes fill. I bend my head and wipe at my sweater so that my hair falls across my face. I tell myself that everything is fine. It's just Reeve being Reeve. He doesn't know anything. How could he? Rennie wouldn't tell anyone. We promised each other. I try to take a deep breath, but it catches in my throat. My bottom lip starts to quiver. I have to get out of here before I lose it in front of everyone.

"For your information, this sweater costs three hundred dollars, which is more than that jalopy you drive around."

I pick up my bag and head for the girls' bathroom. I run in and over to the sink and turn on the faucet. I won't cry. I won't. I will not cry at school. I don't do that.

Except it's not a choice.

I'm crying so hard that my shoulders shake and my throat hurts. I can't stop.

The door opens, and I expect it to be Rennie. But it's not. It's Kat DeBrassio. She drops her bag into the well of the sink next to mine and messes with her hair in the mirror, shaking her bangs out.

I quickly splash my face with cold water to try to hide the fact that I've been crying. But she must see, because she asks, in her gruff way, "You okay?"

I stare straight ahead, at my reflection. "I'm fine."

I met Rennie first, in the concessions stand line at the old movie theater on Main Street. I was ten years old and I felt so grown-up, standing alone with my ten dollar-bill in my back pocket. Rennie told me she liked my flip-flops. They were lavender and pink polka dot. She introduced me to Kat a couple of weeks later. From then on we were a trio. Before Rennie and Kat, I only had Nadia to play with when we came to spend the summer on Jar Island. Now I had two best friends.

Every Friday night we had sleepovers, and we'd alternate houses. We'd spy on Kat's older brother and play with her dog, Shep. At Rennie's condo we'd make microwave peanut brittle, and her mom would give us makeovers. At my house Rennie and Kat would race in the pool, and I'd stay in the shallow end and be the judge. We'd play with my Victorian dollhouse, and then, when we were older, we'd make movies with my dad's camcorder and screen them for my mom and Nadia over breakfast.

I used to be jealous, knowing that when I left Jar Island at the end of August, Rennie and Kat still had each other. In a lot of ways the two of them were alike—both were fearless. I was the scaredy-cat. That's what Kat was always calling me. I never wanted to jump off the high dive, or hold the rudder when Kat's dad took us sailing, or go off with boys we met on the beach. But Rennie and Kat, they both looked out for me. Made me feel safe.

When my family decided to move here for good, it was a dream come true. That summer was a warm-up for the fun we were going to have in high school. But then, at the beginning of August, Rennie finally convinced her mom to let her get a nose job. I never thought she had a bad nose, but once Rennie pointed out the bump on the bridge, I saw it too. When the bandages came off and the scars healed, she was the one who decided we had to be cool in high school. Kat said it was dumb, and Rennie got pissed, and they had one of their blowups. I expected it to be over within a few days, the way their fights usually were, but a week later Rennie was still pissed. She said Kat was immature, she didn't get it. She'd hold us back.

We didn't drop Kat right away. We did our back-to-school shopping together off island, like we'd planned. We went to the movies for Kat's birthday, but Rennie made a big deal about sitting next to me so we could share Sno-Caps, and that was awkward. Afterward we were supposed to spend the night at Kat's house. But as we were walking out of the movie theater, Rennie announced that she didn't feel good, that she wasn't going to sleep over. It was obvious she was faking; Rennie's a horrible actress. I pulled Kat aside and asked, "Do you still want me to come over?" and she said, "Forget it."

I went home and mulled the whole thing over, first by myself, then with my mom. I told her how Rennie and Kat had been fighting, how Rennie didn't want to be friends with Kat anymore, and how I felt caught in the middle. "I mean, if I have to take sides, I guess I'd probably take Rennie's," I said.

My mom said, "Why do you have to take sides? Why not be the one to bring them back together?"

"I doubt Rennie would listen," I said.

"You could at least try," she urged me. "Kat's been through a lot. She needs her friends."

I felt a pang of guilt. Kat's mom had died the year before. Her mom had been sick for a long time. Kat didn't want to talk about it, not to me at least. She talked to my mom sometimes, though, when Rennie and I were hanging out in my room.

"I'll try," I told my mom.

Then I had this great idea. For the first day of school, I would give Rennie and Kat friendship necklaces. It would bind us together again, smooth out the bad feelings.

My mom and I picked them out from the nice jewelry store in White Haven, the place where my dad always gets my mom something for their anniversary. Identical gold necklaces, with a special charm for each of us. I was really excited to give them the black velvet boxes; I knew that Rennie especially would love it.

That first day of school Rennie's mom came to pick me up, and I expected to see both Kat and Rennie in the backseat. They lived on the same side of the island, and I lived farthest away.

But Kat wasn't there, just Rennie in her new jean mini, with the decorative stitching on the back pockets. I climbed into the car, and asked, "Is Kat sick?"

Rennie shook her head.

When she saw her mom eyeing us in the rearview mirror, Rennie leaned in and whispered, "I didn't want to pick her up. I'm over her."

"Did you tell her you weren't coming to get her?" I whispered back. What if Kat was outside waiting for us? What if she was late on the first day of high school?

"She'll figure it out," Rennie said. She touched her nose and asked, worried, "Does it look swollen?"

Even though I'd planned on giving Rennie and Kat their necklaces at the same time, I went ahead and gave Rennie hers right then. She seemed grumpy, and I wanted to start our day off on a nice note. She squealed so loudly, her mom slammed on the breaks. Her charm was a heart. Mine was a tiny gold cupcake. We both put our necklaces on right away.

I put Kat's in her locker. She didn't buy a lock when we went back-to-school shopping. She said she'd just forget the combination anyway. Besides, nobody stole on the island; it was totally safe.

When I saw Kat come down the hallway later that day, her eyes were red, and she wasn't wearing the necklace. Her charm was a gold key. I liked how the key was pretty, but there was also something tough and practical about it. Just like Kat.

She walked right by me.

I tried to bring it up to Rennie later, to see if there was a way we could get things back to how they were before. But she refused. She didn't even want to talk about it. For Rennie it was over. Erased. She had a way of doing that. Erasing the stuff she didn't like. I'd just never seen her erase a person before.

I dry my face with a paper towel. I turn to toss it into the trash, and with my back to her, I say, "Honestly, I never thought your breath stunk. For what it's worth." I realize that these might be the first real words I've spoken to her in years.

Kat stares at me, and I know she's surprised.

And then, from the last stall, there's a sound. Shallow breaths, the kind you have to fight to take when you're crying. Both of our heads swivel toward it. "Who's there?" I call out, panicky, like I've been caught doing something bad.

"Yo. Who's in here?" Kat says.

There's no answer. Then Kat marches down to the stall and kicks the door open with her boot.

CHAPTER FIVE

MARY

I'M PERCHED ON TOP OF THE TOILET, HUGGING MY KNEES to my chest.

The stall door swings open. That spitting girl from this morning stares back at me. The pretty Asian girl is standing next to her, and her white sweater has a big stain across the front.

"Who are you?" Kat demands.

"I'm Mary." I swallow hard. "Nice to meet you."

Kat says, dryly, "You too."

"What are your names?"

This seems to catch them both off guard. "I'm Kat, and this is Princess Lillia."

The Asian girl gives her a dirty look. "It's just Lillia." Then she narrows her eyes on me. "Why are you hiding in here?"

"Umm . . . no reason." It's hard to look her in the eye, since I've been listening to her crying for the last ten minutes. It doesn't seem right, someone so pretty and popular should have anything to cry about. Whatever it is, it must be bad.

Lillia flicks her hair over her shoulder. "You're obviously upset about something. Or maybe you just enjoy spying on people in bathrooms?"

Kat slouches against the open door. "Let me guess. You hooked up with some guy over the summer. You let him feel you up, and now he doesn't even remember your name."

"Not even close," I say, and bite down on my lip. I'm not sure I should tell these girls anything. After all, Lillia is in Reeve's circle. She's friends with him. And Kat . . . well, she's just scary. "I saw someone I used to know. That's all."

"Who?" Kat says. I can tell by the way she slouches against the door that she's not going to let me leave until I tell her.

"This guy. He . . . used to torture me when we were in seventh grade. He basically got everyone in our grade to hate me. He's the reason my family moved away. Anyway, I saw him today, for the first time in four years, and he didn't even recognize me. After everything he did." Some of my hair slips into my face. I push it behind my ear.

"How old are you?" Lillia asks me, quieter and softer this time.

"Seventeen."

Kat asks, "And you're originally from the island? Which middle school did you go to?"

"I'm from here, but I went to Belle Harbor Montessori, on the mainland." I used to ride the ferry every day to school and back. Me and him.

Kat shakes her head and says, "Reeve."

My eyes widen. I'm nervous that she figured it out so fast, but I'm also strangely comforted. "How did you know?"

"Who else could it be?" Kat says, holding to the stall door open for me. "We go way back."

I climb down. Lillia moves back over to the sink and wets a paper towel. "I'm not surprised. Reeve's basically a Neanderthal," she says, dabbing her front. "He ruined my sweater."

Tentatively, I say, "I thought you guys were friends. I saw you together this morning."

Lillia sighs. "We're not friends, but we're not *not* friends."

Kat rolls her eyes. "Great answer, Lillia."

Right away I say, "Please don't tell him you saw me." The last thing I want is to have Reeve hear that I'm still crying over him.

The bell rings, and Lillia pulls a tube of cherry ChapStick out of her shorts pocket and rubs it on her bottom lip. She presses her lips together with a pop. "Don't sweat it. I've already forgotten your name." She looks at Kat and says, "Gotta run," and then walks out.

Kat watches her go, and when the door swings closed, she says to me in a low voice, "Hey. So, Lillia *was* crying, right?"

I look at my sandals. That's private. I shouldn't even have been in here.

"Did you hear her say anything? What was she upset about?"

"No. Nothing."

Kat sighs, disappointed. "Where are you supposed to be right now, Mary?"

"I don't even know."

"Where's your schedule?"

I look in my bag, but I can't find it. "Um, I think I have chemistry now."

She pushes her bangs out of her eyes and peers at me. "Wait, aren't you a senior? Why haven't you taken chemistry yet?"

I wet my lips. "I got really sick at the end of seventh grade, so I was held back a year."

"That sucks. Well, the science department is over on the east side of the building. You're going to have to book it over there to make it in time." She pauses. "Listen, don't let that jackhole Reeve get to you. Karma's a bitch. He'll get his."

"I don't know," I say. "I mean, I wish I could believe it. But Reeve seems fine. I'm the one who's been hiding in the bathroom all morning."

"He's not worth it," she says. "None of these people are. Trust me."

Gratefully I say, "Thanks, Kat." She's the first person to really talk to me today.

I follow Kat out of the bathroom. She makes a left and heads down the hall. I watch her go, discreetly, in case she might look back at me.

She doesn't.

CHAPTER SIX

LILLIA

ALL OF THE GIRLS TRYING OUT FOR THE SQUAD ARE sitting on the football field bleachers in their short shorts and camis. Nadia is in the first row with a couple of her friends. I smile at her, and Nadia gives me a small smile back. I'm relieved she's not still upset about my back handspring comment.

Rennie's standing with Coach Christy in front of the girls, while Ashlin and I sit on the sidelines. We've got our uniforms on, like models. Rennie, too. Sleeveless shells with a *J* sewn on the chest, pleated skirts with bloomers underneath, and the ankle socks with the tiny colored balls on the heels. I have to admit, it feels kind of good to be wearing my uniform again.

When Coach Christy runs back to the gym office to photocopy permission slips, Rennie springs into action. Surveying the bleachers, she says in a low voice, "Okay, here's the real deal. If you want to be a Jar Island varsity cheerleader, you have to look and act the part *full-time.* You're not just representing yourself; you're representing me. This is my squad. I have standards." She pauses for effect. "Fingers crossed, we're getting new uniforms this season, and they're gonna be crop tops. That means I don't want to see one French fry on anyone's plate at lunch. I'm serious. Also, Dori." Dori looks up, startled. "You need to retire that jacket. It makes you look like a soccer mom."

I gasp, and Ashlin giggles behind her hand.

The girls whisper to each other nervously. Rennie looks over her shoulder to make sure Coach Christy isn't on her way back outside, and she snaps, "Did I say I was finished?"

Everyone hushes up.

"There can't be any weak links whatsoever. That means if your friend is slacking, you let her know. Like, just as a for instance, Melanie, you need to commit these three words to memory stat: 'cleanse,' 'tone,' 'moisturize.'" Melanie's eyes fill up with tears, but she quickly nods.

I honestly can't believe what I'm hearing. I mean, okay, Melanie has bad skin, but does Rennie need to blow up her spot in front of everyone? I look over at Ashlin, hoping for solidarity, but she shrugs and whispers, "Forget the three steps. Send the girl to a dermatologist."

Rennie points a finger at Nadia. "I want everyone to check out Nadia's legs. That's the level of tan you need to have. If you don't, go see Becky at Mystic Beach on Sandtrap Street. She'll hook you up."

My sister flushes with pride and lowers her head humbly.

"And I'm not just talking to the freshmen." I see Rennie scan the sophomores and juniors, who are here too. I know exactly who she's looking for. Teresa Cruz. "Don't get too comfortable just because you're an upperclassman. Every girl has to earn her spot here. I will not hesitate to cut any dead weight for the good of the squad."

I see Coach Christy come out the metal doors, so I clear my throat and motion for Rennie to wrap it up.

Finally she smiles. "Last chance, girls. If you don't think

you can hang, don't let the door hit you on the way out."

No one makes a move.

In the locker room it's just Rennie and me changing out of our uniforms. Ashlin and Coach Christy have the other girls running around the track.

I'm pulling my sweater over my head as I say, "So we're going straight to Alex's now, right? He was pretty upset today at lunch."

"Over what?"

"Over the fact that we left the party." At the mention of the party, Rennie's face goes blank. "I told him we'd come over after practice to take down the decorations and straighten up the pool house."

"Will Reeve be there?"

Sourly I say, "I hope not." I bend down and take off my sneakers.

"You know how today at lunch Reeve was going on and on about who his cheerleader should be?" When I don't reply, she keeps talking. "I think that was his slick way of asking me. I mean, it makes total sense, right? Captain for captain."

I pull my hair into a ponytail. "But wasn't he hooking up

with Teresa Cruz a bunch this summer?"

Rennie laughs dryly. "Um, they hooked up, like, twice. Besides, have you seen her thighs? She can barely cross her legs, much less do splits. You really think Reeve would want her repping his number out there?"

"I don't know." I tighten my ponytail.

"You don't know?"

"I think Teresa's pretty." Rennie gives me a look like I'm crazy, but I ignore it. "So you're coming with me, right?"

Rennie rolls her eyes. "Lindy has a maid. He doesn't need us."

"You're not supposed to say 'maid'—"

"Please, no lectures on rich people terminology!" she snaps, putting her cami back on.

My heart is thumping in my chest as I take off my socks and put on my espadrilles. Rennie won't even look at me as she packs up the rest of her things. "Ren, I know you're still upset about what happened with Kat this morning—"

I don't even get to finish. Rennie levels me with a death stare and says, "I couldn't care less about that freak." then she walks out of the locker room, without saying good-bye.

By the time I get to the parking lot, her Jeep is long gone. I end up tracking down Ashlin for a ride to Alex's.

Ash drops me off outside Alex's house. I let out a big sigh of relief because Mrs. Lind's car isn't in the driveway. I was hoping she wouldn't be home, because what if she's mad at me too?

Unbuckling my seat belt, I say, "Thanks for the ride, Ash."

"No prob, Lils. I'm just sorry I can't help you clean up." She makes a sad face and says, "I promised my mom I would go with her to get her hair cut. Last time they totally made her look like an old lady."

"It's fine," I say. I haven't told her about Rennie's and my fight. That's between the two of us.

I hop out of the car, and wave as Ashlin drives off. Instead of going to the front door, I head straight for the backyard. Alex is skimming the top of the pool with a net, trying to fish a red Solo cup out of the water.

"Hey," I say.

He looks up, startled. "Where's Rennie?"

Ordinarily I would offer up an excuse for her, but today I just shrug.

I start gathering up the tiki torches and the beach ball paper lantern lights we strung around the yard. There's no way I can carry everything back to my house. If Alex wants this stuff out of here, he's going to have to drive me home. He still seems pretty mad at me, though. "Did you get to try one of my cupcakes?" I ask.

"Yeah." Alex is sitting on a lounge chair, messing with his phone.

"Was it good?"

"It was all right," he says.

"Did you get one with a Swedish Fish inside? I did that in a few of them."

He finally makes eye contact. "I ate three, and I think one had a fish."

He's warming up to me again, thank God. I offer him a small smile. "Cool. Um, I'm a little thirsty. Can I have a soda?"

He jerks his head toward the pool house. "You know where they are."

Ouch. Okay. So maybe I will have to walk all this stuff home.

The pool house is basically Alex's apartment, complete with a living room, a kitchen, and a huge master bedroom. He has it set up like a bachelor pad, James Bond style. Black leather sectional sofa, big-screen TV mounted on the wall, an actual Coke machine by the bar. And he has a snack pantry that his mom keeps stocked with cookies and chips and anything you could ever want.

His bedroom door is open, and I see one of our plastic palm trees deflated and handing over the back of his desk chair. His room is usually clean, but today it's messy, for Alex. The bed's not made and there are clothes on the floor.

I go to pick up the palm tree, and I stop. There is a small heap of clothes by his bed. A green tank top is on top of the pile. I bend down and pick it up.

My sister's. The one she wore the night of the party, part of her minnow costume. I know because I have the same one, same brand, only one size bigger. There's a crusty pink stain over the front, strawberry daiquiri. I smell it. Rum.

I walk back outside holding the tank. Alex's eyes widen when he sees it. "Why do you have Nadia's tank top?" I ask him.

"Oh . . . someone spilled something on her. I gave her one of my shirts to wear home," he says.

Suddenly I find it hard to breathe. "Was Nadia drinking?" I told her not to. I forbid her. "She didn't do anything stupid, did she?"

"Like what? Like go off with a random guy?" He shakes his head. "No, she didn't do anything like that."

I can feel the blood drain from my face. Is he talking about Nadia . . . or me?

Alex walks away and starts loading the decorations into the back of his SUV. I pick up as many of the tiki torches as I can carry and follow him. He doesn't say anything, and neither do I.

CHAPTER SEVEN

MARY

I'M SITTING ON MY BED, STARING DOWN AT AN OLD PHOTO album that I found in the basement. I age as the pages turn. Posing in front of a blanket fort with a flashlight lit under my chin. At the apex of a swing from the tire hung on the backyard tree, my hair almost white from the sun. Me and my dad with big clumps of seaweed on top of our heads. Practicing clarinet for my parents and Aunt Bette in the dining room.

The book ends with me posing next to the lilac bush for my first day of seventh grade. I'm on my tiptoes, smelling the flowers.

It's no wonder Reeve didn't recognize me this morning. There's only one way to put it—I was fat.

Everyone was talking about the new scholarship student. The Belle Harbor Montessori on the mainland was teeny tiny. There were just twenty kids in our seventh-grade class, and I was the only one from Jar Island. During lunch a few of the boys were debating how smart you needed to be to get a scholarship, when Reeve walked in.

Everyone watched as he moved through the food line. My friend Anne leaned over and said, "He's pretty cute, don't you think?"

"He's not bad," I whispered back.

Reeve was easily taller than every other boy in our class. But he wasn't lanky; he had a bit of muscle to him. . . you could tell he probably played sports at his old school. We didn't have sports at Montessori. We didn't even have recess, unless you counted the foliage hikes we took through the woods.

Our teacher waved him over and showed him where our class was sitting.

"Hey," he said, kind of bored-sounding. He plopped into an empty chair. "I'm Reeve."

A couple of the boys mumbled "Hey" back, but mostly no one said anything. I think we all picked up on his apathetic attitude. He didn't really want to be at our school. He probably had lots of friends back wherever he'd come from.

I felt bad for him. Reeve only picked at his sandwich, not saying anything. It must have been hard coming to a new school. This was the only school I'd ever known. I'd gone to Belle Harbor Montessori since I was in kindergarten.

When lunch was over, and everyone stood up, I saw Reeve looking around, unsure where to put his tray. I leaned over to grab it for him. I don't know why. Just to be nice, I guess. But he snatched it away before I could get my hands on it and said really loudly, "Don't you think you've had enough to eat?"

The boys who'd heard him busted up laughing. I think I might have even laughed too, just because I'd been so caught off guard. Anne made a face. Not one of sympathy either. Just a plain old frown. And not at Reeve. At me.

Reeve, he laughed the hardest of all. He was the first to leave the table, and everyone just followed him, even though he couldn't have known where our classroom was. He left his tray on the table.

I ended up throwing away his lunch with my own.

Before Reeve, I was one of the smart girls, especially in math. I was the shy but friendly one. I was a little socially awkward, sure. The girl with the long blond hair from the island. But after Reeve, I was the fat girl.

I close the album. I'm not that girl anymore. I hadn't been her for a long time. But being back on Jar Island, with Reeve, with my old pictures and stuffed animals and things—it makes it feel so fresh.

I hear Aunt Bette downstairs, quietly doing the dishes.

Our dinner tonight was awkward, to say the least. This morning I imagined telling Aunt Bette every detail about my epic first day—the look on Reeve's face when he saw me again, him trying to talk to me, him trying to find out where I've been for the last four years. She'd let me have a glass of wine, and we'd toast to the start of a great new year.

Since none of that happened, there was nothing to tell Aunt Bette. Needless to say, I didn't feel hungry. It would have been rude to get up from the table, though, so I just sat there quietly while she twirled spaghetti on her fork and read some art journal.

I feel empty inside. Hollow. I just really need to talk to my mom and dad, hear their voices. They'll probably try to convince me to come back home, and I might let them.

The next five minutes I spend pacing around my room with my cell phone over my head, trying to get enough bars to call them. I can't get a signal. When we lived here before, cell service was practically nonexistent on Jar Island. There were a few random spots where you could get reception, like near the lighthouses, or sometimes in the Lutheran church parking lot, but for the most part Jar Island was a cell-phone-free zone. I guess that hasn't changed.

There's a telephone downstairs in the kitchen, but I'd rather not talk to my parents in front of Aunt Bette. I might start crying.

I hear Aunt Bette climb the stairs. I peek out my door and watch her walk to her room.

I guess I could try talking to her. I used to confide in her about all kinds of things. Whenever she'd visit in the summer, we'd walk down the hill and buy hot chocolates on Main Street. Even in August. She'd tell me about things I know my parents would freak over. The month she spent living in Paris with a married man, the series of paintings she did of herself nude. Aunt Bette has lived about a million and one lifetimes. She could have good advice for me.

Aunt Bette is already in bed. Her eyes are closed. But I guess she hears me, because they suddenly open. "Mary?"

I step into the room and crouch by her bed. "Are you asleep?"

She shakes her head and blinks. "I don't think so. Am I?"

Even though I'm on the verge of tears, I laugh. "Am I bothering you?"

"No! Please!" She sits up. "Are you okay?"

I take a deep breath and try to get a hold of myself. "It's strange to be back."

"Yes. Of . . . of course."

"I don't know if I belong, after everything that's happened."

In a low voice Aunt Bette says, "This is your home. Where else would you belong?"

"Nowhere, I guess."

"I've missed you, Mary." A faint smile spreads across her face. "I'm glad you're here."

"Me too," I lie. Then I go back to my room and crawl into bed.

It takes me forever to fall asleep.

CHAPTER EIGHT

LILLIA

My mom's in her bedroom on the phone with our dad, and Nadia and I are watching TV downstairs, sharing a pint of homemade dulce de leche ice cream from Scoops. At first, when I asked if she wanted some, she said no, even though it's her favorite. I knew she was thinking about what Rennie said at cheerleading practice. I brought the carton over to the couch, and she watched me lick the ice cream off the top of the lid. "Just one bite," she said, exactly like I knew she would. All the girls in our family have a sweet tooth.

The dryer dings, and I pause the show we're watching. I go over to the laundry room and stuff the clean clothes into a basket and bring the basket back into the living room. I used extra dryer sheets, and the clothes smell so snuggly. I put my face up to a T-shirt and inhale the warmth. I start folding a stack of T-shirts, and then I see Nadia's tank top. I put stain remover where there was strawberry daiquiri, and it came out. I didn't even bother with my cashmere sweater. I just put it in the dry cleaning bag and hoped for the best.

"Here's your shirt back," I say, handing it over.

Nadia's face goes white. "Um, thanks."

"I got that stain out." I watch her closely. "Alex said someone bumped into you and spilled their drink."

"Yeah." Nadia takes a big bite of ice cream, avoiding my eyes.

"Where's Alex's shirt? I tried to find it in your room so I could wash it and give it back to him."

She hesitates and then says, "It's at Janelle's. Remember I was going to sleep over there after the party? I told her to bring it to school today, but she forgot."

My phone buzzes. It's Ashlin. Everyone's meeting over at Bow Tie tonight after Rennie gets off work.

"Who's that?" Nadia asks. "Are you going out?"

I set my phone down, because this is serious. "Nadia, you tell me right now. Did you drink at Alex's, even though I told you not to?"

"No!" She has two bright splotches on her cheeks.

"Then promise me. Promise on our sister bond."

Nadia won't look at me. "Lillia, cut it out. I already told you."

My heart breaks right in half. She's won't promise because she's lying. She's lying to my face like it's nothing. I've never lied to Nadia. Not ever, not once. I'd never do that to her. "I'm giving you one more chance. You tell me the truth right this minute, Nadia, or else I'm telling Mommy everything."

Nadia's eyes go big and scared. "Okay! Wait! I had, like, maybe a half cup of strawberry daiquiri. I didn't ask for it. One of my friends gave it to me. I thought it was a virgin one. I just took a couple tiny sips, so I wouldn't waste it. It's not a big deal. You drank at parties when you were a freshman!"

Okay. Yes, I did, but it was the *end* of freshman year. When Rennie and I started going to parties, she'd drink beer, drink whatever was around. The guys called her Half Pint, because she was so little, but she could hold her own. Unlike me, I was so scared of getting in trouble, I'd sip from the same cup of beer all night long. "Quit trying to justify it! You lied to me. You straight up lied to my face, Nadia." I fall back against the couch. I can't believe she lied to me. "You're on lockdown now. No parties, no hanging out with my friends, because you obviously can't handle yourself. And if I find out that you drank more than you're telling me, you're done."

"I'm really, really sorry."

It's not even about the drinking. "I didn't think you would ever lie to me."

A fat tear rolls down her cheek. "I won't drink ever again, Lilli! You have to believe me."

"How can I believe anything you say to me now?" I stand up. I feel like I'm going to start crying too. I walk out of the living room and go up to my room.

I never should have left her at that party. This is my fault just as much as it is Nadia's. Maybe more. I'm her big sister. It's my job to look out for her, to keep her safe.

When we got to the other party, there were a ton of people there. No one we recognized, mainly out-of-towners. College kids. There wasn't a theme or anything. Just a bunch of people hanging out, listening to music.

The guys came and found us right away. It was flattering, the way they'd been waiting for us to show up, how they paid us so much attention. At first I kept looking at my phone to check on the time. I didn't want to stay any longer than the hour Rennie had promised it would be.

They asked what we wanted to drink, and Rennie told them to make us vodka and cranberry with a spoon full of sugar, because she knew I could only drink if it was supersweet. Every time our cups were empty, the guys were right there to fill them up again. We were having fun, the four of us, and I stopped checking the time, stopped thinking about the other party we'd left to come here. I remember laughing over every little thing my guy, the tall one, said, even though nothing he said was that funny. I guess that's how drunk I was.

Mike. That was his name.

Around eleven I knock on Nadia's door. She doesn't answer, but I can hear her TV on in the background. Through the closed door I say, "I'm trying to look out for you, Nadia. That's my job."

I wait a few seconds for her to answer. Whenever Nadia gets mad, she holds a grudge, and it's for sure not easy to win her back. I hate when Nadia is mad at me. I hate it more than anything. But I have a reason to be mad too.

I let my head rest against the door. "Let's ride to school together tomorrow, okay? I'll drive, just us two. If we leave early, we can stop at Milky Morning and get raspberry muffins right when they come out of the oven. You love those."

Still nothing from Nadia. I sigh, and go back to my room.

CHAPTER NINE

KAT

My dad, Pat, and I are sitting in the living room with our bowls of chili, watching some motocross show. It's the third day of chili. When my dad makes his hellfire chili, we end up eating it for at least a week. I'm sick of it.

I stand up, and Pat goes, "You do the dishes tonight. I did them last night."

"There were no dishes last night. We used plastic bowls."

He turns back toward the television and rubs his bare feet on Shep's back. "Yeah, and I had to throw them away. So it's officially your turn."

I give him the finger, then I put my dishes in the sink and leave them there. Pat is such a freaking scrub. He's been living at home since he graduated high school two years ago. He takes a few classes at the community college, but he's mostly just a scrub.

Back in my room I check my phone. No missed calls, no texts from Alex. Nothing. I actually did want to talk to him, about how his pal Rennie has no soul, how she deserved that loogey to the face. But I'm not going to be the one to make that call, not when he said he would.

Instead I call Kim at the record store. When she picks up, I can barely hear her over the noise.

"What's going on?" I ask.

"Some indie record label party for a lame-ass band."

"Can I come over? I had the worst day. I freaking hate my school, I hate Rennie Holtz, I—"

"All right, all right," she says, and I grab my overnight bag and start throwing shit inside it. Who cares if it's a school night? I can take the first ferry home in the morning. Or skip. I'm about to thank her, but then Kim puts her hand over the phone and says, "There's another bottle of whiskey in the basement. Go ahead and bring it up," and I realize she's talking to someone else.

"Kim? Please?" I'm whining, but I don't care. I need to get off this island tonight.

She sighs. "Sweetie, I'm not going to be done here until at least two in the morning. Just call me tomorrow when you get home from school, okay?"

"Sure, whatever," I say. I mean, yeah, Kim's busy. I get it. I get that she's twenty-three and probably over all this high school BS. But I really need her. I need somebody.

When I stop and let myself think about what happened today, I can barely even handle it. I freaking spat in Rennie's face. Pretty much the trashiest thing I could ever do. God, what must my mom think? My dad's always worried he's not raising me feminine enough, that my mom is disappointed from heaven. She was really ladylike, really gentle. She must think her daughter is a piece of shit. The lies Rennie's been telling about me since freshman year, I just proved them true.

I bet that's exactly what the witch wanted. To dig my grave and then lead me right into it. She knows my buttons. But you know what, I know her buttons too. It works both ways. No matter how shitty Rennie's been to me, and she's been plenty shitty, I've never sunk to her level. Why not? Who the eff knows. I'm realizing now that I should have put her in her place a long time ago.

I decide to go for a walk and have a smoke to clear my head. I put on my boots and head out the back door. I don't need Pat bitching at me about the dishes again. I'll do them when I get back. If I feel like it.

It's dark outside, and the driveway is full of my dad's woodworking tools, splinters, and bent nails, so I carry Shep in my arms until we reach the sidewalk. A rich couple commissioned one of Dad's hand-carved canoes before they left Jar Island at the end of summer. It'll be done by the time they come back next year.

I head straight into the woods behind my house. I brought Alex here a lot this summer. There's a clearing on the other side where you can park your car and look right out onto the ocean. It's secluded; nobody really knows about it. A hidden T-Town secret. We'd park there and listen to music, or watch the moon. We just liked hanging out with each other. I liked that I could be myself around him. And I think he felt that way too.

I walk, letting Shep sniff anything he wants, while I have a smoke. When my cigarette's burned down to the filter, I crush it underneath my boot, grinding my heel until the butt gets mixed up with the dead pine needles and the sand.

When I look up, I see it—Alex's SUV, parked in the clearing. With another girl inside.

I stumble backward into a tree, then get behind it. Who's the girl? Is it the one from his party, the one he was lying in bed with?

I squint hard. The girl is petite. Dark hair.

Oh my God. It's Nadia Cho. I taught that girl how to tie her shoelaces. That's my first thought.

And my second thought is—*Alex Lind is running game on me? With a freshman?* I don't think so. Clearly he has no idea who he's messing with.

I back up, my heart pounding hard. I reach for my cell phone. I've got one bar. What was her number? I must have dialed it a million times. Three five something something. I stare at the keypad, willing it to come back to me. Three five . . . four seven.

She picks up after four rings. "Hello?"

I keep my voice low, my eyes on his SUV. "Just so you know, your sister is in Alex Lind's car right now. In the woods!" Let's see how stealth Alex is when Lillia's chasing him down, ready to saw his balls off with a nail file.

It's quiet for a second, and then Lillia says, "Who is this?"

"It's Kat. Did you hear me? I said I'm ten feet away from your sister and Alex hooking up!"

"Kat, my sister's at home."

I squint into the dark to try to get a better look. It's hard to see, but I swear to God that it's Nadia in his SUV. "I'm not kidding you, Lillia. They're right in front of me. I wouldn't normally give two shits, except Alex and I are hooking up. Sort of."

"My sister is sitting next to me on the couch. I don't know what you're trying to do, but whatever it is, don't bother. And please don't call me again."

I open my mouth to tell her that her little sister and Alex were in bed together two nights ago, and hear a dial tone. I look again. I guess I can't be 100 percent sure it's Nadia. I mean, I thought it was, but the thing is, Lillia doesn't lie. Lillia Cho might be a lot of things, but in the years I've known her, she's never been a liar. So I guess it's not Nadia. I guess it's just some random dark-haired girl in Alex's SUV. Another girl who isn't me.

I'm in my dad's old VW Rabbit convertible, all the windows down, music blasting so loud I can't hear myself think, which is pretty much the point.

I take a lap around the island, cruising past the lighthouse on the ridge, past the big island cemetery with the creepy old family plots, then over to the one-lane airport strip, then along the marina until I'm back at the lighthouse again. There's nowhere else for me to go. The last ferry pulled out of the harbor hours ago. Otherwise I'd just show up at Kim's apartment, whether she invited me or not. But I'm trapped on this damn island, so I just keep driving that loop again and again.

Why am I even surprised? Whoever that girl is, she for sure isn't going to spit in anyone's face, she's not going to have to work a crappy job that makes her smell like fish to save up for college, no one is going to call her or her family trash. I thought I might have changed Alex's mind about me this summer. That's my bad for thinking he was different. He's not. He's just as bad as the rest of them. He bought into Rennie's lies like the rest of this stupid place.

The next time I look at the clock, it's after midnight and I've only got a quarter tank of gas left. My dad will kill me if I bring his car back on E again. There are only a few gas stations on the island, and I go straight for the one that's cheapest, over by Bow Tie, that crappy overpriced Italian restaurant in Canobie Bluffs the tourists love.

I'm pumping my gas when I look across the parking lot and see them—Reeve and Rennie and PJ and that bobble head Ashlin. No Lillia. I guess she was telling the truth. She really is at home with Nadia. Anyway, they're over by the dumpsters, Rennie's sitting on the hood of Reeve's truck, and they're passing around a wine bottle.

Alex told me about this. Rennie works at Bow Tie as a hostess, and she flirts with the bartenders and they give her free booze. She'll take it out with the trash, and after the restaurant closes up and everyone's gone home, she'll come back with her dumb-ass friends and they'll drink all night.

I should call the cops. I should, but I won't. I'm no narc.

But hopefully someone else will, because they're so loud. I can hear them from where I'm standing, every word.

Two headlights come down the road. Reeve pulls Rennie down, and they crouch behind her car, but then PJ screams out, "Alex!" and the whole group runs into the road and stops his SUV.

"Nadi!" Rennie screeches, and runs up to the passenger window. "Isn't it past your bedtime?"

I knew it. It was Nadia!

Everyone talks for a couple of seconds before Alex starts

beeping his horn to get his friends out of the way. I guess he's in a rush to get Nadia home. It's after midnight on a school night, and Mrs. Cho would kill Nadia if she caught her sneaking out. Mrs. Cho was really cool but she was also strict. Once she sent Lillia up to her room for a whole hour while Rennie and I were over swimming because she thought Lillia was being a fresh mouth.

When Alex drives off, Rennie catches me looking and points me out. She calls, "Umm, sorry, Kat. I don't think that gas station takes food stamps!"

I pretend not to hear her. I can't handle getting into it with her again today.

Reeve whoops and says, "Uh-oh, Kat! You're not going to let Rennie get away with that, are you? Come on! You're a tough guy!" He sputters into laughter. "I know I wouldn't mess with you."

Gas starts to leak out of the nozzle, and I jam the hose back into the cradle, my hand shaking. Rennie thinks that just because she goes with Lillia's family on vacations to St. Bart's or wherever the fuck, that she's on their level. But she's not. She lives in a two-bedroom condo with her single working mom. She works at Bow Tie because she has to. That Jeep she drives was a hand-me-down from her mom's married boyfriend. Rennie might try to pretend otherwise, but we both know the truth: If I'm trash, then she is too.

I'm back in my room when my phone buzzes. It's Alex.

R U awake? I'm around if you want to talk.

I whip my phone across the room. That ass. Like I'd ever speak to him again. He doesn't deserve to hang out with me, and he definitely doesn't deserve to make out with me. He associates with shit bags like Rennie and Reeve. He thinks they're quality people, and as far as I'm concerned, that makes him just as bad as they are. They make me want to barf, every last one of them. They get away with murder on this island. They just do what they want to do, and screw everyone and everything else.

Today I told that girl in the bathroom that Reeve would get his, that karma's a bitch. I meant it when I said it, but now I'm not so sure. When has Rennie ever had to pay for any of the evil shit she's done to me? Never. I'm sick of waiting for karma. Karma can suck it.

CHAPTER TEN

MARY

I'M SITTING IN CHEMISTRY CLASS, AND I FEEL DIZZY from trying to untangle Mr. Harris's blackboard notes. He's written out a bunch of numbers and letters, trying to explain the process of scientific notation. I think it's supposed to be a shorthand way to deal with infinite numbers. Only, I'm infinitely lost. I thought I was studying science, not math.

But the other kids in my class seem to have no problem following what Mr. Harris is saying. They're nodding and scribbling things down in their notebooks. It's been this way all day, in every single class except gym. It seems like the juniors in Jar Island High are smarter than me, and I should technically be a senior. I used to be smart. I always got good grades at my old school. Then my life got screwed up, and since the Reeve stuff, I've always been behind. What if the school decides to put me back another grade? I'll be eighteen and a sophomore? No. That can't happen.

I want to lay my head down on my desk and never wake up. I look over at the guy sitting next to me. Every time Mr. Harris turns around to write on the board, he carves something into his desk with the pointy end of a key. I lean closer to get a better look. It says, *EAT ME.*

After Reeve's first day at my school, I tried to steer clear of him. Which wasn't easy, because we had to ride the ferry to and from Jar Island together every day. Reeve would sit in the galley with the other passengers, and I'd go outside on the deck. Even when it started to get cold, I'd ride outside. I was fine with it. I actually like sitting on the deck, always have. But then one day when it was rainy, he saw me walking outside and called out, "Hey, Big Easy. Come here a second."

Big Easy was the nickname Reeve gave me after a social studies unit on New Orleans and Mardi Gras. It caught on with my classmates really fast. The only person who used my real name at the Montessori was my teacher. I was Big Easy to everyone else.

Who would want to eat lunch with Big Easy? Or be science partners, or have sleepovers together? Nobody. I wouldn't have wanted to be friends with me either. So how could I blame Anne for abandoning me? I couldn't, but it still hurt.

I remember exactly how his voice sounded that morning. Kind of bored. I wondered if he'd noticed me, had thought of me standing out in the rain just to keep away from him. If that was why he'd called me over. Because he felt bad.

I wish I could travel back in time and push myself out that door and into the rain. But no. I walked over, as if Big Easy was my name. I even said "Hey, Reeve," as if we were friends. And I smiled, too. I was appreciative. I was lonely.

Reeve looked up at me from his seat. After a second or two, he said, in a low voice, "Take one step to your right."

I did what I was told.

Reeve slid off the edge of his seat, and it flipped up, the same way the seats do in movie theaters. Then he crouched in front of it on the floor, his back to me, and pulled something out of his pocket.

"What are you doing?" I whispered.

Reeve didn't answer me, but I could see his shoulders start to shake up and down. I heard scratching noises.

I glanced over my shoulder. Behind me the old woman inside the snack booth was reading a newspaper, waiting for customers. I guess she felt me staring, because she lifted her head and smiled at me. I forced a smile back and then turned and pretended to be watching the storm through the windows.

That's when I knew—Reeve was using me for cover.

I didn't want to get in trouble. But also, I felt . . . useful.

When he was done, Reeve sat back on his chair. He flicked the knife open and closed with one hand. "I stole this off my brother Luke," he said.

I wasn't sure what to do, if I should walk back outside, but Reeve added breezily, "If you want, I'll show you what the different blades are for."

And he did, for the rest of the ride.

When the ferry got close to the mainland, Reeve gathered his things and left to use the bathroom. I waited for him to come back. When he didn't, I went to the window. Reeve was already off the ferry, headed up the road to school.

I took my time, walked slow, careful not to catch up.

The bell rings and the room gets noisy right away, as if the entire class has been collectively holding their breath for forty-five minutes, but now they're free to talk to each other. Everyone separates into their groups of friends and heads into the hallway, leaving me behind.

It's not that I expected to come into Jar Island High and be instantly popular. I'm not delusional or anything. At Montessori I didn't have a million friends. But there were plenty of people who talked to me. I had a place to sit during lunch. My life was perfectly fine, until Reeve showed up.

Why did I come back? What did I hope to accomplish, exactly?

It took a long time for me to get better, but I did. I got better. But suddenly it's like the last four years never happened, and I'm feeling all the same terrible feelings about myself that I did back then. I could be at home right now, with my mom and dad. Instead of here, surrounded by bad memories and no friends and the boy who made my life a living hell.

So that's it, then.

I'm leaving.

As soon as I make the decision, I feel loads lighter. I pack up my things. I walk down the hallway and see Reeve at the very end, as cocky and confident as he ever was, taking his sweet time getting wherever he needs to go.

Perfect.

I know exactly what I'm going to do. Yesterday he caught me off guard, but today I'm ready. I will get right in his face, say my name, *my real name*, out loud. Let him see for himself that he didn't break me. I'm here. And then I'll blow him a big fat kiss good-bye and put an end to this chapter of my life once and for all. No more regrets. It's no way to live.

My adrenaline is pumping as I pick up the pace and fight my way through the hallway traffic to get to him. "Reeve!" I shout down the stairs.

But he doesn't turn around. And I can't get close. There're too many people standing in my way. A wall of people.

"Hey, Reeve!" I call out again, pushing my way through. He still doesn't hear me. "Reeve!" I suck in a huge breath. "REEVE!"

A rush of something bursts forth, a wind, and the force of it makes all of the locker doors slam shut in unison. The sound fills the hallway, one big clap of metallic thunder.

Reeve stops and looks around. Everyone does.

"What the hell was that?" someone says.

"How should I know?"

"A storm?"

"Dude, we just came from running laps in gym. It's sunny outside."

The air is quiet for another second, and then the second bell rings. It brings the place back to life. Everyone goes about their business.

I spin and take off in the opposite direction. *I have to get out of here.* That's my only thought.

CHAPTER ELEVEN

LILLIA

I'M DRESSED FOR SCHOOL, LYING ON TOP OF MY BED, MY eyes wide open.

I didn't sleep last night. How could I, when I didn't know where my own sister was? Even after Alex dropped Nadia off, after I heard her tiptoe up the stairs, her door creak open and then closed, even then I couldn't sleep.

I doubt Rennie will pick me up. Not after how we left things yesterday. I wait until ten minutes to eight before I tell Nadia to get in my car, that I'm driving us today.

After that neither of us says a word to the other.

The whole ride I keep trying to find a way for this to make any kind of sense. What could they have been doing together in the middle of the night? Maybe he wanted his shirt back, and he drove her over to Janelle's to pick it up. Maybe I made Nadia feel so guilty, she wanted to go apologize to him for spilling her strawberry daiquiri everywhere, because some might have gotten on his carpet or something. Or maybe they were planning me a surprise birthday party. In the middle of the night. In the woods.

Alex Lind and my little sister. I don't even want to think about it. Because when I do, I feel so mad, I can barely breathe.

Homeroom bell is about to ring when Rennie appears behind my locker door. She's wearing a loose scoop neck top that hangs off one shoulder, leggings, and gladiator sandals, and she's holding out two Blow Pops like they're a bouquet of flowers. "Peace offering," she says. "One for you, one for me."

"No, thanks." Does she honestly think that a Blow Pop is going to make it all better? If she hadn't dragged me off to that party, none of this would have happened.

"I tried calling your cell yesterday," she says. "Guess you were in a dead spot."

Practically the entire island is a dead spot. "Well, I had no missed calls. Why didn't you try my house?"

I can tell she's trying to think up another lie. But I guess nothing comes to mind. She bites her lip. "Okay. Real apology. I'm sorry I left like that yesterday. It wasn't cool. But come on! This is weird. You and I never fight." She leans against the locker next to mine and looks at me, concerned. "I know things have been kinda crazy the last few days, but I promise you, senior year is still going to be awesome."

I take the Blow Pop and slowly unwrap it. I don't even care about senior year anymore.

"So are we cool?"

When I look up, I notice that Kat's lingering in the stairwell, watching me.

"Yes," I say quickly to Rennie. "We're cool."

"Sweet. Will you come with me to Mrs. Gismond's room? I need to drop off my science lab."

I look over Rennie's shoulder. Kat mouths, *We need to talk*, and my stomach turns over.

I say, "Actually, I have to take something over to the office. I'll meet you in homeroom, okay?"

Rennie nods and gives me a peck on the cheek. "See you in a few."

I watch her go. As she passes Kat's locker, she opens it up and tosses her half-licked Blow Pop inside, like it's a trash can.

As soon as she turns the corner, I walk up to Kat and say, "What do you want?"

"Not here." Kat looks around. "I know a place where we can talk in private," she says, like some Mafia don beckoning me into her study.

I let out a sigh. "Seriously, Kat. You need to quit doing drugs. They're destroying your brain. We're not friends, remember? We haven't been for a really long time. So I don't want you calling me, I don't want you trying to talk to me at school. I'm sorry Alex played you for sex, but—"

"I didn't have sex with Alex!"

I shrug. "Okay, but he clearly isn't interested in you, because he's with someone else. But that person is *not* my sister."

Kat groans. "Look, I don't know why you're playing dumb. Alex drove Nadia to hang out with all your friends at the Bow Tie parking lot last night after their little hookup."

What?

Kat continues, but her words come slower and she's watching me really closely. Which is not good, because I am barely holding it together right now. "Nadia and Alex drove up in his SUV, and Rennie ran up to the window and kissed her hello."

I want to say something, I want to tell Kat she's dead wrong, but I can't make words.

Something blooms on Kat's face. A smugness. "Oh. Rennie didn't tell you they were all hanging out together?" She taps her lips with her pointer finger. "Gee. That's weird."

"I'm done talking about this." I start to walk away, but Kat reaches out and stops me.

She says, "We both know it, Lillia." There's something about the way Kat says my name—sad, mad, a bit pleading. "We both know how Rennie is."

It's the pleading in her voice that makes me bite my lip and give her the slightest nod. Then she lets me go.

It's not even five o'clock yet, and the sun is already moving away. Squinting, I tilt my chin up so I can feel the sunlight on my cheeks.

"You want my sunglasses?" Rennie asks from the pool. "They're on top of my clothes." Ashlin's hanging between two pool noodles, and Rennie's stretched out on a raft, and she's got one arm holding on to the side of the pool so she doesn't float away.

"No, thanks," I say.

"Lil, you should wear sunglasses, or else you'll get crow's-feet."

I shake my head. I never wear sunglasses. I don't want to make it feel darker out than it is. I want it to be daytime for as long as possible.

We're at my house, hanging out by the pool. I asked Rennie to come over so we could talk, but then she invited Ashlin.

I'm lying on a lounge chair, trying to figure out what I'm going to say to Rennie. I'll ask her to stay longer when Ash leaves, and I'll give her the chance to explain herself, to tell me what the hell is going on between Alex and Nadia, but then that's it. We're done.

I'm going over it again in my mind when I hear music growing louder. Bass. I put my sweater on over my two-piece and walk to the gate. Through the slats I watch as Alex's SUV pulls into my driveway, with Reeve, Derek, and PJ inside.

I spin around. Rennie's already paddling her arms to get to the ladder.

"Why did you invite them?"

She shakes her head, like I'm being ridiculous. "Reeve texted me before practice and asked what I was doing. So . . . I told him. Why?"

If Nadia was home, I would lock the gate. But she's not. She went to her friend's house to work on cheer routines.

The boys come in, sweaty and grass-stained from practice.

Ashlin runs up and hugs Derek, but quickly peels herself off him. "Eww. You guys stink."

Reeve grins at PJ, and in a second they both strip down to their boxers and dive into the pool. Derek cannonballs behind them, and then Ashlin and Rennie hold hands and jump in too.

As soon as they hit, Alex takes a seat on one of the lounge chairs. Not exactly near me, but definitely closer than I want him to be. I put Rennie's sunglasses on after all, to hide how angry I am.

My mom must hear the splashing, because she comes out the patio door. Right away Reeve and PJ chorus from the pool, "Hi, Mrs. Cho!"

"Hi, boys!" Then she notices Alex sitting by me. "Alex! How are you?" She loves Alex.

He stands up like the fake gentleman he is. "Hi, Mrs. Cho. Did you get your hair cut? It looks nice."

My mom beams at me like, *Wow, isn't he something?* Yeah, he's something all right. "As a matter of fact, I did. Thank you for noticing, Alex."

I keep expecting Alex to try to make eye contact with me. But he doesn't. He looks everywhere but at me. Maybe he's still mad at me. Or maybe it's his guilty conscience.

When my mom goes back inside, the guys come out of the water. Like a king Reeve goes, "Somebody towel me up."

Rennie says, "Lil, you have towels for them, right?"

"Actually, no," I say. "Our housekeeper is doing the wash right now. The most I could give you is a dishrag. Or paper towels. Sorry."

Ashlin and Rennie share a look. PJ makes a sad face at me and starts to shiver. I roll my eyes and throw him my towel. PJ gives me a big smile. "Thanks, Lil!"

"Yeah, thanks a lot," Reeve says.

Ashlin lets Derek borrow her towel. Rennie holds out hers for Reeve, but he declines the offer. Instead he just runs his hands over his abs, wicking away the water, and grabs his clothes. "There's a real shortage of hospitality up in here. You ready, Alex?"

"Yup."

I walk over and open the gate for them. "Bye," I say.

Reeve makes a peace sign at me and leaves, shaking his head. Since when is Reeve Tabatsky the authority on manners? I've seen him pick food out of the garbage. It was at Alex's house, but still.

The boys file out behind Reeve, and Rennie and Ashlin go inside to change. I get up and lean against the fence. That's when I overhear a conversation on the other side. Because Alex hasn't left yet. His SUV is still in my driveway.

I hear Reeve say, "God, Cho is such a bitch. Do you think she knows that you and Nadia had a sleepover?"

I gasp.

"No way. Nadia swore to her that she slept at that girl Janelle's house. There's no way she'd tell her."

"You'd better hope not," Derek says.

Then Reeve says, "Bro, what are you even getting out of all this? I say you just stick with DeBrassio. I give that girl respect. She knows what kind of girl she is."

Alex starts his SUV. "I know what I'm doing."

Rennie comes up behind me and puts her hand on my shoulder. I jump, and say, "Hey. Where's Ash?"

"She's peeing. Lil, I don't know how else to say this to you, but . . . you need to get it together."

"What do you mean?" My mind is still racing. Nadia slept over at a boy's house. Not just any boy. Lindy. Someone I thought was my friend. Who'd never do something like that. I don't know why I've been so naive. Boys, they aren't to be trusted. Not any of them.

"Those guys are our friends, and you don't want to give them a towel? Today is Wednesday. Carlota isn't even here today. I wasn't going to call you out in front of everyone, but come on." She looks around before lowering her voice. "Lil, you need to chill, or people are going to figure out something's wrong."

I can't think straight. I lean against the fence, use it to hold myself up. "You're right," I manage to say. I'll tell her whatever I have to, just to shut her up.

But she doesn't. Her eyes light up. "OMG! I didn't even tell you what happened at Bow Tie last night."

This is it. Finally. "What?"

"Reeve and I kissed! I mean, it was only for a second. He pulled away and told me that I was too important to him to just be a random hookup. Isn't that the sweetest thing you've ever heard? I'm telling you, we're like *this close* to being an official couple." She does a spin, like she's already wearing her wedding dress.

I force a smile. "You guys are perfect for each other. Honestly."

After dinner I hear Nadia in the den, watching television, but I don't join her. I could barely stand to look at her from across the kitchen table. I go straight up to my room, lie down on my bed, and wonder what I'm going to do now that I can't trust anyone.

My phone buzzes, and I reach over to my nightstand to pick it up. It's a text from a number I don't recognize.

This is Karma. I'm a bitch. Can you think of anyone who deserves a bitch slap?

Oh, yes, I can. I can think of a few.

My phone buzzes again.

If so, meet at Judy Blue Eyes, 2am. If not, sit back and enjoy the show.

That's what Kat always said she'd name her boat if she ever got one. After her mom. It was Judy's favorite song.

CHAPTER TWELVE

MARY

IT WASN'T ME. IT COULDN'T HAVE BEEN ME.

Whatever happened back at school, whatever that was—I don't even want to think about it. I just want out of here. Off this island, away from Reeve and everything that reminds me of him and who I used to be.

When I get home, Aunt Bette's Volvo is in the driveway. I quietly set my bike down on the front lawn and walk backward, toward the street. Forget my dresses, my clothes. Aunt Bette can send me everything later. All I know is that I need to be on the next ferry out of here.

At the curb I turn and give the house one last look. I try to memorize the exact shade of gray the cedar shingles are, like the sky right before a summer storm. I count the white shutters bolted to each of the windows. Twelve. I trace the curve of the cobblestone walk through the air with my finger. I take it in, because this is the last time I'll ever see this house again. I'm not ever coming back here. Never.

Then I take a deep breath and start the downhill walk toward the ferry, fighting back tears the whole way. I was crazy to think that Reeve would ever apologize for the terrible things he did to me. I always hoped, somewhere deep down inside, that I mattered to him. That, despite everything, there was something real between us. That he cared about me. That he was sorry for what he did.

I know now, I know for sure, that I was wrong. He's never going to apologize to me, or acknowledge what he did. And so there's no reason for me to stay.

My heart is pounding in my chest as I reach the ferry dock. I'm panting too hard to talk, so when I get to the ticket window, I stand a bit off to the side to give myself a chance to catch my breath. I watch from the shore as one boat docks and lets its passengers on. A woman behind me takes my place in line. She tries to buy a ticket, but the four p.m. ride is sold out. The earliest she can get on is the six p.m.

It gets darker. More people line up to buy tickets, but I don't make a move. I stand and watch and wait. I want to go back in line and buy my ticket. I want to so badly. Everything inside me is screaming *Go, go, go, go*. But I can't. Something's holding me back. Something's keeping me here.

What is happening to me?

CHAPTER THIRTEEN

KAT

THE SKY IS BLACK. I'VE GOT THE TOP DOWN ON DAD'S convertible, and the clock on the dashboard reads a quarter to two in the morning.

I check my cell phone one last time before chucking it into the backseat. No calls, no texts. Nothing. She's not coming.

Why am I such an idiot?

I should have kept this whole revenge idea to myself. Revenge is supposed to be a solitary thing. I think I heard that somewhere. And I don't know what help I thought Lillia could give me. Her mind can't go to the dark places mine does. She's way too pure for that. And even with whatever's going on between Lillia and Rennie, there's no way Lillia would ever betray her. Actually, knowing Lillia, she's probably reading my text out loud and Rennie's laughing her ass off. I got too excited, and now look. I'm going to be done before I even get started.

Screw this. I'm just gonna go home and work on my early decision app to Oberlin. That's the only thing that will get me through this year—the thought of finally getting off this island for good.

I pull into the ferry parking lot to turn around. The lights are off, the place is cleared out, except for one girl sitting on the curb. She's got her elbows on her knees, her head in her hands, and her blond hair over one shoulder.

I think about cruising right past her, but something makes me slow down. As I get close, I see that it's the girl from the bathroom.

"Bathroom girl," I say, pulling to a stop.

"My name's Mary," she says. She's chewing on a piece of hair.

"I know," I lie. "I was being funny." I shake my head and start over. "What the hell are you doing out so late?"

Her eyes are wide and frantic. "I have to get off the island."

"Well, you know it's almost two in the morning, right? There's not going to be another ferry until tomorrow. You missed the last one by, like, three hours."

Mary doesn't say anything. She just stares off toward the piers. You can hardly tell water from the sky. Everything's black. "I think I'm losing my mind."

She says it, and honestly, I believe her. This girl is totally weird. But I should get down to the yacht club. On the minuscule chance that Lillia does show up, I need to be there. "Do you want a ride home or something?" I ask Mary, hoping her answer is no.

"I'm just going to wait. Maybe I'll get up the guts to leave by the morning."

"You're going to sit here all night?"

"It's only a few more hours. And then I never have to see this place again."

"Where's all your stuff? Didn't you move here with anything?"

"I—I'll get it some other time."

This is crazy. Girlfriend is full-on freaking out. "Is this about Reeve?"

Mary lowers her eyes. "It's always been about Reeve."

I'm about to say, *Eff him*—but before I can, I see Lillia's silver Audi fly down the road and take the first right into the yacht club parking lot. I can't believe it. She showed. She actually showed.

"Get in," I tell Mary, because I might be a bitch, but I'm not going to leave her here alone in the dark.

"I—"

"Hurry up!"

For a second Mary looks like she's going to argue with me. If she does, I'm out of here. I don't have time to baby her ass. Lillia might not even get out of the car if she doesn't see me there. Mary hesitates, and then she tries to open the door, but it's stuck. "It's locked."

"Let go of the handle," I say, and push the unlock button, but when Mary tries the door, it still won't open. God. "Just hop in, all right!"

"Who are you chasing?" she asks as I gun it to close the distance between us and Lillia's taillights.

I don't answer her. I just drive.

When we get into the parking lot, Lillia's standing by her car. She's got on a tight hooded sweatshirt, rolled-up pajama shorts with pink and red hearts on them, and flip-flops. Her hair is pulled up into a long ponytail. I think, from the way the moon hits it, that it's wet. She must have just taken her bath. That's a weird thing about Lillia. She always took a bath every night like a kid. I guess some things don't change.

"You're late, Kat," she says. Then she notices Mary with me, and her grip tightens around her car keys.

I hurry out of the car and walk over. I'm excited and relieved that Lillia's here but trying to hide it. "She needed a ride," I whisper. "Don't worry. It's cool."

"Kat—" Lillia's giving me the evil eye. "I'm not saying anything in front of her!"

I guess Mary can hear us, because she calls out, "It's fine. I can go." She climbs out of my car.

I hold up my hand for Lillia to give me a second, and I look back at Mary. I say, "Leave Jar Island tomorrow morning like a scared little baby?"

"I *am* scared. I'm scared out of my mind."

"Of Reeve Tabatsky?" I'm actually pissed now. This girl needs to get a backbone, stat. "He ain't shit. I won't let him touch you."

"That's not what I'm worried about." Mary covers her face with her hands. "It's me. I'm the problem. I—I just can't get over it. I can't move on."

"Well, yeah. You don't have any closure. The wrong hasn't been made right. Reeve's never gotten what's coming to him."

Lillia shakes her head. "Forget this. I'm out." She clicks her car alarm. The headlights flash on and off like a lighthouse, and the doors unlock.

I sidle up to her car door and cover the handle with my back so she can't open it. "Don't leave now. You wouldn't have come here if you didn't want to get Alex as badly as I want to get Rennie."

Mary slowly approaches us. "What did Alex do to you?"

Lillia hesitates before saying, "He didn't do anything to me. He did something to my sister."

Yeah, Nadia and me both. Not that I'm scarred or anything. It was just a stupid hookup. It could have been more, but he screwed that up. I'm over it. Almost.

Mary says, "I'm sorry. I really didn't mean to intrude. I'm going to go. And listen, I promise I won't tell a soul. You can trust me. I know more than maybe anyone else on the island how this kind of thing can weigh you down. I just . . . I think it's really cool you both are going to do something about it." She turns around and starts walking away, back toward the ferry. "Good luck."

Lillia and I look at each other. "Wait!" I call out. Mary turns around. "You want in on this, Mary? Help us . . . and we'll help you take down Reeve." I'm afraid to look at Lillia, because I know she's probably pissed at me right now. But she doesn't say anything. And she doesn't leave, either.

"Why would you do that? You don't even know me."

Mary's staring at me all intense and unblinking, and it throws me off. It takes me a sec to recover. I say, "I don't have to know you to see that you're a total mess over whatever happened, like, years ago. And, hey, it wouldn't be a free ride. You'd have to get your hands dirty too. But we'd be in it together. The three of us."

Mary looks at me and Lillia for a long moment. So long that I start to get antsy. At last she says, "If you help me get Reeve, I'll do whatever you want."

Lillia doesn't move. Her lips are tight and she's shaking her head. "I don't know."

"Think about it," I tell her. I'm so psyched, I'm practically bouncing on my toes. "Mary's new. No one even knows her, much less suspects her. Plus, with one other person, it'll be easier on both of us." She doesn't look convinced. I throw my hands into the air and say, "You trusted me enough to come here, didn't you? All you have to do is trust me just a little bit more. I've got a good feeling about this."

Biting her lip, Lillia says, "So we're going to get revenge on Rennie, Alex, and now Reeve? You're basically asking me to take down everyone in my group."

Maybe you shouldn't be friends with such assholes is right there on the tip of my tongue. But I swallow that down and go with diplomacy. "I hear you," I say, nodding. "You've got the most to lose. I get that. So we'll take care of Alex first." Pointing, I say, "Let's go scheme where we're not out in the open. My boat's parked down that way."

Immediately Lillia says, "No way, Kat."

"You still haven't learned to swim yet, Lil?" I tease.

She flushes. "I just don't see the point."

"It'll be safer if we talk on the water, " I say. "No chance of anyone overhearing us."

Lillia rolls her eyes and unfolds her arms to gesture around. "Who's going to hear us?"

Lillia Cho. Always thinks she knows best. "Lots of rich old men bring their mistresses here," I say. "And also, security. And cops. I mean, if you're willing to risk getting arrested, I—"

"Maybe you should have picked a better place," Lillia snarks back.

"Let's just go to the boat," Mary says. "I mean, we're here now."

"Fine," Lillia groans.

I lead the way along the dock, with the moon at my back. Mary's next to me, and Lillia a few steps behind.

As we walk, my mind is racing with possibilities. How we can do this, what will be the best way to get started. I've already given it some thought, just in case Lillia did show up tonight. But now that Mary's in the mix too, I've got to make a few quick adjustments. All I know is that I have to seem prepared, for Lillia's sake, to put her mind at ease. That girl is as skittish as a cat in a thunderstorm. One hiccup and she'll bolt.

When Mary asks me if I own one of these boats, pointing at the souped-up yachts, I barely hear her. She has to ask me again. Shaking my head, I say, "Not exactly."

Because I work at the club, I get to park my boat for free. But not here with these boats, obviously. Mine's tied up back behind the gas pumps on an older stretch of dock where my boss keeps his junkers, the broken old boats he's bought cheap to strip for parts.

"Be careful," I tell them. "The planks along this dock are half-rotted, and there's lots of rusted nail heads poking up through the cracks. I think I still have a splinter stuck in my heel. This jerk pulled his yacht in too fast and made a wake so big that it rocked me right off my boat."

"That sucks," Mary says.

I nod. "And he barely even said sorry. Rich people never say sorry."

Lillia rolls her eyes but keeps her mouth shut.

I take the tarp off my Catalina daysailer, fold it up, and put it in the hatch. It's been a while since I've had it out on the water. Maybe not even since June, which is crazy. But the thing is, Alex and I would always hang out on his boat, because it had a fridge to keep our drinks cool and leather bucket seats that reclined, and an amazing stereo system. For some weird reason I feel guilty about this. About forgetting who I was before I met him. The things that used to be important to me. Fixing up my boat, hanging out with my real friends. I never thought I'd be one of those girls, those girls that compromise who they are just for a guy. Especially some two-timing wannabe player like Alex Lind.

"Get in," I say, hooking my floodlight up to the battery. It sends a bright beam out through the night, lighting up the caps of the waves. Perfect.

Lillia takes one step on board and freezes as the boat sways. Then she hops off like a scared bunny rabbit. She almost backs right into Mary, who looks nervous too. Crossing her arms, Lillia says, "Let's just talk out here."

Laughing, I say, "I've been sailing ever since I was old enough to turn the steering wheel on my own, for God's sakes! I feel safer driving this than a car."

"I said I'm not getting on that thing," Lillia snaps. "Either we talk out here or I leave."

Under my breath I mutter "Diva," unhook my floodlight, and then join them on the dock.

The three of us sit in a semicircle.

It hits me right then that I've already won. Because Rennie's best friend is sitting here right now, pledging to help me take her down. And Alex is going to get his, too. I could give two shits about Reeve, but it'll be nice to see him get what's coming to him. It's like a freaking three-for-one deal.

I stretch my legs out in front of me. "We've got to set some ground rules. First off, I think each of us has to participate in all three acts of revenge. That way no one can back out or blame someone else."

"Obviously," Lillia says.

I shoot her a look but keep going. "Second, we can't be seen talking to each other in public. Ever."

Mary nods. "Yeah. I guess that makes sense."

I continue, "In fact, I even think texting each other is too risky. Lillia, what if Rennie picked up your phone and saw my number?"

Lillia looks down at her lap. "Not that Rennie's, like, snooping around on my phone, but yeah, I guess you have a point. We're going to have to be careful."

"We have to be *more* than careful," I say. "No one can ever know what we're up to. What we do together lives and dies with us." Then I clear my throat, because this is the most important part. "And if we're really going to do this, no one can bail halfway through. If you're in, you need to be in until the very end. Until we all get what we want. If not, well . . . consider yourself fair game. It'll be open season, and we'll have a hell of a lot of ammo to use against you. If you can't swear to that, we might as well just pretend like tonight never happened."

Mary nods first, then Lillia. I smile, because, holy shit, we're doing this.

"All right, then," I say. "I think that's it. Now we just have to figure out what we're going to do to Rennie, Alex, and Reeve."

"Alex first," Lillia corrects.

We look at each other. No one's saying anything.

"So what's the plan?" Lillia asks.

"Don't expect me to do the heavy lifting," I say, defensive. "I just came up with the rules!"

Lillia purses her lips. "Are you serious? I thought you'd be all over this. I figured you'd already have, like, a notebook with everybody you hate and lists of things you'll do to get back at them." She actually sounds disappointed, which gives me a weird sense of pride.

Off the top of my head, I start riffing. "Okay, well, Alex is obsessed with his SUV. We could spray paint it, mess with the engine—"

"Not big enough," Lillia interrupts.

Mary asks, "Does he have a pet or something? We could kidnap it . . . and kill it!" Lillia and I exchange a horrified look as Mary giggles. "I'm just kidding about that last part. I love animals!"

I keep going. "We could hack into the school computer and mess with his grades. Make it so the only college that will take him is Jar Island CC. His dad will beat his ass if he doesn't get into an Ivy."

Lillia sighs and says, "I don't know how to hack into anything, and I doubt you do either, Kat. Do you, Mary?"

Mary shakes her head.

"I think I have a better idea," Lillia says. I start to bristle, but she goes on. "I want to make it so no Jar Island girl will ever hook up with Alex Lind again. So . . . how do we make that happen?" There's something about the way Lillia says it. Leaning forward in the dark, her eyes are wide open and calm. She means business.

"Hell yeah!" I clap my hands. I can't help myself.

CHAPTER FOURTEEN
LILLIA

AFTER CHEER PRACTICE ON FRIDAY, RENNIE LOOPS HER arm through mine as we walk together through the parking lot. "So, what do you want to do tonight?"

"Oh, you aren't working?" I'd figured she was. I'd hoped she was.

Rennie shakes her head. "Terri said she'd switch with me. I want to do something fun!" She says this last part in her baby voice.

"Hmm," I say, pretending to think. But I just want to go

home, lie on my bed, and dream up more stuff to do to Alex. I kept zoning out in class, imagining how amazing it will feel when we start messing with him. It's, like, therapeutic. I haven't been this happy since . . . well . . . for a while.

During lunch yesterday Rennie noticed me smiling to myself and asked, "What're you all smiley about?" I almost choked on my chicken wrap. I've never had to keep a secret this big before. When my mom planned a surprise fiftieth birthday party for my dad, I worried so much I'd spill the beans that I had a stomachache for two weeks. When my dad tucked me in at night, I would be thinking, *Don't say anything, Don't say anything.* I had this fear that it would just come out because I was concentrating so hard on keeping it to myself.

But I managed to pull it off. I told Rennie I was thinking about where we'd take our graduation trip to in May. That's always been our plan. Go somewhere together, just her and me. I said, "Fiji could be awesome. Or the Maldives."

I'm never going to look at Rennie the same way again, but in a way I'm glad not to have to do anything about that just yet. My true beef is with Alex, and that's where I'm focusing all my attention.

Part of me—the nostalgic part, I guess—wishes I could tell

Rennie what I'm up to. She'd get a big kick out of what we're doing. I bet she'd think of lots of sick, twisted things we could do to Alex, things I'd never come up with in a million years. But of course I can't say anything. Because when we're done with Alex, Rennie's next.

For now I just need to keep playing it cool. The more normal I seem to everyone, the less they'll suspect that I'm behind anything. That is essential. No one can find out. Ever.

Rennie asks, "You want to come eat dinner over at my house, and we can figure it out there?"

I smile and say, "Totally."

I leave my car in the school parking lot, and Rennie drives us to her condo in the Jeep. Her complex is called The Gulls, and the sign is lit up by spotlights. The front entrance is nicely manicured, with flowers and some big bushes of sea grass. But when you pass that and get to the gate, it's a lot less nice. You used to have to punch a code to get in, but the gate has been broken all summer. It's tied open with rope. Ever since there were a few break-ins at The Gulls last spring, my dad doesn't like me coming here.

"Someone should fix that gate," I say as we drive through. I dig a grape lollipop out of my purse and unwrap it. Then I offer it to Rennie for first lick. She shakes her head and I add, "It's not safe. Anyone could just come in."

Rennie shrugs. "The management here sucks. Remember how long it took us to get the shower fixed? Mom's been talking about moving off island again once this year is over."

I stop sucking on my lollipop. "Seriously?"

"Hello! She wanted to move us last spring, when they raised our rent."

I remember. We cried and begged Ms. Holtz to change her mind. We even came up with a plan for Rennie to live with me for senior year. Ms. Holtz finally gave in when she saw how dead set Rennie was on staying.

"Anyway, now she's dating some guy on the mainland. Rick the restauranteur." Rennie makes a face. "He owns a sub shop or something tacky like that. My mom's there, like, every weekend, and she's spending a fortune on ferry tickets. And she's been looking into a real estate class. I bet she breaks her lease on the gallery before June."

"Your mom loves the gallery too much to let it go."

"She does love it, but things have been super-tight lately," Rennie says. "Don't forget I just turned eighteen. That was the end of child support checks from my DBD."

I stay quiet. I never quite know what to say when Rennie brings up her dad. He left when she was three, and she's only seen him twice since then. He used to call on her birthday, but not since he got remarried and had kids. Now he's out in Arizona someplace. Rennie hardly ever talks about him, and when she does, she calls him her DBD—deadbeat dad.

She sighs. "It's just crazy that when we're both on Thanksgiving break from college next year, we won't be living ten minutes away from each other. There'll be an ocean between us."

"You're not moving to another country," I point out, relieved she's not talking about money or her dad anymore. "The ferry ride is no big deal."

"It's a huge deal, and you know it," Rennie says. "Everything will change."

I was thinking about this even before things got so messed up between us. When we go away to college, we'll drift apart. We won't need each other so much anymore. Maybe that's a good thing. If Rennie's not home for breaks, it will just make it easier.

In the complex there are three identical buildings positioned around a small pool in the center courtyard. We walk around it on our way to the front door of Rennie's building. As long as Rennie's lived here, I've never gone into the pool. It feels weird, to swim in front of a hundred people's kitchen windows. And my pool is, like, three times the size. So we always just swim at my house.

Rennie's fumbling for her keys when the door to her condo swings open. Ms. Holtz has her hair blown out smooth, and she's in a gray and white wrap dress, a big chunky beaded necklace, and silver hoop earrings. "How do I look?" She does a spin.

"Cute!" Rennie squints. "But you need different lipstick. Something brighter."

"And I think the tag is still on," I say. I go to the silverware drawer, get the scissors, and clip it for her.

"I should tell your mom about this shop, Lillia," Ms. Holtz says. "It's full of deals on designer clothes. Check the tag. This is a five-hundred-dollar Diane von Furstenberg dress that I got for sixty bucks!"

Rennie groans. "I already told you, Mom. That print is, like, from two years ago. Right, Lil?"

"I'm not sure," I say, even though Rennie's right. My mom has it in the blouse version. She doesn't wear it anymore, though. "It looks great on you."

"Thanks, hon." Ms. Holtz spins me toward her and gives two air kisses, one on each of my cheeks. "Hey! You girls should stop by the gallery tonight. I'm showing an amazing local artist who makes stained glass representations of water." I guess neither Rennie or I look that excited about that, because she adds, "I'll let you two drink some wine if you promise to stay hidden in the back room."

"Maybe," Rennie says, but she gives me a secret look that says *No way*. The booze isn't even a pull. First off, wine is gross. Second, Rennie has at least three bottles of vanilla vodka hidden under her bed. She gets them from the bartenders at Bow Tie.

Ms. Holtz orders us a pizza—half mushroom and onion for Rennie, half cheese for me. Rennie and I go into her room to do our nails while we wait. I pick Ballet Slipper. It's light pink, so pale that it's almost white. Rennie picks Cha Cha, a fiery orange. When her nails dry, she goes to take a shower. I flop onto her bed.

An entire wall of Rennie's room is dedicated to our friendship. There are pictures of Ashlin and Reeve and everybody, but it's mostly us. We are at the center of it all. The strip of pictures we took in a photo booth at the fair one year, a subway card from when my mom took us to New York for my fourteenth birthday. The Broadway Playbill from the same trip. I feel sad looking at it. Like the memories are from a long, long time ago.

Ms. Holtz sticks her head in the door. "Pizza's here, Lil."

"Okay," I say, and beam her a big cheerful smile. "Thanks, Paige." I feel a little weird calling Rennie's mom Paige, but she always insists.

Instead of leaving she slouches against the doorway. "I'm so glad you came over tonight. It's funny I was just saying to Ren this morning, 'I haven't seen my Lillia in forever!'" It's been a week, which wouldn't be strange, except Rennie and I practically live together, we hang out that much. There's a pause, and I'm not sure if Ms. Holtz expects me to explain. But then she says with a funny laugh, "Don't look so scared, honey! I'm not mad at you! I know how busy you girls get with school and cheering."

I nod, like that's the reason exactly.

"You know I love you. You're my favorite of all Rennie's friends, hon. I just want you girls to always stay close."

I nod again. Ms. Holtz tells me all the time how I'm her favorite of Rennie's friends. I mean, it's a nice compliment, but today something about it makes me feel uncomfortable. Or maybe that's my own guilty conscience.

Rennie comes in with two towels, one wrapped around her body and one around her head.

"Pizza's here, Ren," Ms. Holtz says.

"Cool. Thanks, Mom. Have a good night!" Rennie practically closes the door in her mom's face.

She takes the towel off her head and flings it onto the bed. She has to unplug her air conditioner to have an open outlet for her hair dryer. I go open the window so her room won't get too hot. She sits on the floor in front of the mirror hanging on the back of her bedroom door and starts blowing out her hair with a round brush.

"So, what are we doing tonight?" she asks.

I climb off her bed and crawl on my knees over to her. "Let's go to the movies. We haven't been to a movie in, like, forever." That's what Rennie and I would do whenever it rained. This summer there were a million sunny days. Tonight I want to go so I won't have to talk to her or look at her.

"Ooh! Yeah. You want to make it a girls' night? Me, you, and Ash?"

"No. Call the boys." I have to say it, because that's old Lillia. And that's who I need to be.

"Just Reeve and PJ? Or should we call Alex, too? Is he done with his hissy fit about us bailing on his party?"

"I'm sure he's over it by now." I start to braid my hair. "Besides, who else is going to buy me candy?"

Rennie falls backward laughing, and in the process topples me over with her. She starts squeezing my knee, and I can't help but crack up, because I'm so ticklish. Then Rennie rolls on her side and smiles at me. "Lil," she says, before letting out a sigh. "I'm so glad . . ." I don't know if she expects me to finish her sentence or what, but when I don't, she lies back down and says, without looking at me, "You're making the right decision. Letting it go."

I dig my nails into the palm of my hand and feel the almost-dry polish curdle against my skin. "I know," I say, my eyes closed tight.

I woke up to Rennie shaking my shoulder. "Get up, Lillia. Get up!"

It was dark. I was lying on a leather couch, my legs hanging off the side. My tank top and my shorts were gone. I was just wearing my one-piece bathing suit. "What's happening?" I croaked. My mouth felt dry and cottony, and my head was spinning.

Rennie, her eyes as big as I've ever seen them, leaned in close to my face and whispered, "Shh!" Her breath reeked of tequila. She had her shoes in her hands. "We're getting out of here."

I sat up on the couch, and the room was spinning. I was still drunk. Someone was lying in the bed, asleep. My guy, Mike, wasn't in the room. I didn't know where he was.

Rennie was on her hands and knees, feeling around in the dark for my shirt. She found it over by the desk. I quickly slid it over my head, and found my shorts behind one of the couch cushions. Rennie opened the bedroom door a crack, keeping her eyes on the boy in the bed. She let me out first.

The house was totally wrecked. A couple of people were asleep in the rooms we passed, and on a pullout couch in the living room. I didn't even breathe. I was running for the door, and Rennie was right behind me.

We didn't stop running until we were down the driveway. I fell into the mailbox, heaving for breath. Rennie crouched down and put her heels on. I stood next to her, trying to remember what just happened. Where the night went. Everything was blurry in my head.

But then I remembered. Taking the shots of tequila. Following the guys up to the bedroom. They said we were going to watch a movie. Mike, kissing my neck. Picking me up, putting me on the desk. I kissed him back. I liked it. Then I didn't. I said no. I think I said no. Didn't he hear me?

I felt the bile rise in my throat. "I think I'm going to be sick." I started to dry heave, and Rennie guided me over to the curb.

I threw up everything.

"You need to walk," Rennie told me. "My Jeep's blocked in the driveway."

"No!" I said. I was already crying. "We can't walk all the way to T-Town from here! It's too far."

"We have to." She didn't sound sympathetic. She started walking. "Let's go."

I didn't say anything for the first mile or so. I just cried. Rennie stayed a few steps ahead of me, her back ramrod straight. My feet were hurting so bad in my sandals, but I couldn't take them off. There was broken glass on the road. A couple cars drove by, and I wondered if they would stop for us. But they didn't. They didn't even slow down.

I threw up one more time in the grass. Rennie came over and pounded me on the back. "I can't walk anymore," I said, hugging my arms to me.

"Yes, you can. It's not that far."

Rennie started to walk again, but this time I didn't move. "We have to call someone. I think—I think I need to go to the hospital. I think Mike put something in my drink."

"He didn't put anything in your drink." Her hair was whipping around her face from the wind. "You just had too much, that's all."

"That's not all! He—I didn't . . ." I was crying hard, so hard that the tears were going in my mouth. "I could have an STD! I could be pregnant!"

Rennie shook her head. "He used a condom. Don't worry." She looked away. "He came over and asked Ian for one."

"Oh my God. Oh my God." I said it over and over. Like a prayer. A prayer for this to be a nightmare, to wake up and not be here. Anywhere but here.

"Lil, you need to—"

"Did you have sex with Ian?"

"Yeah." She said it softly.

"Why didn't you help me?" I wept. I remembered now, calling out her name. I saw her with Ian in the bed. Mike was kissing me down my neck, pulling the front of my bathing suit as low as it would go. I called out "Rennie." Then I blacked out.

"You were fine! You were having a good time." She started walking away from me.

I ran up to her and grabbed her arm. "No, I wasn't! You knew I didn't want it to happen this way!" With a boy I barely knew, in the same room as my best friend, so drunk I could barely keep my head up. My first time was supposed to be special. With someone I loved. I'd barely fooled around with anybody before. I'd only ever kissed three boys total.

Rennie shook me off. Her eyes were hard diamonds. "Things got out of hand. But we both knew what was going to happen when we went upstairs with them."

"I didn't know!" I screamed it so loud, my throat burned.

"Come on, Lillia! You were in it just as much as I was. No one poured those shots down your throat."

"It—it wasn't supposed to happen like that. Not to me."

Rennie curled her lip. "But it was okay for me? I might not be a virgin, but I'm no slut." I was crying too hard to answer her, and she sighed and said, "Look, it happened but it's over. Let's just forget it."

"I can't," I said, my shoulders shaking. "I mean, what if people find out? What if we see those guys again?" The thought of running into Mike somewhere on the island made me want to die.

Rennie shook her head and put her hands on my shoulders. "They were only renting for the week, remember? They'll be gone by this afternoon." She locked eyes with me. "I'm not saying anything. You're not saying anything. No one will ever know."

It was light out by the time we got to Rennie's apartment complex. I wanted to go home. I wanted to tell my mom everything. She'd know what to do. She'd know how to fix it. But I couldn't tell her. She thought I was having a sleepover at Rennie's. And what would she think of me if she knew? What would my dad think? And Nadia? I would never be the same girl to them. Never, ever.

When I got out of the shower, Rennie was already in her bed, her eyes closed. I crawled in next to her. With our backs to each other, she said, "Tonight never happened. We're never talking about this ever again."

We pick up Ashlin and then drive over to the theater. I don't even know what's playing until we get there. The guys are waiting outside for us. Rennie jumps onto Reeve's back, and he carries her inside. Ashlin and I get in the concessions line and figure out our snack game plan.

"How about popcorn, Reese's Pieces, and gummi bears?" she asks.

I can feel Alex lurking behind me, so I make a big show of saying, "No Sno-Caps? They're the best!" Sno-Caps are Alex's favorite.

Ashlin makes a face. "Sno-Caps are gross, Lil! They taste like dust."

And just like clockwork, Alex comes over and says to Ashlin, "Are you kidding? Sno-Caps are awesome."

"See?" I say to Ashlin. "I'm not the only one who likes them."

To the girl at the concessions stand, Alex says, "One box of Sno-Caps, please."

I put my chin on his shoulder. "You're sharing with me, right?"

"Get your own box," he says. But the backs of his ears are pink, and the corners of his mouth are turned up in a smile.

Just like that, I know I've got Alex right where I want him— thinking everything's cool between us and that I don't suspect a thing.

CHAPTER FIFTEEN

MARY

I'M AT THE KITCHEN TABLE, FINISHING UP MY HOMEWORK. Aunt Bette's on the phone with one of her friends as she does the dinner dishes. She says, "Things are great. Mary's been keeping me company."

Even though things were a little awkward those first few days, now Aunt Bette is really happy to have me here. We've settled into a nice routine. I try to stay out of her way, and not interrupt her while she's painting. And if my bedroom door is closed, she leaves me alone.

When I came home super late from that night at the docks,

Aunt Bette was still up. I begged her to please not say anything to my parents. If they found out, they'd probably pack up the car and come and get me. Aunt Bette didn't say yes or no, but my parents haven't showed up in the minivan, so I'm pretty sure she didn't tell them.

That's the kind of cool aunt she is.

As soon as Aunt Bette goes to bed, I sneak outside to wait for Kat. I sit on the curb with my legs stretched out. The other houses are dark, and far, far down the hill I can just barely make out the moon hitting the water. If I concentrate hard enough, I bet I could hear the ocean.

Eventually Kat's convertible comes up the hill with the lights off, and I jump up from the curb. She pulls to a stop right in front of me. "Hey," she says. "Ready to do this?"

"Totally," I say as I climb in over the door and into the backseat. "I can't wait to get my license." I mean, I love my bike, but with a license I could go anywhere. So long as Aunt Bette let me borrow the Volvo.

Turning around, she says, "Why are you sitting in the back? I'm not a chauffeur."

I flush. "I don't know. I thought I'd give Lillia the front seat."

I feel clumsy and stupid until she starts to drive and then she says, "I'm sure that's exactly what she'd expect. Only the best for Princess Lillia."

"I really don't mind," I say, leaning forward.

Kat snorts. "Of course you don't," but she says it nice, as if it were a compliment.

Pretty soon we're in front of Lillia's house. It's so big and modern. It's not even a house; it's a full-on mansion. Lillia lives on the ritziest part of the island, White Haven. Most of the houses have thick hedges around the yards so you can barely see what they look like. And there's so much space. The houses are spread far apart, with big garages that fit a ton of cars, and fancy gardens and manicured lawns.

Kat shuts off the engine and the headlights. She blows her bangs out of her eyes and says, "She's late. It's so like her to not be considerate of anyone else."

I smile to myself. I don't say what I am thinking—that Kat was late too.

As we sit there in the dark, the wind picks up. Kat zips her hoodie and turns to me. "Aren't you freezing? There might be one of Pat's work shirts in the trunk."

"No," I say, tugging at my pale pink shorts. "I'm not cold at all. Too excited, I think."

That's when Lillia appears. It's so dark outside, all I can see is her face, until she gets a bit closer. She's sneaking down the driveway, dressed entirely in black. Black turtleneck, black leggings, black ballet flats.

Kat busts up laughing. "Oh my God."

Lillia runs up to the car, breathless. "Hey," she says, climbing into the passenger seat.

"Lillia, we're not robbing a freaking bank," Kat says. "This isn't a heist."

Defensively she says, "We have to be careful!" Lillia glances back at me and frowns. "Oh, well. I guess it doesn't matter."

I feel like I've done the wrong thing again. We're the same age, but these girls feel so much older than me.

Alex's house isn't far from Lillia's. Just a couple of miles. It's as big as Lillia's but more traditional-looking, lots of brick. They even have their own dock, and there's a speedboat tied to it. Kat slows down and dims the headlights as soon as we get close. She parks the car a few houses away from his.

I can't believe we're really going to do this.

"Does everybody remember what to do?" Lillia's asking both of us, but she's looking at me in the passenger vanity mirror.

It's been decided that I should be the lookout. I'm relieved I don't actually have to break into his SUV. She might be a cool aunt, but I don't think Aunt Bette could hide it from my parents if she had to bail me out of jail. The way they worry about me, I would be on lockdown for the rest of my life.

Kat rolls her eyes. "We've only been over this fifty times. It's not that complicated."

Kat's job is to look for some special notebook of Alex's. Lillia says he's always scribbling in it, but he never lets anybody read it. She called it his secret diary. She's sure there'll be good ammunition in the notebook, and at the very least he'll freak out over having lost it.

"Whatever," Lillia says, "I was just making sure."

"You just worry about yourself," Kat says as she reaches over Lillia to open the glove compartment. She fishes out a flashlight. "Do you have the Retin-A?"

Lillia lifts up a travel-size bottle of lotion.

"Is that enough?" Kat asks.

"It's a three-month's supply. So, yeah. It's enough."

Kat gives her a sidelong glance. "I didn't know you suffered from acne, Lil."

"My mom uses it for wrinkle prevention," Lillia says, indignant.

The plan is for Lillia to empty out Alex's bottle of sunscreen and fill it with the Retin-A. Retin-A is a zit medicine. It makes your skin hyper-sensitive to the sun. According to Lillia, Alex lathers himself up in sunscreen even if he's just stepping out of the house. Basically, we're going to give Alex the worst sunburn of his life. Blisters, peeling, the works. It'll be a mess.

Kat turns the flashlight on and off a couple of times. We creep out of the car.

As we walk up the driveway, Lillia whispers, "We have to keep a close eye on the pool house. That's where Alex stays."

"I know that," Kat snaps.

"I was talking to Mary," Lillia snaps right back.

"Guys, come on," I whisper. "No more bickering." I crouch beside Alex's SUV, keeping my eyes trained toward the house. The lights are off, but I can see there's one on in the pool house. Kat said Alex would be asleep by now, but it looks like she was wrong.

Meanwhile, Kat and Lillia are already in the SUV. Apparently Alex doesn't lock his doors. Kat's in the front seat, going through Alex's backpack, and Lillia's in the backseat looking for his equipment bag.

"I don't see the bag, Kat," Lillia says, sounding panicked.

"Maybe he left it in his locker."

"How am I supposed to do this lotion switch, then?"

"Quit freaking out! We'll think up something tomorrow," Kat says. A few seconds later she says, "Shit. His notebook isn't here either."

"You're not serious. I thought you said he kept it in his car!" Lillia climbs out of the backseat and joins Kat up front. She rummages through the glove compartment, then the center console, then flips down both of the visors. But Alex's notebook is nowhere to be found.

"We could take his textbooks and throw them in the water," Kat says, holding one up.

"No! Who cares about textbooks? He'll just buy new ones." Lillia looks like she's going to cry, she's so mad. "I'm not leaving without that notebook."

My stomach does a nosedive. It seemed so easy, when we were talking everything out. I take one last look back at the house, and then I dart around the side of the SUV to help search for the notebook.

Lillia's head snaps up. "God, Mary! What are you doing? Get back to your post!" she hisses.

I stiffen. "I was just trying to help—"

But then Kat yelps. "Got it!" She holds up the notebook triumphantly. It was under the driver's seat. Kat and Lillia high-five, and then they grin at me. I give a very relieved thumbs-up.

She and Lillia jump out. Kat closes the door, a little too hard. We both run back for Kat's car as fast as we can. Kat gets into the driver's seat, and I dive into the backseat.

But Lillia's still back by the SUV. She's standing in the driveway, looking toward the pool house.

"What's she doing?" I ask Kat.

Before Kat can answer me, Lillia stoops down and picks up a huge rock from under one of the potted plants that border the yard. And then she hurls the rock through Alex's rear window. It makes a big flash, all the shards reflecting the light of the moon. The sound of shattering glass echoes through the air.

Kat and I both gasp. This was definitely not part of our plan.

The lights in the house start to turn on. First in a room upstairs, then the ones on either side of the front door.

Kat yells, "Fuck! Let's go!"

Lillia makes a beeline for us, her long black hair streaming behind her like a banner. Jumping inside, she screams, "Drive!"

We peel out of the cul-de-sac, tires screeching. When we're a few blocks away, Kat shrieks, "What the hell was that?"

Lillia doesn't answer her. She's turned around in her seat, still looking back toward Alex's house. She is breathing hard, and there is a thin cut on her cheek, where a piece of glass must have hit her.

I say, "Lillia! You're bleeding!"

She puts her hand to her cheek and then looks down at it. "Just a little," she says. Our eyes meet, and she blinks, looking stunned. "I guess I got caught up in the moment, huh?"

Kat goes, "Hell, yeah, you did. That was badass! Looks like someone's taking the bus to school tomorrow!" She cranks the volume on the radio and starts dancing in her seat, wild and crazylike.

I laugh and throw my hands into the air, like we are riding a roller coaster.

"Grab the wheel!" Kat hollers. Music is pumping, and so is my adrenaline. We're flying. "I want to see what's in that notebook!"

Lillia leans over and takes the wheel as Kat opens the notebook up. "This thing is full of *poetry*!" She screams above the music and the wind, "*All your doors are locked. None of my keys fit. The longest hallway leads to you, but I never reach the end.*"

I let out a shriek. "What a cornball!"

Kat continues, gasping for breath. "*Longest hallway. Long, long, hallway. Longest hallway.*"

"Wow," Lillia says. "That's one seriously long hallway."

We howl with laughter.

"So, what are we going to do with it?" I ask.

"I know what we can do. I'll make copies of one of those corny-ass poems," Kat says as she turns down the road toward Lillia's house. "And then I'll put them up all over school."

Lillia cracks up laughing and says, "Kat, I knew you'd come up with something amazing."

I lean forward and ask, "Wait, what are we gonna do about the Retin-A?"

Lillia climbs out of the car. "Well, he'll definitely have his equipment bag with him at football practice tomorrow. They're having two-a-days all week. I'll just have to find a way to sneak into the boys' locker room."

"He's gonna look like a leper!" Kat crows.

Lillia squeals and runs backward toward her house. "Night, girls."

"Good night!" I call out. That's exactly what this is. No, it's an incredible night.

WHEN THE BELL RINGS, I TELL ASHLIN I HAVE TO STAY after and talk to Mr. Franklin about the quiz, and to go on to lunch without me. I wait until she's down the hall before I sprint toward the gym.

The boys' locker room is empty, but the thing I wasn't counting on was that there's no designated football area. I'd figured the football players' lockers would be together, maybe even have their names taped on them. That's how the cheerleaders do it. But there's no way to tell whose locker is whose.

I start randomly opening the lockers without locks, but those are empty. I'd assumed the boys wouldn't use locks, because what do they even have that needs locking up? Hair gel? My heart's beating so fast, I'm afraid it's going to burst. What if someone walks in and sees me? I have zero excuse for being in the boys' locker room.

It feels different, doing this by myself. Like, a whole lot scarier.

Frantically I try a few more lockers before I give up.

I'm sitting on the bottom bleacher at cheer practice, fiddling with the laces on my sneakers and feeling down about messing up my part in the plan.

Rennie's standing up front with her clipboard, getting ready to run down the list of who has to cheer for who for our first game on Friday night. "Most of you guys already know the drill. Everyone is assigned a football player to take care of. You decorate his locker on game day, you bake his favorite cookies, you basically just get his spirits up and his head in the game. I had QB One Joe Blackman from when I was a freshman to when he graduated because he requested me every single year. You wanna know why?"

A couple of junior girls, Teresa Cruz and Lynn McMannis, whisper something to each other and titter. I know what they're thinking, but it isn't true.

Rennie throws an icy glare in their direction, which silences them. "I'll tell you why. Because I'm the best. I gave it one thousand percent every game day. I anticipated Joe Blackman's needs without him having to ask. Sugar-free peanut butter cookies fresh-baked that morning, special cheers when he needed the boost. And honestly, I take pride in the fact that Joe's playing division three football in college, because I know I helped get him there." Rennie starts to pace. "Cheering's not just about wiggling your butt and looking pretty. It's dedication to excellence. And by the way, Paige, your toetouches were looking weak as hell at practice yesterday."

By this point I'm zoning her out. When Rennie starts giving these "inspirational" speeches, she goes on forever and ever.

When her lecture is finally over, Rennie begins to read the list. My head snaps up when she gets to Nadia's name. "Nadia, you have Diego Antunes," she says.

I turn around and look at Nadia, who's chewing on her lower lip and looking disappointed. Standing up, I say, "And just so everyone knows, a freshman getting to cheer for an upperclassman is a serious honor." I say it so Nadia will feel better, but I don't think it helps.

Things have been quiet on the Nadia and Alex front. I still have her on lockdown. She's only allowed to hang out over at Janelle's or at our house. I keep my bedroom door open at night, so I'll hear if she tries to sneak out again. And I checked her phone yesterday morning while she was in the shower, and she didn't have any texts or calls from Alex. Hopefully their hookup was just a onetime thing. If it wasn't, it will be after this week.

Rennie keeps working down her list. I'm listening for Teresa's name, because I'm sure Rennie will stick her with someone who sucks.

"Teresa, you're with Lee Freddington."

Yup. Lee Freddington is a sophomore, and our backup QB. He's not going to get a minute of playing time, not with Reeve as QB One. Teresa stares Rennie down, and for a second I wonder if she might actually say something. But of course she doesn't. No one ever does.

Rennie hands me her clipboard. "Everyone come see Lillia, and she'll tell you your player's info. We're only giving this out once, so make sure you write it down someplace where you won't lose it." To me, she says, "I'm going to get a bottled water. Be right back."

I look down at the list of the boys on the football team, with their birthdays, favorite cookies, home addresses, cell phone numbers—and their locker combinations, both gym and regular.

I want to kiss this piece of paper. Alex Lind, you are so dead.

On Tuesday Alex's skin looked pink and tender. Today is Wednesday, and it's cracking. He looks like the lizard Nadia found on our family vacation in Hawaii a few Christmases ago. I almost feel sorry for him. It's hard to look him in the eyes, even. His eyeballs look so white against his skin. So do his lips. They're chapped and blistering.

We're at the lunch table. Rennie leans close to me and whispers, "Alex's skin is making me lose my appetite."

I take a bite of my sandwich. "It's not that bad," I lie.

"Then you sit across from him," she says.

He's so miserable, it seems like it hurts him to eat. I didn't realize it would be that painful. I'd thought it would be purely cosmetic. Alex catches me looking at him, and I quickly glance away.

As soon as Alex gets up to get a soda, I say to Rennie and Ashlin, "Do you guys think it could be contagious?"

Ashlin looks horrified, and Rennie practically gags on her celery stick. "Oh my God. I'm switching seats," she says. She moves her stuff two seats down, next to PJ. Ashlin moves with her.

When Alex comes back with his Coke, it's just me and Reeve at this end of the table, and Alex definitely notices. Reeve must have too, because he says, "Dude, what the hell is up with your skin?"

Alex barely looks up. "It's the sun," he says. "Coach needs to calm down on the two-a-days."

"I've been out there the same as you," Reeve says, gulping down milk. "Maybe you should go to the doctor or something. Get that situation checked out."

"My mom already made me an appointment for tomorrow," Alex says. "It's probably just an allergic reaction. I think our cleaning lady started using a new laundry detergent. That could be it."

"You should put some aloe on it," Reeve says.

I sweetly offer, "My dad has an aloe plant. I could cut you off a piece."

"Thanks, Lillia." Alex sighs. "First my car window gets smashed; now this. It's been a crap week."

"Dude, that was a blessing in disguise. Now you can get those tints you wanted for the windows." Reeve throws his arm around Alex and says, "Hey, you know what? Maybe you shouldn't be going to a dermatologist about your skin. Maybe you should go to a gyno. You could have caught some crazy kind of herpes from DeBrassio!" He bursts out laughing.

Alex's head jerks up. He glances at me before growling, "Shut up, Reeve."

"Hey, I give her credit. She's a player just like me."

I turn to Reeve and say, "Oh, so you're saying you have herpes?" Reeve just laughs harder.

"Kat's not like that," Alex says, his eyes fierce. Then he gets up and throws his lunch into the garbage can.

"I was just kidding," Reeve calls after him.

I watch Reeve get up and follow Alex out of the cafeteria. It's surprising, the way Alex defended Kat. Kind of sweet, even. But then I remind myself that this fake chivalrous Alex also cheated on Kat by taking advantage of my little sister, so really, what right does he even have to defend anybody? He's not fooling me. Not anymore.

CHAPTER SEVENTEEN

KAT

AFTER SCHOOL ON WEDNESDAY, I TAKE THE FERRY OUT to see Kim at the music store. When I called to ask if I could use their copy machine, Kim put me on hold and made sure the owner, Paul, wasn't going to be around. When she came back on the line, she said they were pretty low on paper so I should bring what I think I'll need. I stole a whole ream of it from the library. Five hundred sheets to humiliate Alex.

As amped as I am about doing this, it's sort of annoying. I mean, basically my whole night is going to be spent doing this crap. I wouldn't care, but Mary hasn't done much of anything so far. I don't blame her for not having any ideas yet—she doesn't know Alex. But she's going to need to pick up the slack and earn her place. Lillia's been all right, I guess. Although her ideas have been pretty weak. The Retin-A thing was fine, but if it were me, I'd have put Nair in Alex's shampoo or something. Go big or go home.

Whatever. We're just getting started. Hopefully by the time it's my turn and we've got Rennie in our cross hairs, we'll be a well-oiled revenge machine.

Kim perks up when I walk through the door. Even though there's a customer waiting in line to be rung up, she pulls me behind the counter and gives me a big hug. The guy's a punk with a full-on Mohawk, so I guess Kim thinks he doesn't give a crap about customer service.

"Kat!" she says. "I've missed you, bitch!"

"Missed you too," I say. Actually, I guess I haven't. I've been too caught up in this revenge thing.

The summer before my junior year, I spent hours and hours perusing the racks at Paul's Boutique, checking out bands I'd never heard of at the listening stations. There was one where the headphones had an extra long cord, and I could sit on the floor. I wouldn't listen to a song here or there but whole albums. Five, six, seven.

Kim kicked me out a few times. She'd be ready to lock up for the night, and I'd be on the floor with my eyes closed, the volume turned up as loud as it could go, with no clue what time it was. It wasn't that I didn't have other things to do. I was always welcome to hang out with Pat and his friends. But I could only handle dudes-who-love-dirt-bikes talk for so long before I wanted to lock the garage doors, rev all the engines, and die from carbon monoxide poisoning.

So Kim was, rightfully, annoyed with me back then, because I really was a terrible customer. I'd mostly just hang around all day without buying anything. If I were her, I would have barred me from the store along with the shoplifters.

I'm not sure what made her eventually take pity on me, exactly, but it happened like this—I went up to the register and tried to buy a ticket to see this band called Monsoon in the garage space, even though the show was for people twenty one and older.

Kim called me out right away. She leaned over the counter and looked me up and down. "What are you, like, thirteen?"

"I'm sixteen," I said, shifting my weight from one foot to the other.

She laughed in my face and held up the ticket. "I don't think I heard you right. How old are you again?"

It took me a second to figure it out. I cleared my throat and said, "Twenty-one."

She arched one of her thick-as-hell eyebrows. "Where's your ID?" I bit my lip. I didn't have an answer. Luckily, Kim gave me one. "You left it in the car, didn't you?"

I nodded. "Yup."

She gave me the ticket. I tried to hand her ten bucks, but she wouldn't take it. "I've got an extra comp ticket."

"Wow," I said. "Thanks."

"Don't thank me. Nobody else working here wants to see them, so I'll be working the show alone. Monsoon sucks, if you didn't already know. And you're going to help me take down the set when it's over."

She was right, of course. Monsoon sucked big-time. But it was still one of the best nights of my life.

Kim peels herself off me so she can look me in the eyes. "Hey. Sorry about having to be so quick on the phone last week. It was a crazy show. The last band showed up late and so drunk they could barely get through their set, and Paul's been a complete prick lately. You caught me at the worst time possible. It's been—"

"It's totally fine," I say, cutting her off. Kim's day doesn't sound half as terrible as mine was, and anyway, I've got to get this done before the last ferry back to Jar Island. "Can I just chill in the office?" That's where the copier is, and the store computer. They've got programs loaded on it to make flyers for shows. I helped Kim make them a couple of times. I'm going to lay this thing out real nice. But not so nice that it gets back to me. I'm thinking a scan of Alex's handwriting with some cheesy clip art of two unicorns touching horns or something.

"Yeah, sure." Kim rings up the Mohawk guy, and then he leaves. "What's this school project about?"

"Umm, it's more like an art thing."

"Oh. Cool. And how's your boy Alex? You guys riding off on a golf cart into the sunset?"

I feel a pang at the sound of his name but quickly try to cover it up. "Eww!" I say. When Alex was on his fishing trip, I came to the store almost every day. And I know I talked about him a lot. God, it's crazy how much can change in a few weeks. I start walking backward, away from Kim, because I really don't have time to chat.

"But he was so nice, Kat. You need a nice boy. And he liked you, I could tell. I think you'd be good couple."

I roll my eyes. "I just can't wait to finish this year out and get to Oberlin. I'm ready to, like, start my life, you know? If I had to live around here for another year, I swear I'd kill myself."

Kim's mouth gets thin. "Yeah. I hear you."

I can tell she's mad, but I wasn't talking about her. Of course I wasn't. Kim is, like, the coolest person I know. "Kim, I didn't mean—"

"I don't know if you ever caught on, but Paul and I are screwing. Well, we *were* screwing, until his wife found out. So now he's being a huge prick and bitching about how the register's off by a dollar or that there's never any toilet paper in the store bathroom. Dude is trying to fire me and kick me out of the apartment over the store. I know it."

"Damn," I say. "That sucks." It really does. I met Paul once. He's kind of old. And gross.

"Yup," she says, and the *P* makes a pop sound. "You know where the copier is. Just try not to make a huge mess."

I feel like an ass. But I am in a rush. And when Kim gets

in a pissy mood, it's best to just leave her alone.

As the computer warms up, I take out Alex's notebook and start flipping through it, because maybe there's another poem even more lame than "The Longest Hallway." Though I doubt it. That was so wack.

Near the front of the book, I see something called "Red Ribbon." God, he is such a weirdo.

> *Winter stars fall so I keep wishing.*
> *I love the way you look in sweaters.*
> *Can we Eskimo kiss all night long?*
> *'Cause your red ribbon has me tied up in knots.*

Red ribbon? What the hell is that? Some kind of menstruation metaphor?

Oh, yeah. This is so it.

CHAPTER EIGHTEEN

LILLIA

IT'S SATURDAY NIGHT. REEVE GOT THE KEYS TO ONE OF THE empty summer houses his dad's company takes care of, so everybody piled into cars, and now we're in some random person's house in Middlebury. Reeve just told us to take our shoes off so we don't track dirt on the carpet, but then he helped himself to a brand-new bottle of gin from the bar and mixed it with a bottle of their Sprite. How considerate of him, right? He poured cups for everyone but himself, because he has to have his game face on for football practice on Monday.

He's so very moral about not drinking during the season.

I'm sitting on the living room floor, my legs stretched out in front of me. I'm super-sore from the last week of cheer practice. Rennie choreographed a new halftime routine, and she made us run through it a million times. A few of the guys from the football team are lying on the floor too, talking about some new defensive strategy.

I'm halfway falling asleep when Rennie bursts into the room, Reeve right behind her. "We just had an amazing idea," she announces. She holds up an empty bottle of beer and does a little dance. "Who wants to play spin the bottle?" she shrieks.

The guys perk up. I'm wide awake now too. No way am I sticking around for this. Quickly I scramble up and say to Ashlin, "I'll call you tomorrow."

"Everybody sit in a circle, boy-girl-boy-girl," Rennie's saying. "Ash, go get the people in the Jacuzzi."

Ashlin covers her mouth and giggles and says, "Seriously, Ren? What are we, in the seventh grade again?"

Rennie glares at her. "Hello, it's retro. And hello, it's our senior year. It's called making memories." In a lower but not altogether quiet voice, she adds, "Perfect opportunity to make out with Derek, Ash."

Ashlin's face splotches, and she jumps up. From the other side of the sliding door, I hear her call everyone inside.

I give Rennie a quick wave good-bye, hoping she won't notice, but before I can slip out of the room, she grabs my arm. "Lil, you have to stay," she hisses, giving me a meaningful look. She looks over at Reeve and back at me. "Please. I need you."

"I have to get home before my curfew."

"It's Saturday night! Your mom always lets you stay out a little later on Saturday nights." Rennie takes my hand in hers, and I know she's not going to let me leave. "Just till midnight, okay?"

"Fine," I say with a sigh, "but I'm only watching. I'm not playing."

She gives me a grateful kiss on the cheek and pulls me over to the group that's already formed on the floor. Alex is there, sitting next to Ashlin, his hair damp from the Jacuzzi. Jenn Barnes and Wendy Kamnikar, two juniors that Derek is friendly with, plant themselves across from them. I sit down next to Tyler Klask and PJ, a part of the circle but not completely. I'm checking my hair for split ends when Rennie says "Lillia first!" and thrusts the bottle at me.

My mouth falls open. "Rennie!"

"Don't be a spoilsport, Lil," Rennie says, smiling at me. "Everyone has to play." I narrow my eyes at her, but she just keeps smiling a sunny smile. "Hurry up and spin."

"Come on, Lil. Just say yes or she'll never leave you alone," PJ says in a low voice, nudging me.

Reeve, who's watching me with this bemused look on his face, starts pounding his fists on the carpet. "Lilli-uh! Lilli-uh!" Everyone joins in.

I glare at everybody. "God, you guys! So immature."

Ashlin spins the bottle and shouts, "This one's for Lil!"

It lands . . . on Reeve.

I can feel my cheeks heat up as our eyes meet. I'm about to say *No freaking way* when Reeve reaches out and adjusts the bottle so it's pointing at Alex. "I think it was going more in this direction," Reeve says with a lazy grin.

"Hey!" I object. "Interference!"

Alex clears his throat and jokingly says, "Look, I don't know what you've heard, but contrary to popular opinion, I'm not contagious or anything."

"I—I don't think that! It's just, those aren't the rules." I don't want to kiss Reeve, and I definitely don't want to kiss Alex. In fact, I don't want to kiss anybody. Maybe I don't want to kiss anyone ever again. At least not for a long time.

Reeve raises an eyebrow. "I had no idea you wanted me so bad. I'm flattered, Cho."

"That's—that's not what I'm saying, and you know it," I say. I can feel myself getting flustered. Reeve's always doing that. Twisting my words around.

Derek says, "Reeve, just kiss her already."

"Guys, don't pressure her," Rennie says hastily.

Oh, *now* she's looking out for me? Give me a freaking break. Just for that, I'm doing it.

As I crawl to the middle of the circle, I can't seem to get a good deep breath. I sit on my knees, and I keep my palms flat on the ground to steady myself. Reeve leans toward me oh-so-slowly, dragging out the moment for as long as he can. He's grinning at me, that smug self-satisfied grin I hate. I feel myself start to panic, but I try with all my might not to shrink away from him. If I freak out right now, everyone will see it and wonder why, and I can't have that. I have to be normal. I have to pretend I'm the same girl I was.

Reeve tips my face up, and that's when something in his face changes. The grin drops and he's staring into my eyes like he's trying to puzzle something out. At the last second, instead of kissing my lips he plants a kiss at the top of my head, the kind my dad used to give me when he'd come in to say good night. I don't know if I should feel grateful or insulted.

"No fair," Ashlin says, shaking her finger at Reeve. "It has to be on the mouth! Those are the rules."

PJ nods sagely and says, "Ash is right. Them's the rules."

"Give it a rest," Alex says. "He kissed her."

Reeve claps his hands together. "Who's next?"

I crawl back to my spot. I just want to go home.

Loudly Rennie says, "It's Reeve's turn."

"Yay for me." Reeve rubs his hands together and spins the bottle. Part of me hopes the bottle will land on Rennie so I can get out of here faster, but another part hopes it won't, so she doesn't get what she wants. The bottle doesn't land on her. It lands on Josh Fletcher, and everyone busts up laughing. "Come on, Fletch. Don't be scared," Reeve says. "I'll do you like I did Lillia."

"You'd better spin again, man," Josh warns. "I don't know where your lips have been."

Reeve ends up spinning again, and this time it does land on Rennie. Grinning, he leans forward for a quick kiss. But Rennie has other ideas. She gets on her knees and inches across the circle until she's right in front of him. She grabs a wad of his T-shirt and pulls him toward her. Then she kisses him like she wants to eat his face off. It starts close-mouthed, but a second later they are actually *kissing* kissing. She even puts her arms around his neck.

Everyone starts whooping and screaming and freaking out. It's so sad and gross. Rennie's making a total fool of herself in front of everybody. Especially Reeve. He already let her down easy. It's obvious he doesn't want to date her, but it only makes Rennie want him more. It's pathetic.

CHAPTER NINETEEN

MARY

Senor Tremont is lining up a bunch of plastic vegetables on his desk and asking for volunteers to role-play a scene at a Spanish marketplace, and all I can do is smile at Alex's empty seat.

That night was maybe the most fun I've ever had. Sneaking out with Lillia and Kat, laughing our butts off, speeding through the darkness. When I got home, I crept back into bed and tried to sleep, but that was pretty much impossible. I just lay there in the dark, tracing the flowers on my wallpaper with my finger and thinking how this was even better than what I'd hoped to accomplish that first day. This isn't just about Reeve. It's about me, and it feels like fate or magic—the girls coming into my life, right when I needed them most.

Through the window I spot Alex getting out of a car. A woman—his mom, I guess—waves good-bye and drives off. I watch him run all the way to the main doors. I hear Alex's feet pounding the linoleum, over Senor Tremont haggling with the girl sitting behind me over how many pimentos he can buy for three euros.

"I'm sorry I'm late, Senor," he says, rushing in. "I had a doctor's appointment."

Senor Tremont frowns. Then he puts a hand up to his ear, pretending like he can't hear Alex. "En español, Senor Lind. Por favor."

Alex is halfway to his seat. He stops, his shoulders sag, and his eyes roll to the back of his head. I have to cover my mouth to keep in a laugh.

"Yo . . . yo soy . . . ," Alex tries.

I lean forward on my elbows and cradle my chin in my hands.

I really, really, really wish Lillia and Kat were here to see this for themselves.

Alex is trying to conjugate the verb "apologize" for the third time when the fire alarm goes off.

CHAPTER TWENTY

KAT

ONCE THE FIRE ALARM STARTS GOING OFF, I FLICK MY hand so that the cap of my Zippo lighter snaps closed. Just in time too, because I think I'm almost out of butane. Plus the metal case is blazing hot. I blow on it, jump off the radiator in the girls' bathroom, and crouch down at the door. The top part of the door is wood, but the bottom is covered in thin slatted vents. I watch the hallway light get sliced by pair after pair of legs hurrying their way to the nearest exit. I hear one of the teachers say, "We didn't have a drill planned for today, did we?"

Another teacher says, "I think this might be the real deal." They instruct their students to hurry along with urgent *This is not a test* voices.

Yeah. Hurry the eff up. I've got work to do.

I shrug off my book bag, slide my arms through the straps so that it hangs in front of my body, and open the zipper. Inside are the photocopies I made last week. I've also got a roll of masking tape I stole from the art room. I take that out and rip pieces off, sticking them on my arms so I can move fast.

Jar Island only has a volunteer fire department, so I figure it'll take them at least ten minutes to get here. It takes one, maybe one and a half, for the school to empty. As soon as the coast is clear, I push open the door and start running.

The senior hallway will do the most damage, so that's where I start, slapping up the photocopies every few feet. On classroom doors, on lockers, on the spout of the water fountain.

I know this is supposed to be Lillia's revenge, but I have to admit, this feels pretty freaking awesome. Alex has tried calling me a few times in the last week. Not that I bothered to answer, or to call him back. He doesn't deserve to ever speak to me again. That's how it is with me—you do me wrong, you're dead to me.

Except for Lillia. I'm making a temporary exception in her case.

At the end of the hall, I kick the door of the stairwell open and take the stairs two at a time, putting up copies as I go. The alarm is so loud, my ears are about to bleed. The emergency lights are giving off big bright flashes. I remember my brother's friend Luke pulling the fire alarm my freshman year. He got suspended for a week, and he had to pay a big fine for wasting the volunteer fire department's time. I hustle even faster.

When I reach the landing, I duck so I'm out of sight at the window, then sprint the rest of the way up to the second floor, where the freshman lockers are. Adrenaline pumps through me, and I feel like I could run forever.

I think about Nadia coming back in, seeing Alex's face and reading his stupid poem, and being completely mortified. I doubt she'll ever want to go for rides in his SUV again. I freaking love it. I love that Alex is going to get dumped by a freshman, that everyone in school is going to laugh at his corny ass.

I get another stretch of hallway done, though it takes me a lot longer this time because I have to stop and rip off pieces of tape. Then I hear the sirens.

I don't have much longer. Which sucks, because I've got

more than half the school left to cover. So I screw the tape and just start throwing sheets everywhere like confetti. Which is way faster. I do the science wing and the English hallway. When I slide down the banister of the back staircase, I toss papers over my shoulder.

I'm just about on the first floor when a team of firemen burst through the doors. They've got their hard hats on, flashlights beaming, walkie-talkies crackling.

Luckily, I'm right in front of the auditorium. I duck inside and hide myself in the folds of the big American flag. A second later two firemen bound in. I hold my breath and watch their flashlights hit the walls, the ceilings, the stage.

They yell "Clear!" and duck back out into the hall, continuing their search for a fire.

They won't find one, but Alex is gonna get burned.

CHAPTER TWENTY-ONE

LILLIA

I DIDN'T EVEN HAVE TIME TO GO TO MY LOCKER AND get my jacket. The teachers were freaking out, pushing us along through the hallways like the building was really on fire. It's super-bright outside, but it's freezing, especially for this early in September. I'm shivering, huddled close to Ashlin, who puts her arm around me.

PJ says, "You want my jacket, Cho?"

I nod. "Yes, please!" PJ shrugs it off and hands it over. I put it on, and Ashlin zips me up, hopping from foot to foot. It smells as mildewy as PJ's basement, but it's better than nothing.

"Do you think there's a real fire?" she asks me hopefully. "Maybe we won't have enough time left for the quiz."

We had a fire drill last week. This doesn't feel like a drill. The teachers didn't seem to know anything about it. I wonder . . . could this be Kat's doing? She said she'd get those posters up, but even for her this is gutsy.

"Maybe," I say as the volunteer fire truck comes barreling into the parking lot. Some of the freshmen start clapping and chanting "Let it burn! Let it burn!"

So juvenile.

We're in the parking lot for another half hour while the firemen check out the building. I can't feel my toes. The firemen finally come out and give the all clear, and the teachers start ushering us back inside.

I'm walking down the senior hallway when I see them. Our posters, with Alex's smiling face and his poem right next to it— on lockers, on walls. They're *everywhere*.

Alex has seen them too. He's stopped short in front of a whole cluster of them on a set of lockers. Slowly he says, "What the . . ."

Reeve tears a sheet down and starts reading it out loud, doubling over with laughter. *"Winter stars fall so I keep wishing. . . . I love the way you look in sweaters. Can we Eskimo kiss all night long? 'Cause your red ribbon has me tied up in knots!"*

That doesn't sound like the poem Kat was reading in the car. "The Longest Hallway" one.

I take down a sheet and read it over.

Wait.

Red ribbon?

It was Christmastime, my freshman year. My whole family was at Alex Lind's house for their annual holiday party. Since we'd moved to the island full-time, Alex's mom and my mom had gotten to be pretty good friends. They went to lunch together, shopping off island, that kind of thing.

The parents were downstairs drinking and talking and mingling by the fireplace. Elvis Presley was playing on the stereo, and us kids could hear it upstairs in Alex's room. This was before he moved into the pool house. He used to have the whole third floor to himself. It was basically one big rec room, with beanbag chairs and a foosball table and a dartboard. For the party Alex's mom had set up a table of kid food, things like chicken fingers and popcorn shrimp and mini pizzas, probably so we wouldn't come downstairs and bother them.

The little kids, my sister included, were fighting over who got to play darts next. Nadia nearly got into a scuffle with an eight-year-old boy, a cousin of Alex's, I think, and I had to break it up. Since Alex and I were the oldest, we were in charge. I hadn't even wanted to come, since Rennie wasn't going to be there, but my mom had insisted we go as a family.

Alex put in a DVD for the kids, and they quieted down for the most part. I was sitting at Alex's desk, doing stuff on his computer and eating a Christmas cookie. It was a reindeer with a Red Hot candy for a nose. Alex was lying in his hammock a few feet away, strumming on a guitar. He wasn't too bad at it. Out of nowhere he said, "Hey, cool headband."

I looked up, startled. "Oh, thanks," I said, touching the crown of my head. "It's actually a ribbon." My mom had wanted me to wear a dress, but I would have felt dumb showing up at Alex Lind's house dressed up. So I wore a kelly green sweater and a tartan skirt, plus the red ribbon, for a festive touch.

"Cool," he said, looking back down at his guitar. "You look nice in red. Like, uh, that shirt you wear sometimes."

"What shirt?"

"I don't remember." His freckly face turned the same color

as his hair. He kept strumming the guitar. "I think you had it on last Monday or something?"

The only red I wore on Monday was during gym. "That was my PE uniform from my old school," I told Alex.

"Nice," he said. Now his face was as red as my ribbon. "Yeah, we don't wear uniforms here."

"Yeah, I know," I said.

It was awkward for another second or two. Then Alex got up and went to the bathroom and I went back to the computer.

Oh my God.

That Christmas party was freshman year. He remembered? All this time? That can't be.

I look at him, and he's looking at me. He drops his eyes right away. So it *is* about me.

Next to me Ashlin covers her mouth with her hand. "Oh, my gosh," she says, giggling. "I had no idea Alex was a poet!"

I feel dizzy.

"Who did this?" Alex demands. He's all flushed; he's definitely upset.

Reeve is practically falling on the ground, he's laughing so hard. "Bro, this is that song you've been working on, isn't it?

Come on. Don't be ashamed. This is good stuff. You've got talent."

"Shut up, Reeve." We watch as Alex starts taking down the posters. I wonder how Kat managed to get them up so high.

"Alex, man, can we Eskimo kiss all night long?" Reeve asks, sputtering into laughter again and throwing an arm around him.

Alex shoves him away. "Did you do this?"

Shaking his head, Reeve says, "No way! I swear on your red ribbon!"

Alex tears the rest of the posters down and stalks off in a huff, throwing them into the garbage on the way.

Reeve starts singing the poem, and everyone's laughing. I walk up to him and snatch the poster out of his hand. "You're such a jerk," I say loudly. To Ashlin I say, "Let's go back to class."

Ashlin and I are walking away as Reeve calls out to me, "You need to work on your sense of humor, Cho."

I don't turn around. I just keep walking. Ashlin's talking about Alex's poem or song or whatever it is, but I'm barely even paying attention. I can't stop thinking about the look on Alex's face when our eyes met. Does he really like me that much? But if that's true, what is he doing with my sister? It just doesn't make sense.

CHAPTER TWENTY-TWO

MARY

I FEEL LIKE I'M A COMPLETELY DIFFERENT GIRL. WHEN I see Reeve in the hallway, I don't go out of my way to avoid him. I just walk right by with my head held high, because I don't care if he notices me or not. Even if he did suddenly recognize me the way I wanted him to that first day of school, make a big deal over how different I look now, it wouldn't make any difference. Even if he apologized, he's still going to get his. The wheels are already in motion.

I've held myself back for way too long. I'm not going to do

that anymore. So when I walk down the hallway, I make sure to smile at the people I don't know. In bio class, when James Turnshek turns the Bunsen burner up too high and makes the beaker shatter, I laugh along with everyone else. I don't even care that we'll have to start over on the lab.

Near the end of the day, I pass Lillia in the hallway. I'm on my way to math, and she's at the water fountain, holding her long black hair back with one hand, leaning into the stream of water. I would keep walking, but she does something when she sees me looking at her. She makes her eyes go real big, double the size they usually are, and jerks her head just slightly, like she wants me to walk over.

I try not to be too obvious when I stop and double back. Hugging my books to my chest, I meander over and pretend to look at some student council announcement taped up to the wall.

As soon as I'm next to her, Lillia lets go of her hair. It falls and covers her face, and a few of the ends get wet in the basin of the water fountain. I guess she does it so no one can see her talking to me. She whispers, "Meet after school at the pool, okay, Mary?" in a voice so quiet, I have to strain to hear it.

I nod, and then we head off in opposite directions.

* * *

The swimming pool is in a separate building, and right now it's closed for repairs. They're doing work on it for the winter, when swim season begins. The door is wedged open, so I slip inside.

I'm the last one here. Lillia and Kat are sitting together on top of the lifeguard chair. They're both leaning in to look at something on Kat's cell phone. Lillia's twirling a lollipop around in her mouth. Kat's picking the shredded parts of her jeans.

"Hey," I say. "What are you guys looking at?"

Lillia jumps down from the perch, and her pleated skirt lifts up just the littlest bit. She shifts the lollipop so the white stick juts out of the corner of her mouth. "Kat took a video of some people singing Alex's song in the cafeteria today."

Kat jumps down next, and her boots make a slapping sound on the concrete deck. She holds her phone up for me to look. "These kids were doing it like a rap. But I heard other people singing it like a jazzy number, heavy metal style—"

"Jeez," I say. "Maybe Alex is a good songwriter? I mean, it's in everyone's head."

Kat rocks back with laughter that fills the entire building, bounces off every wall, every tile. "That shit is catchy, I give him that much." And then she gets a cigarette out from her pocket and lights it up.

I'm worried that Kat shouldn't be smoking in here. But I'm not about to tell her to put it out. So instead I ask, "Do you think anyone suspects we're behind it?"

Kat rolls her eyes. "No one suspects us. And no one even knows who you are."

I guess I look hurt, which I am, but then Lillia says, "Yup. That's why you're our secret weapon!"

I joke, "Yeah, I'm silent but deadly."

"Like a fart!" Kat cracks up.

I laugh too, and then I give her the middle finger. I think it might be the first time I've ever done that.

Kat grins. "Aww, look. Sweet little Mary's turning into a hell-raiser."

"Am not!" I squeal, louder than I mean to, and I cup my hand over my mouth.

"I'm only kidding," Kat says. "But seriously. We're scary good at this."

"Better than good," Lillia corrects, and pulls her lollipop out. The inside of her mouth is a deep cherry red. "We're amazing."

She looks down at her cell phone and starts tapping the screen. Without looking up she says, "I mean, we could even quit now, if we wanted."

Both Kat and I look at her.

"What?"

Lillia slips her phone into her purse. "I'm just saying . . . we could quit while we're ahead, and just get started on Rennie or Reeve." Her voice is a bit quieter than before.

"No way, dude!" Kat says. "Tomorrow's going to be so epic. First football game of the season. Everyone watching our plan go down. This is going to be our best work yet. I bet I won't sleep a wink tonight. It's like freaking Christmas Eve."

Kat isn't taking Lillia seriously, I can tell. She's just grinning, thinking about tomorrow. But I see the look in Lillia's eyes. Something's different.

"What's changed?" I ask her.

She bites her lip. "I don't know. Nothing."

"The football game is tomorrow," I say. "We've already done so much work."

Impatiently Kat says, "Lil, quit with the guilty act."

"I thought this was my revenge," she says, sliding her hands into her pockets. "Shouldn't that mean I get to say when it's over?"

"Why would you want to chicken out now?" Kat demands. "Did you tell someone? Did you say something to Rennie?"

"No! God, it's not like that. Look, I'm pretty sure that whatever went down between my sister and Alex is over. So, Kat, feel free to start up with Alex again. Whatever keeps him from sniffing around my sister is fine by me."

"Don't you bring me into this!" Kat's pacing. "This is your thing, not mine."

"Oh, please. Don't act like you aren't benefiting from it. You like Alex, he hooked up with my sister, and now he's back on the market. Congrats."

Kat glares at Lillia. "Get it straight, Lil. Your baby sister had *my* sloppy seconds. "

I step in between them. "Um, what are you two talking about?" Alex and Kat? They were a thing? "Why didn't either of you tell me!" I start shaking my head. "This is seriously screwed up. We can't keep secrets from each other!"

"You're right, Mary." Lillia spins toward Kat so hard, her hair whips from one shoulder to the other. "Kat, what were you and Alex, exactly? Boyfriend and girlfriend? Texting 'I love you' every night? Or just a one-night mistake."

Kat's eyes flash with fire. But before she can say anything

back, the door to the pool building closes with a sickening thud.

A deep voice calls out, "Hello? Who's in here?"

I gasp. So does Lillia.

Kat sinks down and grinds her cigarette out on the floor. She lifts her chin and nudges it toward a door. The three of us run over, and she opens it, revealing a small electrical closet. We squeeze inside together, and then Kat closes the door except for a crack, so we can see out.

"Who is that?" Lillia hisses, but Kat holds up a finger. I think we all stop breathing.

Through the wedge of light we watch one of the construction workers look around. He's a big guy, with dirty jeans, work boots, a yellow hard hat, and a ring of tinkling keys. He calls out "Yo! Who's in here?" again. And then he starts sniffing the air.

The cigarette smoke.

Next to me Kat closes her eyes.

We stay absolutely motionless, watching the construction worker walk over to the pool, looking around suspiciously. He walks over to where we're hiding, and then pushes the door closed, trapping us in the dark.

It takes a second for my eyes to adjust. Slowly I start to make out Lillia standing next to me. I think she's about to faint. Her eyes are closed, and she's shaking out her hands really fast. Kat sees her too, and she grabs one of Lillia's hands and holds it, trying to calm her down. Lillia doesn't open her eyes.

It's quiet for a few more minutes, and then we hear the pool door open and then close again. We wait for a few more seconds before we leave our hiding spot.

"Shit," Kat breathes. "That was close."

Lillia doesn't look relieved. She's still pretty shaken up. "You shouldn't have been smoking in here, Kat."

Kat brushes it off. "Whatever. It's not like we got caught. Besides, I'm not the one who was screaming."

Bristling, Lillia says, "See, this is what I'm talking about."

I can tell they're about two seconds from going at it again. The thought of me not getting revenge, of this whole thing falling apart before I get to Reeve—it's unthinkable. But if it's this hard for Lillia, I know it'll be even harder for me. I'll just have to keep reminding myself that Reeve deserves this. He deserves everything that's coming to him, and then some.

In a strong, clear voice, I say, "Guys. Stop it."

They both look at me in surprise.

I continue. "I believe in this, in what we're trying to do. Just knowing that Reeve is going to get what's coming to him, I feel more peace than I have in years." I take a fast breath, in case they try to interrupt me, but they don't. They're actually listening. "I know you two have a complicated history, and there's a lot of stuff in your past. But none of that matters anymore. We're all here because somebody hurt us." I turn to Lillia. "If I had a sister and someone took advantage of her, I'd want to get them back tenfold. There's nothing wrong with that. I think that's being a good big sister. What you're doing right now, it's protecting your sister. I—I wish someone had done that for me."

Lillia's chin trembles. "That's all I want. To protect Nadia."

Kat clicks her tongue at her. "What are you talking about? You're a good big sis, Lil. You always have been."

Lillia pulls her ChapStick out of her purse and dabs it on her lips. "Let's just go over the plans for tomorrow's football game. There's a lot we need to cover."

That fast, we're back down to business.

CHAPTER TWENTY-THREE

KAT

IT'S FRIDAY, JUST AFTER SEVEN. THE ORIGINAL PLAN was to pick up a part for Ricky's bike from the auto shop, but it was already closed and now we're just driving around. Me, Ricky, and Joe in Joe's hatchback. Ricky and Joe are guys I know through my brother, Pat. They were both a year ahead of me in school. Joe hasn't graduated yet because he never goes to class, and Ricky's at community college now. Lillia would probably consider them losers, but they're good guys.

I'm sitting shotgun, and Ricky's asleep in the backseat. To Joe I say, "Where are we going?"

"Where are we *ever* going?" Joe says, his eyes barely open. "Nowhere."

Ricky sleep-mumbles, "That's why she stopped hanging out with us this summer."

"Shut up. I did not." But I did. I was with Alex, most of the time. I turn around and punch Ricky in the shoulder. "Wake up! Come on. It's Friday night. Let's do something."

"You have a real restless spirit, Kat," Joe says. "You should chill out."

I am restless, because the football game will be starting soon. I lean forward in my seat and drum my hands on the dashboard. "Hey, I've got an idea. Why don't we stop by school? There's a game tonight. Let's go laugh at people."

Joe gives me a look like I'm crazy.

Ricky sits up and says, "A football game? No way."

"Come on, guys," I wheedle. "I mean, what else are we going to do? Drive around all night?" I open up my bag and dangle a bag of weed I stole off my brother. "You guys smoke. I'll drive."

It's an offer they can't refuse.

Half an hour later we're standing underneath the bleachers by the end zone. The game is just about to start. Lillia's warming up on the sideline, doing kicks and jumps. I catch her eye, and she gives a nod before she bends into a stretch. So that means she got it done. Good. I was kind of worried after that conversation in the pool yesterday. I need to chill out on pressing her buttons. Because the truth is, if Lillia decided to walk away, there's nothing I could do to stop her. Even if I went around telling everybody at school what she did to Alex, nobody would care, not after they found out her reasons. It kills me to say it, but I need her more than she needs me. If it wasn't for Mary, we would have imploded yesterday, and where would that leave me?

I take a drag off Joe's cigarette, and that's when I spot Mary in the bleachers. She waves at me excitedly. I look away—but not before I see the flash of hurt cross her face.

I feel bad. She's sitting alone up there. But it's not like I can ask her to join me and Joe and Ricky. They'd ask questions; they'd want to know who she was. And Mary would probably faint at the sight of a j. It's better this way.

CHAPTER TWENTY-FOUR

MARY

YIKES.

I avert my eyes and sink low into the bleachers. I'm such an idiot for waving at Kat with all these people around. So much for flying under the radar. Also, waving at someone and them not waving back at you is *sooo* embarrassing. Hopefully no one noticed.

I do think Kat and I could be friends, when this is over. Lillia I'm not so sure about. I mean, I hope we'll talk once in a while. But she's so popular. She doesn't need another friend. I guess the best I can hope for there is that we'll be able to stop pretending not to know each other when we're in public.

Down near the front of the bleachers, the Jar Island band kicks into a fight song. I can't see the band from where I'm sitting, up in the very top row. Just the rims of their shiny brass instruments moving side to side in unison and the white feathers sticking up from the tops of their hats.

Everyone around me sings along. They flap their arms like seagull wings and stomp their feet on the bleachers to make thunder.

I don't know the song.

Lillia and Rennie are down on the football field in their cheering uniforms. Rennie has a megaphone with a big *C* painted on the side, I guess because she's the captain. The other cheerleaders on the squad stand in a perfectly straight row, the toes of their Keds just touching the white chalk sideline. Lillia, Rennie, and Ashlin walk the line and inspect each of the other cheerleaders closely—adjusting the curls of white satin ribbon that tie up everyone's ponytails, straightening their sweaters, dotting lip gloss on the girls who need it. When they reach the end of the line, Rennie and Lillia confer. Then Lillia runs off and grabs Rennie's stubby white pom-poms for her, and together they shake them, along with the rest of the squad, and try to get the people in the bleachers pumped up.

I watch Lillia and Rennie do a quick choreographed dance with each other, smiling and laughing in each other's faces. More and more I realize how hard this must be for her—to act like she's friends with Rennie while she's about to help Kat stab her in the back. I mean, really, everyone we're taking revenge on is one of Lillia's friends.

The opposing football team arrives and shuffles into the stadium on the opposite side of the field. They have their cheerleaders and their band, but they don't have even half the number of fans that our side has. Probably because they had to come in on the ferry to get here. It's a hassle, which is lucky for us. I guess that's why they call it home field advantage.

Our band kicks into another song, and our cheerleaders change formation, making two long lines near the gates. Then Lillia and Rennie unroll a tube of craft paper across the end zone. They've painted Fight, Gulls, Fight! across it in bright bubble letters.

A few seconds later the doors to the boys' locker room fling open, and a pack of football players comes exploding out, helmets clutched in their hands. Reeve leads the charge, bounding in long strides, with the rest of the senior players falling into step behind him, and he's the first one to burst through the paper with a pop.

Reeve's got black stripes painted under his eyes, and his hair is wet and slicked back. Everyone in our bleachers gets on their feet and cheers. He grins and points a finger at the stands, as if he's singling out a person he knows in the crowd. Like his mom or dad, dedicating the game to them. Only he does it the whole length of the bleachers, pointing at everyone. And they cheer like Reeve is doing it just for them.

Reeve Tabatsky, adored by all.

It was raining hard that day. The ride back to Jar Island was rocky, and the ferry shook from side to side. When we docked, Reeve's dad wasn't there to pick him up. He never came to pick Reeve up, but I just figured he would because of the rain.

I saw my mom's car right away, in the same place where she always parked. Shyly I asked Reeve if he wanted a ride, but he said no. He was just going to wait until it let up. As I ran over to my mom's car, I kept looking over my shoulder. Reeve was trying to stand under the awning by the Jar Island tour booth, but his book bag was getting wet. His shoulders, too. Then there was a crack of thunder so loud, it echoed in my chest. When I got to the car, I asked my mom if we could give Reeve a ride home. She said yes.

He seemed grateful when we pulled up.

Reeve sat in the back. "Are you sure this isn't too much trouble?"

"Not in the slightest, Reeve. I'm just glad I've finally gotten a chance to meet you." I didn't dare turn around and look at Reeve. I was scared he'd think I was telling my mom and dad about my nickname, how mean he was to me. I hadn't told them anything about that. Only the nice stuff.

"How about we go through the drive-through window at Scoops and get some ice cream?" my mom suggested.

I mustered up the courage, turned around in my seat, and looked at Reeve. "Do you have to go straight home?"

Reeve shook his head, but he whispered, "I don't have any money."

"It's fine," I whispered back with a smile, because I knew my mom wouldn't let him pay anyway.

Mom got her favorite chocolate chocolate chip, and Reeve got moose tracks in a waffle cone. I usually got a scoop of peppermint patty and a scoop of peanut brittle, but this time I got a rainbow sherbet, because the flavor board said there were less calories in sherbet.

When we dropped him off, Reeve didn't run straight into his house, even though it was pouring. He came over to my window and thanked my mom and said, "See you tomorrow!" Then he ran up his walkway.

We waited until he was safely inside, then we headed home.

I couldn't stop smiling the whole way home. Reeve liked me. He was my friend. Everything was going to change.

Things did change after that day. Reeve stopped racing off the ferry and leaving me behind. He waited for me, and we walked to school together.

Three girls are sitting in front of me, decked out in Jar Island school colors. I watch one girl lean over to the others and say, "God, Reeve is so fine."

"Is he single?" another of the girls says. "Or is he still hooking up with Teresa Cruz?"

I hold my breath.

"That's way over," the third girl says. "Rennie and Reeve are a thing now. I mean, at least I think they are. I heard they've hooked up a few times."

That first day, Reeve was the one to console Rennie after Kat spit in her face. He even gave her his shirt to wipe her face on.

Could they be together?

I look out at the field. Rennie's climbing onto the very top of a cheering pyramid. She's so tiny. She probably weighs, like, ninety pounds, max. I watch her sneakers grind down on the backs of her teammates as she pulls herself higher and higher. A few of them wince.

Girls like Rennie get whatever they want. They don't care who they step on.

It's not right.

I let out the breath I'm holding. At that very moment Rennie stumbles as she's rising up to the very top. The whole crowd sees it happen. Some of them gasp. She ends up falling straight backward and crashes into the arms of her spotters, who then lower her gently to the ground, unhurt. Rennie looks pissed that she didn't make it up to the top. Pissed and surprised. The rest of the girls in the pyramid climb off each other, and Rennie screams at them for having bad form.

My heart is racing and I'm breathing hard. I know I didn't just do that. I couldn't have.

Even though Rennie deserved it. Even though just for a

second I wanted her to fall. But just because you want something to happen, that doesn't mean it will come true.

Or does it? That day in the hallway, when I was chasing down Reeve, I wanted so badly to get his attention. The lockers . . . did I make them all slam shut?

I inch back in my seat and sit on my hands. No. There's no way. It's an impossible thought.

While everyone else stares at the field, I turn and face the shed that's at the very top of the bleachers. An old man takes a seat behind a microphone. The cord of the microphone is plugged into a mixing board, which is hooked up to speakers mounted underneath the eaves of the roof. He takes a sip of water, clears his throat, and says, "These, ladies and gentlemen, are your Jar Island Fighting Gulls!"

He opens up the folder in front of him and traces his finger down a list of names. The list Kat and I put in the announcing booth early this morning, before anyone got to the stadium.

"Let's give a warm welcome to our seniors, who are taking the field for their last season." As the words echo out of the speakers, Reeve, Alex, and the rest of the senior boys pull apart from the pack and face the bleachers. The senior cheerleaders step forward too and stand behind them.

"Quarterback and captain, number sixty-three, REEVE TABATSKY."

Hearing his name, Reeve hops up onto the team bench and waves to the crowd. They scream for him rock star style. Rennie turns a bunch of back handsprings the entire length of the bench.

"Your kicker, number twenty-seven, PJ MOORE!"

Everyone cheers for PJ as he steps up onto the bench with Reeve. He pulls his leg back and then swings it forward, simulating a kick. Lillia leaps up and does a toetouch.

The applause dies down, and I suck in a breath, because I know what's next.

"Wide receiver, number forty-six, ALEX LIMP."

A few people clap, but mostly there's just snickers and people whispering, "What did they just call him? *'Limp'*?"

Alex drops his head to the side, like he maybe didn't hear right. His face is red, redder than it is normally with his skin issue. Redder than I've ever seen a face get. The blond girl who's Alex's cheerleader has her pom-poms up over her head and, she's about to lean into a handstand. But she doesn't. She freezes.

I guess because Alex doesn't climb up onto the bench, the announcer says his name once again. "ALEX LIMP!"

This time everyone hears.

Reeve pitches forward laughing. PJ too. One of the players standing behind Alex taps him on the back. When Alex turns around, everyone in the crowd sees it. The back of his jersey doesn't say "Lind." It says "Limp."

Lillia's brilliant idea. She swapped out his old jersey with this new one, bought from an athletic store online that makes jerseys in our school colors. She sent them a money order so the order couldn't be traced to her, and then she had it overnighted.

"Oh my God," the girls in front of me squeal. "Alex Limp? Eww! That's so gross!"

I watch Lillia. She's covering her face with her hands, pretending to be shocked. Her sister had started jumping around and clapping when the announcer first called out Alex's name, but now her hands are dropped to her sides. She takes a few steps backward, and hides behind the other cheerleaders standing around the bench.

Alex starts turning in circles like a dog chasing his tail, trying to see or get his hands up on the back of his jersey. I burst out laughing, because it's just too funny.

Reeve eventually hops down from the bench and tries to help Alex, even though he's laughing at him pretty hard. Well, maybe that's what Reeve wants to do. But I guess Alex just sees his friend laughing at him, because he lowers his head, drops his helmet, and rushes Reeve, wrapping his arms around Reeve's waist. He tackles him down on the ground with a big thud.

No one in the stands is applauding anymore. The whole team swarms around the boys wrestling on the ground, and the coach puts his whistle into his mouth and blows it a bunch of times, rapid-fire. The announcer keeps announcing the names of the other senior boys, but no one's getting up onto the bench. They're all trying to pull Alex off Reeve, to stop him from punching Reeve in the face. I see Alex get a real good shot in, right against Reeve's jaw. My hands fly to my face.

Kat and her friends run up to the fence, shouting, "Fight! Fight! Fight!" Kat climbs up onto the fence a few links, trying to get a better look.

Finally Alex gets pulled off. Reeve is there in the grass, lying on his back. One of his teammates holds out a hand to help him up, but Reeve swats it away and gets to his feet on his own. It takes him a second, though. His jaw is red and swollen. And his jersey is dirty.

Alex is standing a few feet away, with Derek trying his best to keep him from lunging at Reeve again. Alex is shouting something I can't hear from where I'm sitting, and he's jabbing his finger at Reeve over Derek's shoulder. Reeve isn't even listening. He turns his back on Alex and walks down the sideline. Rennie's trying to get to Reeve, to see if he's okay, I guess, but Ashlin is holding her arm. She won't let her go. Two of the coaches run up, looking concerned, and check Reeve's throwing arm. No one goes to Alex to see if he's okay. But the head coach does storm over and scream at Alex so hard, spit goes flying out of his mouth. Derek forces Alex to sit down on the team bench before he walks away too.

"What is Alex thinking?" one of the girls in front of me cries. "Reeve is our QB. Alex could have just ruined our whole football season!"

"I bet he's still pissed at Reeve for that Red Ribbon thing."

"Poor limp Alex," the third girl says, and the rest of them laugh.

The game starts shortly thereafter, and if Reeve was shaken by the whole Alex fight, he doesn't show it. It only takes two or three plays before he lobs a touchdown pass into the end zone. By then everyone's back to cheering for Reeve again, as if the fight never happened. Alex is on the bench, looking upset.

At halftime I get up to buy some Diet Coke, but the line's too long. Kat's already gone. I saw her and her friends leave not long after the fight. I wonder if I should stick around or not.

I walk past the cheering bench. The girl who cheered for Alex is a few steps away from the other girls on the squad, pleading with Rennie and Lillia.

"Come on, you guys!" she whines. "Isn't there someone else I can cheer for?"

"Are you serious?" Lillia says, folding her arms.

"Please! Every time I do my player cheer, people are yelling 'Go Liiimp!'"

"Don't worry about it," Rennie says. "He probably won't even get to play tonight."

The girl gasps. "What if he gets kicked off the team? I won't have anyone to cheer for!"

At that moment Nadia comes over. Quietly she says to Rennie, "If Wendy doesn't want to cheer for Alex, I will. We can trade. I don't mind."

Lillia's mouth drops open. She crosses her arms. "No one is changing players. Rennie put a lot of thought into the assignments."

Nodding, Rennie says, "Lillia's right. What I say, goes. Wendy, you made a commitment to Alex. You're going to honor that. If you don't like it, quit." She grabs a mirror out of her duffel bag on the bench and fusses with her hair. "There are five college scouts in the crowd for Reeve tonight, and I need to be bringing my A game for him, not worrying about this nonsense. We're done here."

Rennie turns and walks away from Nadia and the other cheerleader. Lillia follows her, and as she passes me, she gives me a nod.

I give one back. Mission accomplished. And not a moment too soon, because honestly, I can't wait until we start in on Rennie.

CHAPTER TWENTY-FIVE

RICKY, JOE, AND I DITCH THE FOOTBALL GAME AT halftime. Football is so unbelievably, mind-numbingly boring. We go get cheese fries and coffee from the Surf Diner, drive around for a bit more, and then I tell the guys to drop me off.

Even though it's Friday night, I end up doing my homework just to get it out of the way. But I think a lot about Alex too.

I bet he got in trouble for the fight with Reeve. His mom probably sent him to his man cave without supper, took away his phone or some other ridiculous attempt at a punishment. The way she fawns over Alex, buys his clothes, it's clear she wanted a girl. She'd be mad about the fighting, for sure. She's pretty Waspy, and Alex was an animal.

I never would have thought Alex was capable of being so raw. And I definitely didn't expect him to throw a punch at Reeve. It wasn't graceful, that's for sure, but he aimed in the right place, and he did hit the mark. I debated calling Alex and telling him to lean into his punches a little more next time. If he had, I bet he could have knocked Reeve out cold.

But I won't call him. And I won't answer his texts, or his e-mails, either. Not until I'm sure he's learned his lesson. That I am not someone to mess with. That he was an idiot for hooking up with Nadia when he could have been hooking up with me.

That night, I come up with the idea of asking Ricky for a ride to school on Monday. Because there's nothing like another guy in the picture to make boys wish they had you back. Or, in my case, the illusion of another guy.

It's how my mom ended up with my dad. They dated for a few months, and when he wouldn't get serious, she showed up at his favorite bar with her gay friend, Albert, with a roll of quarters for the jukebox. It only took one slow song before my dad tapped Albert on the shoulder so he could cut in. My mom was slick like that.

Not that I'm trying that on Alex. I'm just living my happy life, while he lives his miserable one.

It's not hard to imagine Alex standing alone in the parking lot. No one to talk to, all his friends totally shunning him for the fight he had with Reeve. Rennie would pick Reeve over him any day. I know it. He'll be a lost puppy, a friendless little kid. And then I'll come roaring in on the back of Ricky's bike. I'll take off the helmet and shake my hair out, slow-mo.

And, boy, will he be sorry.

I bet he walks right over. Either then or when I'm at my locker. He'll beg for my forgiveness, tell me Nadia meant nothing to him. That there's no girl in this whole school like Kat DeBrassio. And once you go Kat, you never go back.

On Monday morning Ricky picks me up on his motorcycle. I'm glad it's the Japanese import he tricked out with racing shocks so he can jump sand dunes. That's the one I said I wanted to ride. Not his mint-green Vespa. No one's going to think I look hot climbing off the back of a mint-green Vespa.

He flips up the visor in his helmet as I come out the front door. "Damn, Kat."

I bound down the walk, and my hair bounces, shampoo commercial style. I curled the ends this morning. Not enough to where someone might think I was trying to look good. More like I went to bed with it wet last night and I woke up with sexy bed head. I've got on my skinniest black jeans, a black tank, and my mom's black stilettos. The heels might be a touch too much, but who cares. And anyway, there's a senior assembly today with some college admissions counselors. I could always say I dressed up for that, if anyone says anything.

"Thanks for coming to get me," I say, and climb onto the back of the bike. First I put my arms around Ricky, but then I think better of it, lean back, and hold on to the seat. It's a slightly more badass pose.

"No worries. My first class isn't till nine thirty. Here," Ricky says, twisting around to pass me his helmet. It's a racing one, sleek with red stripes and a blacked-out visor. "Wear this. I forgot to bring an extra for you."

I wave him off and say, "I'm cool." After all, the high school is less than a mile away. And I don't want my hair to be flat.

"Kat, come on." The way Ricky says it, I know he's not going to drive me anywhere until I do.

I put it on, and he peels out down my street. The bike is loud. Way loud. The muffler is made that way. I smile, because everyone's going to hear us coming.

"Faster," I tell Ricky, and put my arms around his waist. He'd be cute if he wasn't such a pothead. I feel Ricky tense up, and then he revs us forward. He switches lanes, into oncoming traffic, so we can blow by a slow-moving bus on the way to the high school. Faster. It's one of those words that guys love to hear.

Ricky pulls into the parking lot. He says, "I can't believe I let you bring me here twice in the last three days."

I see Alex's SUV. "Over there," I tell Ricky.

I get off the bike exactly like I planned. One hop. Then I pull the helmet off and shake out my hair.

That's when I see Alex, leaning against his car door. But he's not alone. He's talking to Reeve and Rennie. Actually, Rennie seems to be the one doing most of the talking. She's using her hands a lot, and she keeps pointing at Reeve and then tenderly rubbing his shoulder. I bet she's trying to convince Alex that Reeve had nothing to do with the pranks we pulled.

She seriously can't stay out of anyone's business.

I'm not sure Alex is buying it. He's not making eye contact with either of them, but when Rennie is done, he slaps hands with Reeve, and then they walk into school together.

Reeve doesn't have a bruise on his face where Alex clocked him, which bums me out. But not as much as knowing they're still friends. And the fact that Alex totally missed my bomb-ass entrance.

"All right," Ricky says. "I'm gonna take off."

I hand him his helmet. "Thanks for the ride," I say.

He looks at me and smiles. "Anytime." And then he drives away.

"Love the outfit, Kat!" Rennie calls out to me through her cupped hands. "Biker whore is the perfect look for you!"

There's nothing stopping me from charging Rennie and spitting in her face again. At this point I wouldn't even care what Alex thought of me. But I don't have to do that. Rennie's going to get what's coming to her sooner rather than later. All I have to do is trust that Lillia and Mary are going to have my back, just like I have theirs.

On my way into school, I pass Rennie's jeep, parked in a choice spot. I can't help myself. I mosey up to it, crouch down beside the front tire, and unscrew the cap. I saw Pat do this once, take the air out of a tire when we got stuck in the snow. But he had a tool to do it, something to depress the little air valve. Damn.

And then I realize—my freaking stiletto. I slide one of them off and stick the heel so it sinks down inside the valve. It takes a few tries, but then I hear the hiss. It doesn't deflate as fast as I'd like, though. More like a very slow leak. The bell for homeroom rings out, but I just get comfortable, down there on the ground. I can be late, no biggie.

CHAPTER TWENTY-SIX

LILLIA

RENNIE AND I DECIDE TO SHOP FOR HOMECOMING dresses off island. I don't tell my mom that we're going, because I know she'll make me bring Nadia with us. Instead I sneak my mom's platinum card out of her wallet when she's in the shower. It's not like it's stealing. She already told me I could order a dress off the Internet.

I wanted to ask Ashlin, too, but Rennie insisted it should just be the two of us.

We duck out of cheer practice early to make the five o'clock ferry. We leave Ashlin to co-lead the rest of practice with Coach

Christy. Rennie tells Coach Christy that we have to help her mom with something at the gallery. Ash gave us a suspicious look but she didn't say anything.

Regular passenger tickets for the ferry aren't that expensive, but it's more than a hundred dollars for a round trip with a drive-on. Rennie opens her wallet. It's stuffed with cash, a bunch of crinkled old bills. I know she's been saving up her hostess salary for a nice homecoming dress. She has a separate dress fund she puts money into every paycheck.

"Don't worry about it," I say, and hand the guy some cash.

I'm sure Kat would be pissed at me for doing that, but it's not like she'll find out. Rennie says "Thank you" about a hundred times, which is nice of her.

We drive her Jeep onto the ferry and park on the freight deck. Most of the tourists get out of their cars and take the ride up on the upper deck, but not us. Rennie and I stay in her Jeep, listening to the radio and looking through some magazines I brought along for dress ideas. Rennie wants something tight, hopefully with sequins. I want strapless with a sweetheart neckline in white. Or maybe blush.

Nobody can walk a mall like Rennie. I get turned around easily. Even though we hardly ever come here, Rennie knows where the best stores are, and the fastest way to get from one to the next. We only have a couple of hours to find our dresses, eat something, drive back to the docks, and make it on a not-too-late ferry back to Jar Island.

The first store we hit is a bust, and the second one isn't much better. They both have tons of sweaters and corduroys now that it's fall, but not too many dresses. Or, at least, not ones fancy enough for Jar Island homecoming. Maybe for the underclassmen. But the senior girls always get the most dressed up. It's basically the pre-prom.

But in the third store we have some luck, and both Rennie and I end up with our arms full of possibilities. We take dressing rooms that are side by side.

"You know that new junior girl?" Rennie asks.

I'm halfway into a dress, but I stop cold. *Mary.* A million thoughts race through my mind. Could Rennie have seen us talking in the hallway? Probably not, because I'm careful about that. But maybe she saw me nod at her at the football game. That would be just perfect. To have the whole Alex thing blow up in my face right when we're finished.

I look down at the beige carpeting. Rennie's red toenails are facing the shared wall between us.

"Who?" I say.

"I'm sure you've seen her, Lil. Our school's not that big. Anyway, a bunch of the junior boys were saying that she's sooooo hot." The way Rennie drags out the "so," I know she's being sarcastic. "They're all going to vote for her for homecoming court. But she's not that pretty, if you ask me. Definitely not homecoming-caliber pretty. I bet her hair isn't even really blond. I bet she dyes it."

Even though I'm glad, obviously, that Rennie hasn't noticed anything, I bristle at what she's saying. Mary's pretty. A little weird, sure. But she *is* pretty. And it makes me glad to know that other people, boys especially, see it too. The girl hasn't had the easiest go of things. I still don't know exactly what it was that Reeve did to her, but it clearly screwed her up bigtime.

I hear the rustle of material as Rennie pulls a dress over her head. "Ooh! This one's cute. You ready to model?" The door of her dressing room swings open and then closed.

I hurry up and get the dress on. I don't even like it. The color's not flattering on me. But I step out of the dressing room anyway.

Rennie's standing on the box, up on her tiptoes, modeling in the three-way mirror. I see her eyes move off her reflection and onto me. "Champagne doesn't work for you," she announces.

"I know," I say. I sit down in one of the overstuffed chairs near the mirror, because I suddenly don't want to try on dresses anymore.

"This one is hot, but I don't know." Her voice sounds sad. "I wish I'd tried it on last."

The dress is tight, silver and covered in sparkles. It's exactly what Rennie said she wanted from the get-go. I swear Rennie always gets what she wants. "What are you talking about?" I say.

"Because it's only the first one I've tried on, and I feel like, if I bought it, I'd be settling, you know? The first dress is never the perfect dress."

I don't answer her. I just look at my nails.

"Lillia!" she whines. "What do you think? Is this *the one*?"

I purse my lips, pretend to consider it, and then sigh, "Yeah, sure. I guess," even though the dress does look amazing on her.

Rennie huffs, disappointed with my apathy. She looks back at the mirror and smiles again. She knows how good she looks. She doesn't need to hear it from me. What I say, what I think, doesn't matter to her at all.

She turns around and checks out her butt. "I guess what I

should be asking is, 'Will Reeve like it?' His opinion matters the most, as my date."

I sit up straight. "Wait. Aren't we going in a big group?" That's how it's always been, since our freshman year. There's no couples. No one asks anyone to go specifically with them. For prom maybe, but not homecoming. We just roll in a big group.

"Not anymore. Ash is going with Derek, PJ's taking that cute sophomore girl Allie. And I'm going with Reeve."

"You asked him already?" When did all this happen? When did everyone pair off without telling me?

"Not yet. I mean, it's a given that he'll say yes." Rennie messes with her strapless bra, trying to create more cleavage. "I'm telling you, Lil. It's going to be our night. He'll be looking hot, I'll be looking hot. You saw what happened during spin the bottle. Fireworks."

I feel myself sweating. "Then, who am I going to go with?"

She hops down from the box and says, "Go with Lindy," before disappearing back into her dressing room.

Oh my God. Is she serious? This is just so Rennie, to not even consider the fact that Nadia has hooked up with Alex, which she totally knows and still hasn't admitted to me! It's unbelievably insensitive. And there's no way I'm going to go to homecoming with Alex if there is even a remote possibility that he likes me. Especially not after the things I did to him. That would just be way too awkward.

"I'm not going with Alex," I say. "I'll just ride with you guys in the limo."

From the other side of the door, I hear her say, "We're all going to be paired up. It would be weird if you were alone, just tagging along with no date. Besides, Alex doesn't have a date yet either. It's going to look like you guys are going as a couple anyway."

I honestly don't care what it looks like. "I said no," I say, my voice rising.

"Fine, whatevs. I was just looking out for you. By all means, do whatever your little heart desires."

I go back into the dressing room and force myself to keep trying on the dresses I picked. The last one is maybe cute. It's black, which I hadn't considered, but the cut is just what I wanted. Strapless, with a sharp sweetheart neckline, and a short poufy skirt. It's sophisticated. I come out of the dressing room and ask Rennie what she thinks. "With peachy-nude heels?" I ask.

Rennie taps her finger against her lips. Considering. It used to be that I would wait for Rennie to decide before I could. Whether or not something was good, I mean.

"I think I'm going to get it," I say. I'll wear my hair up, I decide. I step off the platform and go back into the dressing room.

I slide the dress off. And then put it back on the hanger. It's expensive, more expensive than I thought for a plain black dress. I'm standing there, in my underwear, wondering if my mom will kill me, when I see Rennie's hand waving underneath the wall.

"Hey, let me try that last dress on."

You already found your dress, I want to say. *And also you can't afford it.*

Instead I pass my dress under the door, change back into my clothes, and wait while Rennie tries it on.

I hate that she looks good in it too. I decide right then and there that I'm definitely buying it.

"This *is* cute," she says, admiring herself. "Which one do you like best on me, Lil?"

I want to scream. But I don't. Of course I don't. Instead I change the subject. "Hey, did you hear that Melanie Renfro is, like, hard-core campaigning for homecoming queen? I saw her talking to the track guys."

Rennie rolls her eyes. "I'm not worried about Melanie Renfro. I'm telling you, Lil. I've got this in the bag." She cocks her head to the side, and then nods her head decisively. "The silver one. That's a homecoming queen's dress."

It hits me. The best way to get back at Rennie.

The whole ferry ride home, I can't wait to tell Kat that I've got the perfect plan for her revenge—we'll find a way to keep Rennie from winning homecoming queen.

Once we get back to Jar Island, I'm more than ready for Rennie to drop me off. But instead she drives right past my block. I turn in my seat, and she says, "I'm going to swing by Alex's place. I want to talk to Reeve about homecoming."

"Right now? Can't you take me home first?"

"No." She puts a hand on her heart. "I've got this feeling like it needs to happen tonight. It'll take, like, five minutes."

Again. What I want doesn't matter to her. "I'll wait in the car."

"Just come inside with me. Keep Alex company while I talk to Reeve."

We park, and Rennie takes a minute to touch up her lip gloss. Her hand is shaking, she's that nervous. I follow her into the pool house with my arms folded. I'm sure I don't look happy, because I'm not. In fact, I'm hoping Reeve shoots her down.

Reeve and Alex are on the couch, playing video games. I guess what happened on the field is already old news. It's funny. I don't think boys even know how to hold a grudge. I'm sure Reeve denied he had anything to do with the jerseys or the song and Alex took his word for it. Hopefully, Alex won't go looking for the person who did.

I stay near the door while Rennie walks up and stands right in front of the television. "Reevie," she says sweetly. "Can I talk to you for a second, in private?"

Reeve tries to look past Rennie at the screen, and when he can't, he pauses the game. "Of course."

Rennie slides her arm through his and leads him off into Alex's bedroom. "BRB, Lillia!"

Alex turns around and sees me. "Hey, Lillia."

"Hey, Lindy." I sit down on the far end of the sectional. Alex's face is barely red anymore. I guess he finally stopped using that lotion. "Your skin looks a lot better."

Alex turns so he's facing me. "Rennie's asking Reeve to homecoming, huh?"

Surprised, I say, "How did you know?"

"Well, because Ashlin asked Derek today. And I think PJ's gonna bring some sophomore girl." I notice that Alex is blushing. It's coming up from his chest, creeping up his neck. "No one's asked you yet, right?"

Oh, no. Oh, no. Rennie's probably already told Alex to ask me! I quickly get up from the couch and walk over to the window. "God, I don't understand why we can't just go in a big group the way we always do. Why change things now? It's so dumb. I mean, we'll be hanging out together anyway."

Alex comes over near to where I'm standing. Not too close, but close enough. He nods, like I've made a good point. "Yeah. I guess you're right." But I can tell he's disappointed.

Rennie pops out of the bedroom and hops her way over to the glass door I'm leaning against. Her cheeks are flushed, and her smile practically fills up her entire face. "Okay, Lil! Let's go!" she sings.

Rennie always gets what she wants. But not this time. Not when it matters the most.

CHAPTER TWENTY-SEVEN

KAT

I'M SITTING IN BED WATCHING A MOVIE ON MY LAPTOP when I hear the knock at my window. For one crazy second I think it could be Alex. Shep, who is curled up on a pile of my laundry, barely even lifts his head. Dumb dog. I hop off my bed and go to open it. It's not Alex. It's Lillia. "What the hell?" I say, heaving the window open. "I have a front door."

She climbs inside, her cheeks pink. "It's one in the morning," she reminds me. "I didn't want to wake up your dad. But I knew you'd still be awake." Lillia's got on a short puffer coat even though it's barely cold outside. She gasps when she sees Shep. "Shep!"

Shep jumps up and bounds over to her. She bends down and hugs him and strokes his back and ears. "Shep, I missed you!"

"His breath probably stinks right now," I say. "He just had a bone."

Lillia ignores me. "Shep, you remember me! I can tell you do." My dumb dog is drooling all over her, panting and wagging his tail.

She gives him one more pat and then walks right over to my dresser like she owns the place. "I remember this!" she exclaims, picking up the porcelain doll my mom gave me for my seventh birthday. "Her name is Nelly, right?"

Yeah, her name is Nelly. So what. I sit back down on my bed, my arms crossed. "What's up?"

"Will you please close the window first? It's cold."

I want to tell her to see a damn doctor, because something is seriously wrong with her body temperature. But I need to be nicer, so I just do it.

"Thanks," she says, and blows on her fingers. "So, I have an idea for how to get your revenge on Rennie. It's perfect."

I'm having major flashbacks, the way she keeps touching

my stuff, picking up candles and sniffing them, winding up my jewelry music box. Lillia used to love poking around Rennie's and my rooms when she came back for the summer. Like, she wanted to see what parts of our life she'd missed out on when her family left each school year.

She turns back around, a flash of gold dangling from her hand. "You still have it," she says, her eyes wide and surprised. It's that stupid key necklace she gave me the first day of school freshman year.

I leap up and snatch the necklace out of her hand. "Quit touching my shit," I snarl.

"I'm just surprised you kept it," Lillia says with a toss of her ponytail.

"Don't flatter yourself. I just haven't gotten around to pawning it yet," I say, tossing it back into the jewelry box and slamming the top shut.

Under her breath Lillia says, "Since the ninth grade?"

Lillia's mom called Rennie's mom and asked for a playdate. A playdate, for God's sakes. We were eleven years old, not six. Rennie's mom said yes, and then Rennie begged me to come with her. She wanted us to ride our bikes over, so we could leave in case it was boring, but my mom said no, White Haven was too far away. Lillia's house was on the other side of the island—only a ten-minute drive, but still. Our friends lived within walking distance; we ran in and out of each other's houses all day long during the summer. Lillia's house felt a world away.

That first day we played out in the pool for the afternoon. Rennie and I practiced swan dives and cannonballs while Lillia splashed around the shallow end and pretended to be a mermaid. Her mom brought her little sister, Nadia, out and she had swimmies on her arms. Her mom said, "I'm going to fix you girls a snack. I'll be right back. Lillia, you watch your sister." Not long after she went inside, Nadia floated too close to the deep end, and Lillia started to scream. Nadia got scared and burst into tears, so I quickly swam over and pushed her back to Lillia, who was practically crying too. She was, like, "Thank you so much."

That's when Mrs. Cho came outside with a tray of Brie and crackers and Orangina. I perked right up. My mom never bought Brie. She only bought American cheese for sandwiches and Velveeta for macaroni and cheese.

As soon as she saw her mom, Lillia jumped out of the pool and ran over to her and put her arms around her waist. "Nadia went over to the deep end, and Kat saved her life!" Then Mrs. Cho kept gushing over what an amazing swimmer I must be, and I felt embarrassed but also kind of proud, even though I didn't really do anything.

When we were over at the deep end and Lillia was still sitting next to her mom, Rennie whispered, "Let's call your dad soon. I think Reeve's brother is taking the boys out on his boat to go tubing today."

In a low voice I said, "We can't leave now. That would be rude."

Later, when Mrs. Cho and Nadia went back inside and it was just the three of us again, Rennie started talking about how she couldn't wait for school to start. "I hope we both get Miss Harper for science," she said. "Also PJ told me that his sister told him that Mr. Lopez is the easiest math teacher."

I remember feeling awkward, because Lillia was quiet. She didn't know any of these people. I asked her, "What's your school like?"

She said she went to a private all-girls school, they had to wear uniforms, and it was boring. Rennie made a face and said, "I don't know what I would do if there weren't boys at school."

When the sun went down, Lillia's mom asked us if we wanted to stay for dinner. She was making a fish called mahimahi with some sort of pineapple salsa. She said we could make s'mores for dessert on the fire pit outside. I was all *Hell yes,* but before I could say it, Rennie lied and said she had to go home.

In my dad's car Rennie told me she wanted to come over to my house for dinner. We wouldn't be having anything nearly as good as mahimahi and s'mores. My mom was sick, so my dad was in charge of dinner those days. Frozen pizza, hot dogs, or hellfire chili. I could've killed Rennie for making me miss out on actual food.

Later, Rennie was stretched out on my bed, shuffling a deck of Uno cards. Shep was dozing in her lap. He was a puppy back then, and Rennie loved coming over to play with him. Her condo didn't allow pets. "I mean, why would anyone need three refrigerators? Her family isn't even that big! Plus, they only live there three months out of the year!"

"One is for Korean food," I said from my hammock. Another present from my dad. As if a hammock and a dog could make me forget that my mom was dying. But whatever. It was really comfortable. "And then that other one was just for drinks, remember? Lillia's mom told us to help ourselves."

"Well, I think it's weird."

"She's rich. Rich people buy all kinds of stupid stuff."

"Exactly. Don't you think she was kind of bragging a lot? Like, okay, we get it. You're, like, a millionaire."

"I don't think she was bragging," I said. "You're the one who wanted to look in her closet."

"I guess." Rennie scratched a bug bite on her leg. Her legs were always covered in them. "But, like, why did we have to take our shoes off at the door?"

"I think it's an Asian thing," I said. "Also, their whole house is white. They probably don't want people tracking in outside dirt."

"But seriously, three refrigerators?"

"Chill out on the refrigerators, Ren." I hopped out of my hammock. "Just deal the cards."

When Lillia invited us over to her house again a few days later, I made Rennie come with me. "Just give her a chance," I said. I was hoping we could watch TV on that huge flat-screen in the rec room, and maybe Lillia's mom would give us more Brie and invite us to dinner again. Also, I liked Lillia. Sure, she was kind of princessy, but it wasn't her fault she was rich and pretty. She was generous, at least. Rennie could be kind of stingy with her stuff. Not Lillia. She had a makeup case with every nail polish color you could think of, organized like a rainbow. When I picked up a glittery purple one called Black Magic Woman, she told me I could have it. I said "That's okay," which I regretted immediately. Especially when Rennie painted her toes neon pink and Lillia said the color never looked good on her and Rennie could have it if she wanted. I figured Rennie would tell her no like I did. But she didn't. Her eyes lit up and she said thanks, and she stuffed the nail polish into her pocket like she was scared Lillia would change her mind.

It happened slowly. The shift. From me to Lillia. Most people wouldn't have noticed it. I don't even know if Rennie did. But when you know someone as well as I knew her, you can just feel it. When we went to Scoops for ice cream, Rennie used to always split a hot fudge sundae with me, but after Lillia, she started wanting to split the strawberry sundae with her. Or when we rode the bus to the movies, there were seats for two. She'd sit next to Lillia, and I'd be in front of them. Lillia would ask me questions, try to make sure I didn't feel left out—but it only made me feel worse. I didn't need her pity. I was the one who brought her in, not the other way around.

At the end of that first summer, when Lillia left for her real life, I was sure things would go back to normal. And they did. But when Lillia came back the next summer, Rennie stuck to her like glue. The way she used to do to me. It pissed me off, but by this time my mom was really sick, and I needed my best friend, however much I could get of her. When Lillia came to live on Jar Island for good, and Rennie and I had that stupid fight right before school started, that was it. We were over.

The hilarious thing is, I was the one who set the whole thing in motion. After that first time we went to Lillia's house when Rennie wasn't sure about her, I could have gone along with it. But I didn't. I was the one who said "Give her a chance," and Rennie listened. Back then I was the only one Rennie would listen to.

On the first day of freshman year, Lillia left a necklace in my locker. It was from that fancy store in White Haven, the one with a doorbell to get in. She bought one for Rennie, and one for herself. They were supposed to be friendship necklaces. Too bad the friendship was already over.

I honestly don't know why I kept it.

"What's your idea for Rennie?" I sound barely interested, because I doubt her idea will be good. I mean, everything we did to Alex was fine, because Alex is a sensitive guy and he's easier to mess with. With Rennie I'm going to need to go bigger, badder.

Lillia claps her hands together like the cheerleader she is. "It's so perfect. What's the one thing Rennie always wanted?"

I shrug. "Boobs?"

She giggles. "Well, those, too. But that's not what I had in mind." She pauses for effect. "She's always dreamed about being homecoming queen. Remember?"

Slowly I nod. "Yeah." Back when we were in middle school, Rennie used to talk about this kind of stuff 24/7. Being crowned homecoming queen just like her mom. Prom queen, too. Rennie wanted it all.

"Ren's been on homecoming court every year. She thinks this year's crown is a lock. Not that she's fully admitting how bad she wants it. But I'm telling you, she really, really wants it. So all we have to do is make sure it doesn't happen." Lillia pokes me in the shoulder playfully. "Say 'Thank you,' Katherine. This one's for you."

I laugh. Classic Lillia, wanting credit for every little thing. "We can tell Mary tomorrow at school."

Lillia says, "Let's just go over there now." She stoops down and pets Shep and whispers something into his ear.

"Seriously?"

"Yeah! Why not." Lillia starts to climb out my window again, and then turns around and says, "Does your dad still belong to that popcorn of the month club?"

She remembers the weirdest things. First Shep, then Nelly, now my dad's favorite snack. "Yeah."

"What is it this month?" she asks.

"Salty caramel."

Her face lights up. "That was my favorite kind! Can we bring some with us?"

"You know you can't eat that way in college, right? Freshman fifteen, beotch."

With a sniff Lillia says, "All the Cho women have really fast metabolisms." Like that's something to be proud of. "There isn't one overweight person in my family. On either side."

"All right, all right. I'll see if there's any left." Pat smoked up in the garage tonight, and he gets munchies really bad. If we're out of popcorn, I can grab some Oreos or whatever.

We're almost out my bedroom door when I remember something. "Wait," I say, turning back. I reach under my bed and fish around for what I'm looking for. Alex's notebook.

Lillia hesitates, so I push it into her hand. "Think of it as a trophy," I tell her. "You earned it."

CHAPTER TWENTY-EIGHT

MARY

I HAVE NO SENSE OF TIME, BUT IT HAS TO BE HOURS NOW that I've been in the dark. I'm lying on top of my bed with my eyes wide open, in my pj shorts and a camisole. Although I'm tired, and it feels like years since I had a good night's rest, I can't bring myself to fall sleep. It's like I've forgotten how.

So I think about my mom and dad, why Kat wears all that eye makeup when she has such pretty eyes, what Lillia puts in her hair to make it so shiny, on to Friday's geometry test, and last what to wear to school tomorrow. I think about everything and anything to keep Reeve out of my head. But it never works. It's as if he's in here with me, in this room, haunting me.

I roll onto my back and stare through the dark at the beams in the ceiling. I should ask Aunt Bette if she knows a special candle or some sage or incense I could burn to get rid of this negative energy. Aunt Bette's into that New Agey stuff—smudging, tarot cards, crystals. Mom thinks it's silly, but she still wears the moonstone ring Aunt Bette bought for her fortieth birthday. Moonstone is supposed to bring positivity and healing to your life. I could probably use some of that, too.

But I know I can't do it. I can't ask Aunt Bette to help me, because then we'd have to talk about what happened all those years ago. Neither of us want to do that. Her just as much as me.

Something pings my bedroom window and interrupts the quiet. I lift my head off the pillow and watch the glass without breathing. It happens again, this time while I'm looking. A pebble bounces off the pane.

I get up and walk nervously to the window, peeking just past the sheer white curtains. Lillia and Kat wave at me from down on the ground.

With a big sigh of relief, I step out from my hiding spot, smile, and wave back.

"Come out and play, Mary!" Lillia calls up.

And then I hear Aunt Bette's bedroom door creak open from down the hall. I quickly hold up one finger to the girls, jump back onto my bed, and pretend to be asleep.

I open my eyes a teensy bit and watch as Aunt Bette pushes my door open with her bare foot and looks around my room. She's in her nightgown, and her long thick hair is wild and puffy.

She tiptoes past my bed and over to the window. Hopefully, Lillia and Kat have ducked out of sight. I'd rather they didn't meet Aunt Bette like this. I'd rather she had a chance to at least comb her hair and put lipstick on. Plus, it's a school night. Aunt Bette's been really cool, but I don't want to press my luck.

Aunt Bette stares out my window; her hot breath makes a tiny cloud on the glass. Then she gently pulls my curtains closed and goes back to her room.

I know I should wait a while for Aunt Bette to fall back asleep, but I don't want Kat and Lillia to leave. So after a minute or two, I grab a sweater and creep down the stairs, as quiet as a mouse.

Kat and Lillia are sitting underneath our huge pine tree in the backyard. Both of them have their backs up against the trunk.

Kat's legs are outstretched; Lillia's hugging her knees to her chest.

"Hey," I say. "Sorry that took so long. My aunt . . ."

Lillia yawns. "Was that her up there? She looks . . . kind of witchy." Kat clicks her tongue, and Lillia quickly adds, "Sorry."

It makes me sad to hear Lillia say that, but I know she's right. I sink down to the ground. Aunt Bette is my favorite aunt for sure, but she's had problems with depression for forever, according to my mom. I don't quite understand why, because Aunt Bette has had the kind of life I've read about in books. She's traveled the world, selling paintings and meeting all sorts of interesting people. She was beautiful once, and she knew how to play every single card game you could think of. But when the dark times would come, she became a whole other person. She could barely get out of bed some days. It's why she once came to live with us here in the house for a whole summer.

"My mom says that when they were in high school, Aunt Bette could get any boy on the beach to buy them ice cream. They never had to bring change with them." I thread some of my hair behind my ears.

Kat tucks a cigarette between her lips. "No kidding," she says, and the words make the flame of her lighter dance.

And then there's a long, somewhat awkward pause.

Lillia clasps her fingers together and puts on a big smile. "So, Kat and I came up with a way to get revenge on Rennie at homecoming."

"Oh! That's great," I say, and then force a swallow. "Is she, like, dating Reeve? I heard some girls talking about that at the football game."

Lillia shakes her head. "No. I mean, she definitely has Reeve in her crosshairs, but I don't know if he sees her that way."

"Oh," I say, sitting up straighter. "I was just curious."

Kat leans in and says, "All right, back to business. Homecoming ballots are passed out the week of the dance. Everyone votes, and then the ballots are put in the locked box they use for student council elections, which is pretty effing ridiculous, if you ask me. What we're gonna do is break into that box and change enough ballots so that Rennie loses homecoming queen." She cackles. "It will be the greatest disappointment of her sad little life."

Lillia puts her hands on her cheeks and says, "I can't wait to see her face!"

"And then Lillia wins, right?" I say.

"No!" Lillia says, shaking her head. "I don't want to win."

"Why not?" Kat says, surprised. "Rennie will freaking short-circuit with jealousy."

Lillia bites her lip. "I think it'll be even worse if someone else takes her crown. Someone she would never think could beat her. Like Ashlin."

"Oh, yeah! Ashlin. My replacement. I always forget about her. Does she even have a personality?" Kat asks.

"She's a nice girl," Lillia says, glaring at Kat. "And she'll be happy to win."

Kat shrugs, and takes a drag off her cigarette. "Fine, whatever. But we still need a plan to get Reeve." She blows out the smoke in a long, thin line. "Did you have any ideas, Mary?"

I shake my head.

"Okay," Lillia says patiently. "Well, what do you want to have happen to him? Let's start there."

I chew on my nail and think. All the anger I've got starts to bloom up inside me. This is part of the reason I try not to think about Reeve, if possible. It's a Pandora's box. I'm afraid to open myself up and relive exactly what happened. But maybe that's the only way I'll know what kind of revenge will make me feel like justice was served.

After a deep breath I say, "Whatever we do has to be big. It has to be cruel. It has to hurt him on the level that he hurt me." If that's even possible.

Kat and Lillia look at each other, startled by my intensity, I guess. I know what's coming before Lillia even says it.

"What did he do to you?" she asks, her voice barely a whisper.

"You can trust us," Kat says. "We won't tell anyone."

Lillia moves her hair over to one shoulder and makes a little cross over her heart. "Promise."

I drop my chin to my chest and let my hair fall around my face. I know I have to do this. I have to tell someone the whole story of what happened.

I lift my head and wet my lips. "Reeve had a special nickname for me." I feel the words come into my mouth, hot and metallic. "Big Easy."

I can tell by the way Kat's face wrinkles up that she was expecting something worse. "What's the story there?"

"I looked different back in seventh grade. I was fat. And we were studying New Orleans in social studies."

"Seriously? You were heavy?" Lillia's surprise is like a compliment.

I nod, and push the sleeves of my sweater up to my elbows. "Huge, actually."

"So he made fat jokes about you," Kat snarks, her top lip curling into a snarl. "How totally Reeve."

I twist around and look back up at my bedroom window, to make sure Aunt Bette isn't watching. She's not. The curtains are still closed. I turn back around and keep going, sure to keep my voice low. "You remember how Reeve and I went to the Belle Harbor Montessori, right? Well, we were the only two kids in our grade from Jar Island, so we both had to ride the ferry back and forth every day. I tried to stay away from Reeve, because we didn't get off on the right foot on his first day."

Then I tell them the story of that day in the cafeteria, when Reeve made the joke about me eating off his tray. How he made it so nobody wanted to be seen with me in public. Kat and Lillia don't interrupt, but every so often they *tsk* or shake their heads. Each response is a bit of encouragement that helps me keep talking. I tell them about the pocketknife day and the time we went out for ice cream, too.

"After that we developed this weird kind of . . ." I take a second to pick the right word, but nothing seems to fit, so I just go with, "friendship," even though that's not exactly it. "The ferry ride was kind of our time-out. Reeve used to say, 'Us islanders have to stick together, right Big Easy?'"

"Whoa, whoa, whoa," Kat says, rapid-fire. "Wait up. You let him call you 'Big Easy' to your face?" She's fired up, rolling onto her knees and leaning forward.

It's hard to look at her. "It was different when we were on the ferry, just the two of us. It didn't sound as mean, for some reason." I pull my sweater tight around myself. "But once we'd get to the mainland, thing would change. He wouldn't talk to me in public. Well . . . except to make fun of me."

"What a two-faced bitch," Kat says. "He's worse than Rennie!" She grinds her cigarette out in the dirt and then immediately lights another.

Lillia's staring at me, unblinking. "Why would you let him do that, Mary?"

"Because he'd tell me things," I say. "He'd complain about his dad, who I think was a pretty bad alcoholic. He'd tell me how his dad would drink, and then his dad would yell at Reeve and his brothers. I felt bad for him."

"You felt bad for *him*?" Kat says incredulously.

"He hated his dad. He said his dream was to get a scholarship to go to a big university off Jar Island and never come back."

Lillia scoffs. "Scholarship? Reeve makes Bs and Cs! He only gets As in gym."

Kat shakes her head. "You don't know because you didn't grow up here," she tells Lillia. "Reeve used to be the smartest kid in our grade. I remember him getting sent to that fancy school on a scholarship. It was a big deal, because his family wouldn't have been able to afford it otherwise. Our teacher threw him a good-bye party with cupcakes and stuff."

"It wasn't because I was special to him, or anything like that," I clarify. "We were just passing the time together. I knew how hard the other kids at school worked to get his attention. Everyone was a little in love with him. I guess I felt a weird sense of pride for getting to spend some time with him every day."

Lillia grumbles, but Kat says, "Lil, you have to admit Reeve can be a charming bastard when he wants to be."

"All right," she concedes. "I guess I could see that."

I stare at the dirt and say shamefully, "I let myself think that there was something real between us, that I knew Reeve in a way that no one else did. But really, the Reeve I thought I knew didn't exist. He was just setting me up, tricking me into letting my guard down, so he could hurt me even worse."

Before I know it, I'm crying. I guess because I know what happens next. The story I've never told anyone.

The wind suddenly picks up, like a storm might crack open

the sky above us. My hair whips around my face, stinging my cheeks. Lillia zips up her coat; Kat tucks her hands inside her sleeves. Neither of them move.

A voice inside me tells me to stop talking, because once I tell Kat and Lillia, there's no turning back, no pretending it didn't happen. But I swallow the fear down and keep going, because holding on to this secret for one second longer suddenly feels like it's going to kill me.

I didn't expect to see Reeve that afternoon. Ms. Penske kept a few of us after school to discuss plans for the student mural we'd be painting in the gymnasium. I missed the three o'clock ferry, and figured I'd catch the three thirty. But Reeve had stayed late too, playing basketball with a few of his friends. When I walked by the fence, Reeve sank the last basket, and everyone started grabbing their books and putting on their jackets. Reeve saw me. I kept walking toward the water, but slower than I had been, and eventually he caught up with me.

We'd almost reached the dock when a bunch of guys he'd been playing basketball with ran up from behind us. They had a notebook in their hands, one Reeve had apparently left at the courts. When they saw us, their mouths dropped open. Reeve and Big Easy walking together? It didn't make any sense.

Reeve didn't say anything to me, but he suddenly picked up his pace. I walked faster too, to keep up with him. The boys called out, "Hey, Reeve! You forgot your book!" but Reeve pretended he didn't hear them. He practically sprinted the last few feet to the ferry, like he was afraid he might miss it.

The cars and trucks had already driven onto the freight deck, and it was just the people left, lining up to climb the plank onto the ferry. Reeve and I took our place at the end, him first and me right behind him. Then the boys from class came up and stood a few feet off to the side. They handed Reeve his notebook, and Reeve mumbled a thank-you. They started to walk away.

I don't know where this surge of courage came from. Maybe because things had been good between us. Maybe because I wanted to put Reeve in a spot where he'd have to admit what was going on. Maybe because I knew he didn't really care about what these guys thought of him, from our conversations.

There was one thing I did know for sure. Reeve had started the Big Easy thing, and it had caught on like wildfire. But if he showed everyone in class that we were cool, I knew it could end just as quickly. That's how big a deal he was.

I stepped forward so Reeve and I were side by side, and

shouted at the boys, "So what? We're friends!" as loudly as I possibly could. Then I threw my arm around Reeve's shoulder and smiled at him.

Reeve stared at me with unbelieving eyes. Once he blinked, though, he looked furious. He shouted, "Get the hell away from me!" And then he lunged. His palms went straight into my chest, and, throwing all his strength behind it, he shoved me toward the guys.

The force of it was unbelievable. I didn't have a chance. My sneakers skidded over the gravel. The boys quickly stepped out of my path, revealing the edge of the dock. I tried to just fall down, to keep myself from going into the water, but I kept flying backward. At the last second I put my arms out to try to stop myself from going over the side of the dock, and tiny splinters embedded in my palms. The pain had me gasping for air, my last breath before I plunged into the water.

It was so cold, I could barely move. I could tell my hands were bleeding by the way the skin burned despite the chill of the water. I could hear their warbled laughter above me.

"Yo, she looks like a manatee!"

"Hey, manatee! You need a net?"

"Swim! Swim for shore, manatee!"

I flailed my arms and kicked my legs, trying to get to the surface. But my clothes weighed a hundred pounds, and I barely managed to get my head above water. I was gasping for air, and I kept swallowing mouthfuls of salty water.

The dockworkers came running, and one of them tossed me a life preserver. It took two of them to pull me out. The ferry passengers leaned over the edge of the deck to watch.

As soon as I was on land, I threw up a gallon of that salty water. That was when the boys finally stopped laughing and shrank away from the spectacle. The only one who wasn't there was Reeve.

My hands were bleeding, my clothes were soaked and stiff and speckled with gravel, and there was vomit on my shoes. It took me a minute before I realized that my white T-shirt was completely see-through, clinging to every one of my fat rolls. I started shaking, but I wasn't cold. I was about to lose it. And then I did. I started crying, and I couldn't stop.

One ferry worker helped me up to the galley, then left to find me a blanket. He came back with a stack of brown paper towels from one of the bathroom dispensers. I tried using them to dry off, but as soon as they got wet, they disintegrated into ropy bits of pulp.

The whole time I was sobbing.

Reeve was there, in the galley too. He sat in the first row of seats near the deck windows, the seat he'd carved his name in. He looked straight ahead, out the window at Jar Island off in the distance. He didn't acknowledge me, or what he'd done. He didn't even turn around once. No matter how hard I cried.

When we reached Jar Island, Reeve took off right away. I waited for the other passengers to disembark, and then I snuck off the ferry and hid behind a delivery truck that was waiting to drive aboard for the return trip. I could see my mom waiting there. As Reeve ran off the boat, she waved at him. He didn't wave back. He pretended not to see her.

If she didn't see me, I knew she'd stay and wait for me to come in on the next boat. I couldn't stand her seeing me that way. I didn't want her to know that the boy I'd told her so much about, the boy we took for ice cream that rainy day, had done this to me.

I decided to sneak home, change my clothes, and pretend to have come back by the next boat. She would never have to know what happened. Dad, too.

I crouched down and used different cars for cover. Once I was out of the parking lot, I huffed it up the hill to our house, my sneakers squishing with every step. All I could think about

JENNY HAN AND SIOBHAN VIVIAN

was how he'd acted all those times when we were alone. Like he cared about me. Like we were friends. I couldn't imagine facing him the next morning. Both because of what he'd done to me, and because I knew I'd never get that back again. As pathetic as it was, Reeve was the only friend I had left.

I went up to my room and opened my closet with the intention to change clothes. Really. But instead of doing that I found myself staring up at the beams on my ceiling. Then I got a rope from the basement and, after a couple of tries, looped it over a beam and tied it into a noose. I dragged my desk chair over, slipped the rope over my neck. And then took a big step off the chair, and dropped.

But as soon as I fell, I realized that I didn't want to die. I started to fight, kicking my legs to try to get the desk chair to roll back to me. But the rope was so tight, and I couldn't breathe. My weight swung me like a pendulum, and my feet kept knocking into the wall. I was starting to black out, lose consciousness.

Luckily, my mom came home. She heard the tapping of my feet against the wall. She came in and screamed at the sight of me. She got me down, slipped the rope off my neck, and laid with me on the floor while she called 911, stroking my hair, until the paramedics arrived.

Kat and Lillia stare at me, horrified.

"As soon as I was stable, my parents had me transferred to a different hospital, one far away from Jar Island. I was out of school for a whole year doing therapy and stuff. I had to live on a psych floor for months, trying to convince the doctors and nurses that I didn't want to kill myself anymore. And the truth is, I didn't want to. The one thing that kept me going was the thought of coming back here one day and making Reeve own up to what he did."

I let out a breath, and already I feel lighter, just a little bit lighter.

"Well, that's that," Kat says. "We have to kill Reeve."

I can't tell if she's joking or not. I hope she's joking. "I don't want to kill him," I say, to be clear. "I just want him to feel one ounce of the pain I felt." I'm not even sure if that is possible.

"We'll help you, Mary. We'll make him pay for what he did." Tears are spilling down Lillia's cheeks, but there's fire in her eyes.

"Thank you," I whisper.

Kat's legs are shaking. "I want to drive over to Reeve's house right freaking now, and punch him in his face. But I know we can do better, hurt him worse if we wait and think this through. We've got to take Reeve Tabatsky down in a major way."

Lillia wipes her eyes. "So, what do we do?"

"You know him the best of all of us," Kat says. "What does he care the most about?"

Automatically Lillia says, "Football. He cares about football more than anything."

"That's it!" I cry out. "Even back at Montessori he used to talk about how he was going to be some big football star when he got to high school!"

"Done," Kat says. "We'll get him kicked off the team."

"How?" I ask. Is that even possible? Reeve's the star quarterback. There's no team without him. Even I know that.

Lillia's face lights up. "Drugs! Jar Island has a super-strict no-tolerance policy. Ever since that kid from Menlow High got caught smoking weed, our coaches have been watching us really carefully, making sure we don't do anything stupid. If we could somehow plant drugs in Reeve's locker or something, he'd be kicked off the team for sure, even if he is the quarterback."

"But what if he says the drugs aren't his, and the school believes him?" I say. "He could take a voluntary drug test to prove it."

"I guess we'll have to slip him the drugs without him knowing," Kat says. "Acid or ecstasy or something that will make him trip out."

It's one thing to plant drugs in the guy's locker; it's another thing to actually drug him. I look over at Lillia, expecting her to protest.

But she doesn't. Instead she nods and says, "Let's do it at homecoming, when everyone will be watching. He'll definitely get homecoming king. We might as well knock him and Rennie out at the same time." Twirling her hair around her finger, she says, "He might even get expelled. Then you'd never have to worry about him again, Mary."

"What do you think?" Kat asks me. "This is your kill."

"Let's do it," I say. I pinch my hand hard, the web of skin between my thumb and ring finger, just to make sure I'm not dreaming.

CHAPTER TWENTY-NINE

It's Friday night. Everyone and their mom is off island for the first away game, and I'm down at the ferry dock, waiting for my brother's drug dealer to come in on the eight o'clock. It's so perfect, it's almost cliché. If only someone was here to take a picture for the yearbook. Kat DeBrassio: Most Likely to Drug the QB.

My back is up against a dock post. I'm smoking a cigarette as the ferry comes in on black waves of water. Right on time.

I feel for the wad of money stuffed into my front pocket.

Sixty dollars in fives and singles, enough for two hits of ecstasy. I didn't bother asking Mary for money, because after that story she told us, it wouldn't feel right to ask her to pay. But I did ask Lillia. We met up in the girls' bathroom this morning. She unzipped her little pink purse and took out an even littler pink purse and unzipped that too. All she had in there was her ChapStick; a golden Chanel lip gloss called Glimmer, Rennie's signature color; Lillia's driver's license; a red Jolly Rancher; and two credit cards.

I told her drug dealers don't accept plastic.

Lillia felt bad, I could tell, and she promised to pay me back. I told her she could buy me a carton of cigarettes or maybe something for my boat, but then she started whining that her mother goes over her charges each month, so I said forget it. I got it out of what I saved from my summer job. Whatever. It's not like sixty bucks will make or break my college fund.

When Lillia went into a stall to pee, I opened up her purse and took out Rennie's precious lip gloss. What a wannabe. She probably spent half a night's pay on it. Whistling to myself, I dumped it into the trash can.

Cars parked on the freight deck click on their headlights and drive off the ferry. I watch other passengers, men in suits,

JENNY HAN AND SIOBHAN VIVIAN

cleaning ladies, people in supermarket uniforms, file down the plank. It's lit by tiny white Christmas lights.

I get pissed when I don't see Kevin, but he's the last one off. He's wearing the same beat-up jean jacket he always does. I think he's had it since he was my age. He strolls down, stops halfway to light his cigarette, and then keeps going.

I straighten up and walk toward him. He looks at my boobs first, then my face. Classic Kevin.

"Kat?" he says, squinting through the dark. "Is that you?"

"Hey," I say, and shove my hands into my back pockets. "Pat sent me down to pick up his stuff."

"Oh, did he now?" Kevin grits his cigarette between his teeth and gives me a dry laugh.

"Yeah," I say breezily, trying to hide the fact that I'm lying my ass off. While Pat was in the shower, I used his phone to text Kevin for the drugs. Pat's friends, my friends too, use Kevin. Mostly for weed. He makes the trip to the island every Friday to make deliveries to his customers. Even though Pat lets me smoke up with him sometimes, he'd freaking murder me if he found out I'd called Kevin on my own for harder stuff. "Pat's up at the garage, working on his bike. He cheaped out and bought a rebuilt starter, and now he can't get the thing to turn over. I told him to just return the piece of crap and get a new one, but you know how he is. Anyway, he sent me down here." The way I say it, I make it sound complain-y. "Asshole."

"Pat doesn't really strike me as an ecstasy kind of guy."

I'm not sure if Kevin's on to me or just trying to chat me up. Either way, I have to think fast, because Kevin's right. Pat is a stoner, through and through. "He's finally hooking up with some girl," I say. "Only, she's not cute. So . . . maybe he needs help."

Kevin laughs hard at his, so hard he coughs. Then he lifts his arms up in a deep stretch. "Well, I couldn't get regular E from my supplier. So I got the liquid stuff instead. I'd better call that SOB and make sure he's cool with that."

Liquid ecstasy? I didn't know that existed. That'll be even easier for Lillia to slip into Reeve's drink. "It works just the same as regular E?"

"Actually, it's stronger." Kevin reaches for his cell.

"Nice. I know Pat'll be cool with that." I quick take out the money from my pocket and hand it over to Kevin, before he has a chance to dial.

He shoots me daggers. "Not here," Kevin barks, and looks over both of his shoulders. "Walk with me."

So I put the money back into my pocket and follow him into

town, feeling pretty stupid. We go over to the restaurant where Rennie works, Bow Tie, and head for the back door, where the kitchen is. You can hear all kinds of restaurant noise inside— dishes getting washed, pots and pans clanking around, guys shouting out orders. I'm figuring Kevin wants to do the deal here, because it's pretty shadowy. I reach for my money again, but he waves me off and asks, "What's your poison, Kitty Kat?"

Gross. "They aren't going to serve me here."

"I do business with some of the bartenders. We'll be okay. So . . . let me guess." He looks me up and down. "You're a Sex on the Beach kind of girl."

I roll my eyes. "Whiskey," I say.

His face lights up. "Don't go anywhere."

"Wait. Can we do the deal here? I should get back to Pat. I don't want him to freak out."

"Come on my rounds with me tonight, and I won't tell your brother you're buying E off me and trying to use him for cover." He sighs and looks around. "This island is so damn boring. I don't know how people live here. Come on. Keep me company. You're my friend's baby sister, so I ain't gonna try nothing. Hey, I'll even knock five bucks off what I'm charging you. Come on, Kitty Kat. What else are you doing tonight?"

I'm not doing anything, but that's beside the point. I just want my ecstasy and to go the hell home, not keep Kevin company on his drug runs. But I'll take one for the team. For Mary. "All right, deal."

I wait while Kevin struts into the kitchen. He comes out a few minutes later with two drinks from the bar. A beer for him and a whiskey for me. The glass is small, but the brown liquid is poured to the very top. I doubt it's top shelf. Probably well booze, the cheap stuff.

"I like it with ice," I say, just to be a snot. As I take the glass, some of the whiskey drips over the edge and onto my fingers. I lick them clean.

Kevin grins out the side of his mouth. "You are a sassy little Kitty Kat, aren't you?"

Flirting with Kevin makes me want to barf, but I know that's what I have to do to get what I want. And whatever. I'm good at it. I hiss and pretend to swipe at his face with my claw.

I expect Kevin to sit down with his beer. Instead he starts walking away from the restaurant. He tucks his beer up the sleeve of his jean jacket. "Next stop, the Jar Island Retirement Home." I guess I make a face, because he says, "I've got a bunch of glaucoma patients in there who need the weed."

I guess that's sort of a mitzvah or whatever. Helping sick people smoke up. Noble, almost.

"All right," I say. I take a sip of my whiskey and pick up the pace. "We don't want to keep the grammys and grampys waiting."

I spend two hours with Kevin and then walk him back to the ferry. The island's dead, and I don't have anything to do, so I decide to drive over to Middlebury and stop by Mary's house. She keeps creeping into my mind, after that story she told us. Poor thing. It's honestly a miracle that she doesn't have PTSD or some shit.

I park outside her house and walk up the front steps. There's a soft light on in the living room and the flashing light of a television. I press the doorbell and wait.

The volume goes down, but nobody comes to the door. I press it again, then lean over the railing and peek in the windows.

The house doesn't look lived in, more like it got hastily closed up at the end of summer. There's a telescope collapsed and lying on the floor. A chair with a sheet draped over it. Stacks of unopened mail sorted into teetering piles, some newspapers and catalogs. And about ten big black trash bags bulging with God knows what.

And then Mary's aunt darts past the window, like she's trying to hide. I get a prickly feeling in the small of my back as I shrink away from the glass. I lean over the railing and look up at Mary's bedroom. A light is on, but it immediately clicks off.

I practically sprint down the stairs and back to my car.

CHAPTER THIRTY

On Monday morning Mr. Peabody passes out the homecoming ballots during homeroom.

No real surprises. There's Rennie, who is the obvious shoo-in. Even if she wasn't campaigning so hard, she'd still have it. She's the queen of Jar High, just like she always wanted. Then there's my name. Anybody who would vote for me will vote for Rennie. Even my own sister. There's Melanie Renfro, who is known to be slutty, so she'll probably get some votes from random guys. Carrie Pierce, who is way into theater and basically only got nominated because people wanted an "alternative" homecoming queen. Last there is Ashlin. Ashlin who wants this almost as bad as Rennie, but she could never say so, at least not out loud. She wouldn't dare. Ashlin will get a good number of votes, because she's nice to everyone—to their face. She's never beaten Rennie at anything. Until now. I'm actually happy for her, that she'll get to beat her this one time.

I'm about to check off Rennie's name, when, next to me, Rennie raises her hand.

"Yes, Ms. Holtz?" Mr. Peabody says. He has his arms crossed; he looks amused already. Teachers love Rennie. They think she's a spitfire, a ball of energy.

"Can I just say one thing, Mr. Peabody?" She doesn't wait for him to say yes. She swivels around in her seat to face the rest of the class. "Before everybody votes, I just want to remind you guys of something. Homecoming queen isn't a beauty contest, and it's not about popularity. It's about dedication, and school spirit, and making this a better place to go to school."

As if planning parties not everyone is invited to makes this school a better place. Ugh. She's so transparent, I can't believe everyone else doesn't see through her.

Rennie lowers her eyelashes, fake-humbly. "So please

consider that when you vote, you guys." As soon as she's done with her speech, Rennie whispers to me, "This is so mine."

"Nobody deserves it more than you," I whisper back, showing her my ballot with her name checked off.

She reaches over and squeezes my knee. "You're the best, Lil."

My knee socks keep falling down. I wanted to wear sweats or leggings, but Rennie kept saying how knee socks are part of the powder-puff tradition. I was like, can't we just dress up for the actual game? This is just practice. But no.

Like always, powder-puff is the day before the homecoming game. That's when the senior girls play flag football, and the senior boys dress up like cheerleaders.

As soon as it came out that Reeve was coaching one team and Alex was coaching the other, Rennie volunteered to be captain on Reeve's team. Ashlin's the other captain and she won the coin toss, and I was praying that she would pick me, which she did. Obviously, I hate Alex, but Reeve is disgusting. I used to think his ego, his cockiness was a put on. No one could be *that* into himself. But now I know that it's all true. I wonder if he's thought about Mary once since that day. If he even realizes the hell he put her through. I doubt it. I doubt he'd even remember her name. Honestly, I think death would be going too easy on that monster.

Across the field Reeve blows his whistle. I watch him throw his head back and scream, "Suicides! I want suicides, men!" He's loving this. Obviously, their team is going to win, since Reeve is Mr. Football, and both he and Rennie are super-competitive.

Alex doesn't even have a whistle. Our team is basically just throwing footballs at each other, dropping them more often than we catch them. Ashlin yelps every time the ball comes near her face, and I can't even get my whole hand around the thing. I don't get why we can't use a Nerf. People could get hurt.

"Girls!" Alex says, clapping his hands. "Run a few laps to get warmed up, okay? Then we'll practice some plays."

Some of the girls obey, but I ignore him and toss the ball to Ashlin again. It lands nowhere near her, and she goes running for it. "Sorry!" I call out.

I feel a tap on my shoulder. I turn around. It's Alex. "Cho. I need to talk to you for a second."

I can barely stand to look at him. Yesterday I saw him and Nadia talking in the courtyard. And I felt pretty stupid about the fact that I almost bailed on the Limp jersey plan. If anything,

I wish we'd done more to Alex. But it's not my turn anymore. "Um, I'm trying to practice," I say.

"Now!" he barks, and stalks over to the bleachers.

I make a face at Ashlin, and she shrugs and jogs after the other girls on the track.

I follow Alex over to the bleachers and cross my arms. "Yes, Coach?" I say it as bitchy as I possibly can.

In a low, urgent voice he asks, "What is your problem with me?"

I stare at him. I just thought he was going to yell at me for not doing laps. "I don't have a problem with you, Coach," I say, but I'm glad he knows I'm angry. "Can I go now?"

"Stop calling me Coach! I thought we were friends, but lately you're acting like you hate me. I don't get it."

Is Alex honestly this dumb? I probably shouldn't say anything, but I can't help myself. I look around to make sure no one's in earshot, and then I say, "You want to be my friend? I'll tell you how. Don't call my sister. In fact, don't talk to her ever again." Alex opens his mouth like he's going to defend himself, but I keep going. "Don't come to our house in the middle of the night and get her to sneak out, don't give her alcohol at parties, don't—"

"You've got it all wrong! I didn't give her any alcohol."

"Hello! I found her shirt. And I know that she slept over your house that night. She's fourteen, you pervert!"

Alex's jaw goes slack in disbelief. Then he rears up and says, "Pervert? You need to get your facts straight. First of all, I never gave her any drinks. She was sneaking rum with her friends, and by the time I caught them, she was already drunk off her ass. While you were at some other party, I was cleaning up her throw-up and making sure she didn't leave and get caught by your parents!" His Adam's apple is bobbing up and down, and his fists are clenched. "Her friends left her, so she had to spend the night. I stayed up the whole time to make sure she didn't drown in her own vomit. So, you're welcome."

I cross my arms. "If that's true, why were you sneaking off with her in the middle of the night on the first day of school? Don't bother trying to deny it. I saw you drop her off."

"Because she called me crying! She wanted to make sure you never found out she was drunk that night. She made me promise not to tell you. That's how much she cares what you think of her." He lets out an impatient breath of air, shaking his head. "I told her that you had every right to be upset. And that I was going to be watching her too. And that if she ever had a drink in front of me, I was going to make sure you knew about it."

I don't say anything. I just look back over at the field where all the girls are running laps. I'm shivering now.

"I can't believe you would ever think that of me, Lillia. You and I have been friends since the ninth grade! Our families are friends! Nadia's practically my kid sister. I would never think of her like that!" He pushes his hair out of his eyes. Now that the sun isn't as strong as it was in summer, his hair is looking less blond and more coppery. And longer. "That's, like, sick."

"I'm sorry." I don't know what else to say.

"Don't worry about it." I feel this sudden urge to confess everything to him. To really apologize, the way he deserves. But I can't. Because it's not just me. It's Kat and Mary. I had them put themselves on the line for nothing.

I'm shaking, because I'm cold and because I'm sick over what I've done.

Alex takes a step toward me. He unzips his windbreaker, shrugs out of it, and drapes it over my shoulders. It has a clean laundry smell.

"Okay?" he asks, standing close to me. So close we're almost touching. "I can't handle it, you and me not being friends." Quietly he adds, "You mean a lot to me. Always have. Always will."

I open my mouth to speak, but before I can say anything, he starts to back away, back toward the field. Jogging, he calls, "Don't think I'm letting you out of running those laps, Cho!"

I run them. Every last lap. Because if I stop, I'll have to start thinking about what he said, and how I felt when he said it.

On Thursday, game day, PJ surprises me with a Tupperware full of snickerdoodles. I'm pretty sure his mom made them, because they are wrapped up in wax paper, and they are so perfectly chewy and soft, but I'm fine with that. All Ashlin gets from Derek is a sleeve of Chips Ahoy!, not even the whole box. Still, she is excited because she likes him and she'll take anything he gives her. Reeve made Rennie some kind of protein cookie. They are as hard as bricks and they look like manure, but Rennie makes a big show of eating them at lunch.

A ton of people show up to watch us play. Not as many as an actual football game, but still. The boys from the team dress up in cheerleading uniforms and wigs and cheer along the side. It's pretty funny. PJ wears a long black wig, and he keeps trying to do toe-touches, my signature move.

Just like I predicted, Rennie and Reeve's team wins. Rennie scores the only touchdown, and she just about clotheslines

Teresa to make it to the end zone. After the game is over, Reeve throws her over his shoulder and carries her off the field, screaming himself hoarse. As if they won the gold medal at the Olympics or something.

They better enjoy it while they can. Because they're about to lose, big-time.

CHAPTER THIRTY-ONE

MARY

ACCORDING TO LILLIA, COACH CHRISTY KEEPS HER
office locked at all times. Ten minutes and thirty-three seconds
ago, she entered her office with the box of homecoming ballots.
Her door is open a crack. She's been typing on her computer
for the past seven minutes and ten seconds. I know because I've
been watching the clock at the end of the hallway the whole
time. I'm leaned up against some lockers, and Kat is pretending
to text on her phone by the water fountain.

At exactly four o'clock Lillia comes flying past Kat and me, her ponytail swishing from side to side. "Coach Christy!" she calls out frantically. "You have to come right now! There's a cheer-mergency in the girls' locker room!"

"What's going on, Lillia?" Coach Christy asks, stepping out of her office.

"Please just hurry!" she says, tugging on Coach Christy's arm. "I think one of the freshman girls is having a breakdown or something. She's totally freaking out!"

The two of them disappear down the hallway.

Kat and I grin at each other, and after a quick glance around to make sure no one's watching us, we slip inside. I stay crouched by the door while Kat makes a beeline for the ballot box. She said Pat taught her how to pick locks when she was a kid. All you needed was a piece of a soda can. It seemed crazy to me, but she opens it in almost five seconds. She dumps the contents out on Coach Christy's desk.

"Looks like Reeve won without our help," Kat grunts as she sifts through the piles.

"I'm not surprised," I say. "He's definitely the best-looking guy in the senior class." Kat gives me a weird look, but it's true. She stuffs some slips of paper into her messenger bag. Votes for Rennie, I assume. Rennie won't get to stand up there on that stage with him now. Too bad for her. Maybe she shouldn't be such a bully.

I train my eyes back on the hallway. Lillia and the coach could be back any minute. "Are you almost done?" I whisper.

"I'm just counting to make sure Ashlin has enough votes," she says, her head down.

That's when I hear Lillia's voice coming down the hallway, high and hyper. "Oh, my gosh. I thought she was crying, but I guess she was just laughing!"

"Kat!"

Kat's head snaps up. "I'm not done counting!"

I shake my head. "We have to hide!"

Kat stuffs the ballots back into the box and then looks around the room frantically before she sees the supply cubby. She gestures at me to follow, but when she opens the door, we see that it's way too small for both of us.

Lillia is babbling, and now they're right outside the door. "It's so weird! I mean, I think I even heard rumors she was a cutter or something, but I guess not! Maybe it's just multiple personality disorder." She giggles nervously. "We've all been kind of crazed, with all the stress of homecoming."

I dart behind the office door, and peek out to the hallway

through a tiny sliver between the door hinges.

"Well, I appreciate you keeping me in the loop, Lillia. It's important that I know what's going on with my squad."

"Oh, totally."

"Is there anything else?"

Through the crack Lillia's and my eyes meet. Hers go huge. And then the phone sitting on Coach Christy's desk rings.

"I've got to get that," she says. Coach Christy grabs a hold of the door. I see her fingers curl around it. She's going to close it, take the phone call in private. If she does, I'm done for. I am trying so hard not to breathe. I curl my feet in as tightly as I can and close my eyes. We're going to get caught, and it will be my fault.

"Wait!" Lillia cries out.

"Just a minute, Lillia," Coach Christy says. "I'll be right with you."

Coach Christy stops talking suddenly, and my heart almost stops. I open my eyes. But Coach Christy hasn't seen me after all. She shouts, "Lillia!" and rushes out.

I peek through the crack again. Lillia has fainted. She is a small heap on the floor of the hallway. Coach Christy is shaking her, trying to wake her up. Lillia flutters her lids. "I don't feel so good," she whispers. "Can you take me to the nurse's office?"

Coach Christy practically sweeps her off the floor, throwing one of Lillia's arms around her shoulders. And then they're gone.

"They're gone!" I whisper loudly to Kat.

She crawls out of the cubby. "That was way too close." I figure she'll go back to the ballots, but instead she runs into the hallway. I follow her.

"Boo-yah!" Kat yells when we get outside.

"I thought she saw me for sure."

"Well, obviously she didn't!" Kat pumps her fist in the air. "I just wish I could've seen Lillia's performance." She mimics, "'I don't feel so good.'"

I try to smile, but something doesn't seem right. "Did you make sure there were enough votes for Ashlin to win?" I ask.

Kat brushes me off. "I'm sure it's fine. There were plenty of votes for her, and I grabbed, like, twenty of Rennie's votes." She sticks both her hands into her bag and pulls out two big fistfuls of ballots. "We got this. Trust me."

CHAPTER THIRTY-TWO

THE LAST SECONDS TICK OFF THE SCOREBOARD IN WHITE round bulbs. Three, two, one. The referee runs out to the angry seagull painted on the fifty-yard line and reaches for the air horn clipped to his belt. I don't hear it blare because of all the cheering.

We killed them.

Jar Island 38, Tansett 3. A homecoming victory.

Reeve leads our team off the football field, holding his helmet high over his head. He's soaked with sweat, and it makes his hair darker and picks up the curl. There are a bunch of scouts on the sidelines, men wearing different college windbreakers, holding clipboards and video cameras. One of them smiles proudly at Reeve, as if he's his dad or something.

All of the cheerleaders jump up and down and hug each other. I look around to find Rennie. She's by Nadia's side, ruffling the top of her head. It messes up Nadia's ponytail, but Nadia doesn't care. Then Rennie turns a bunch of back handsprings. I'm surprised she's not totally nauseated by this point, since she's been doing them all game long. Rennie put on such a show cheering for Reeve, it was like she thought his scouts might offer *her* a scholarship to be his personal cheerleader.

I give my pom-poms a halfhearted shake. We always have a big crowd for homecoming. Practically the whole school is here, teachers, parents, some alums, too. Everyone joined in our call-and-response cheers, and they knew every word to our fight songs.

Reeve *did* have an amazing game. Perfect pass after perfect pass. He even ran one in for a touchdown himself. Our fans screamed their throats raw, chanting his name, but not me.

I don't know if Mary came to the game or not. I didn't see her in the bleachers. I hope for her sake, she stayed home.

JENNY HAN AND SIOBHAN VIVIAN

As PJ walks past me, I pat him on the back. He's not even sweaty. "Good job, PJ," I say. I do a quick tuck jump.

He smiles and pumps his fist in the air.

Alex trails behind him. As he passes our bench, he turns so he is jogging backward and, with a big smile, calls out, "Thanks for the great work tonight, ladies!"

Smiling, I shake my head at him.

Nadia yells, "You're welcome!" Her friends fall over each other in a fit of giggles.

A few weeks ago that would have ruined my night. But now, after talking to Alex, I know I don't have to worry. I believe him when he says he's not interested in Nadia. He'd never do something I didn't want him to. And, in that way, I guess my revenge was a success. We've gone back to the way things used to be. When Alex would do anything I asked him to. Only this time I'm not going to take advantage of it. He's a person with feelings too.

The boys gather up their equipment and head toward the field house. Everyone but Reeve, who is immediately surrounded by the scouts. The band finishes the fight song, and the bleachers start to clear out. Some of the girls start putting away their pom-poms in the big team duffel bag.

Rennie sees this and turns red. She storms over and shouts, "You cheer until every last player is off the field!"

I don't remember this being a rule. Apparently Ashlin doesn't either, because she gives me a confused shrug. By this point Reeve is the only guy left, and it feels weird for us to keep cheering for him, because he's talking to the scouts. I guess Rennie realizes this too, because she eventually sighs and tells the new girls to take down the banners and load the equipment into the back of her Jeep. She lets Nadia be in charge of her keys.

On the ride home Rennie is bursting with energy. She has on a CD of cheer dance tracks, which are club songs sped up even faster. Her radio volume is turned way up, and the bass makes her speakers crackle and buzz. I turn it down.

"Wasn't that game amazing, Lil?"

"Totally," I say. I worry for a second that I don't sound like I mean it, so I cheerfully add, "Everyone's going to be in such a good mood for the dance tomorrow."

Rennie nods. "We should start thinking about a new halftime routine for play-offs. Just to keep things fresh." Then she reaches into her backseat, trying to find her purse. We nearly veer off the road.

JENNY HAN AND SIOBHAN VIVIAN

I swear, Rennie is the worst driver. I push her arm back toward the wheel and say, "What do you need? I'll get it for you."

"Can you call Ash?"

I do. I call Ashlin, put her on speaker, and hold my phone up between us.

Rennie says, "Hey, Ash. I don't know about you, but I am *soooo* amped up right now. Let's go do something."

"Come over!" Ashlin offers. "You can finally see my new sauna!"

I like the idea. I went in a sauna a few times, when my mom took Nadia and me for a spa day. It would be nice to relax and unwind a little, especially because, the closer tomorrow gets, the more I feel nervous about our plan.

I glance at the clock on Rennie's dashboard. It's ten thirty. Mary and Kat are supposed to come over later to go over everything, and Kat's bringing the ecstasy with her. But there's plenty of time before that happens. I told them to come at two in the morning, because I know my mom and Nadia will be asleep by then.

"Sounds good to me," I say.

"Yay!" Rennie says. "Ashlin, you call PJ and Alex and Derek. I'll call Reeve."

Glumly Ashlin says, "Derek can't come. He has a family thing."

I put my hand over the phone. "Why can't it just be us girls?"

Rennie laughs at me. "Don't worry. No more spin the bottle. I promise. Bye, Ash!" I hang up, and Rennie nudges her chin at me. "Now call Reeve."

I find his name in my phonebook and press send.

He answers after a few rings. "What up, Cho!" Apparently Reeve's already celebrating. "Are you calling to congratulate me? This really is my lucky night."

Before I can answer, Rennie takes a hand off the wheel and pulls the phone out of my hand, and squeals, "Yay for Reevie!"

Thirty minutes later, the six of us are at Ashlin's house, drinking beers in her sauna. Her dad had it built onto the pool house. It's a huge room lined with wide cedar planks. Wooden benches are built into the walls, and there's a big glass door that looks out onto her backyard pool and Jacuzzi. The light is soft inside, and the heat is making me sleepy.

Ashlin's in one of her bikinis. She offered Rennie and me ones to wear too, but Ashlin has huge boobs, and there's no way either of us could fit into her top. So I'm in my underwear and a big

T-shirt I borrowed from Ashlin's younger brother, who's, like, six feet tall even though he's only in seventh grade. But Rennie's just in her bra and panties, lying down on one of the wooden benches with her eyes closed, like she's in a men's magazine.

I've known these guys for years, but it feels weird for Rennie to be in her underwear in front of them. And the dry heat is starting to give me a headache. I take a sip of my beer and hold the bottle up to my forehead.

"I should get Coach to put one of these in our locker room," Reeve says. "Good for the muscles." Reeve's in his black boxer briefs, and beads of sweat trickle down his abs. Alex and PJ are on opposite sides of him, in their boxers, with towels over their heads.

"Seriously!" Rennie says. "I bet you Coach would do it, if you asked. You're his star player, after all, the one who's taking us to State this year!" Rennie gives a big "Woooo!" that fills the room.

PJ clears his throat. "Ahem. Don't forget about the kicker. Remember, for every six points Reeve scores, I'm popping a seventh up there. Right, Lil?"

"Right," I say.

"Seriously, Reevie," Rennie says. "Every one of those scouts wants a piece of you. How are you going to decide where to go?"

"It's gonna go like this." Reeve puts down his beer. "First off, it's got to be a decent school with a good communications program. After that I'll consider the reputation for parties. And then it's location, because I want to be somewhere warm and sunny." He rips the towel off Alex's head and puts it on his own. "And then I've got my *Playboy* college campus edition to refer to, in case of a tiebreaker."

I shudder, crossing my arms over my chest. "It's nice that these schools are willing to overlook your grades," I say to Reeve, because I can't help myself. Sweetly I add, "I mean, if it wasn't for football, who knows where you'd get in, right?"

PJ laughs loudly; so does Alex.

Reeve answers right back. "It's a shame we can't all be Asian, huh, Cho?"

Everyone laughs this time. I take another sip of my beer. A big sip.

We talk awhile more about the game, and Rennie goads Reeve into rehashing his plays for us, highlight reel style. I'm watching Rennie's beer bottle, hoping that once she's finished, she'll be ready to take me home. I'll never hear the end of it from Kat if I'm late. Plus, I have curfew.

PJ has a watch that beeps every hour. When it turns one in the morning, I start yawning, every minute or so. Sometimes they are real, but sometimes they are fake. This one is fake.

"You tired, Lillia?" Alex asks me.

"Yeah," I say. And then I make eye contact with Rennie. But Ashlin gets up and pours a ladle of water onto the hot rocks, filling the place with sizzling steam.

Alex stands up and stretches. "I don't think I can take this heat much longer," he says.

Rennie tells him, "Then get me another beer," and cracks up hysterically.

"You shouldn't stay out too late," I say to her. "Tomorrow's going to be a big day for you. You don't want to have tired eyes."

"But I'm so relaxed," she says, glancing over at Reeve. Her words run into each other.

"Come on," I say. "Let's go, Ren. I'll drive."

Rennie makes a face at Reeve and says, "Is something wrong with her ears? Can she not hear me?" She looks back at me and says, "Testing, testing. One. Two. Three."

I want to slap her.

"I'll take you home, Lillia," Alex offers.

"Awesome," I say, before pushing open the sauna door and stepping outside. Rennie can do what she wants. Why should I care? She's not my responsibility. Just like I wasn't hers.

Ashlin's backyard is dark, and the night air feels good against my skin.

Alex walks out behind me. I tell him, "One second. I'm just gonna go put on my clothes." I run inside Ashlin's house and change back into my cheering uniform.

When I get back outside, Rennie's standing next to her Jeep, wrapped in a towel. "I thought you wanted to stay," I say.

She opens her mouth to answer me, but then Reeve calls out of the sauna, "Come back inside, Ren. Just let Lindy take her home. I'll drive you later."

Rennie shifts her weight and looks back toward the sauna. "I think I will stay. See you tomorrow!" And then she runs off, leaving tracks of wet footprints on the blacktop.

I turn and see Alex, sitting in his SUV with the lights off. I climb inside. "Thanks for giving me a ride. I don't think I can watch Rennie throw herself at Reeve for another hour."

Alex shrugs. "I don't see him complaining."

He starts the car up and I buckle my seat belt. "Of course not. He's an egomaniac." I fiddle with the radio. "I mean, it

302 JENNY HAN and SIOBHAN VIVIAN

doesn't even matter who the girl is, as long as she's as obsessed with him as he is with himself."

Alex doesn't say anything, and I feel embarrassed. Maybe I took it a little too far.

At exactly two in the morning, I go downstairs and open the front door. Kat and Mary are both there. I hold my finger up to my lips and lead them into the living room.

"How was the game?" Mary whispers to me.

"Whatever," I say. "We won." I ask Kat, "Did you get the stuff?"

Kat's walking around the living room, looking at the pictures on the wall. The one of Nadia and me in our Easter dresses at our grandmother's house, the family portrait my mom had commissioned by some famous Boston artist. She's seen them before, but maybe she doesn't remember. "Yeah," she says, lingering at my mom's cotillion portrait. "I got it." She hands me a small glass vial.

"What's this?" I thought we were buying a pill.

"Liquid ecstasy. It's a lot stronger than the regular kind."

I unscrew the top. The liquid inside the vial is clear. I hold it under my nose and sniff, but it doesn't smell like anything. "Are you sure this guy didn't rip you off?"

Kat glares at me. "What do you take me for? I know drugs, Lillia. A couple of drops in Reeve's drink, and he'll be tripping balls. It should only take about fifteen minutes to kick in, so wait until Reeve gets to the dance before you do it. If he starts wigging out before you get there, one of your friends might lock him in the limo until he sobers up."

"How long will it last?"

"Reeve will be riding pink elephants for at least eight hours." Kat snorts. "Mary, as soon Reeve starts to get crazy, find one of your teachers and point Reeve out. I'll do the same thing. Then they'll already be watching when he peaks."

"Senor Tremont is one of the chaperones," Mary says. "We did this whole thing in class today about Spanish dancing."

"Perfect," I say. "I think he almost failed Reeve in Spanish II last year because he wrote his final paper on the *Three Amigos* movie. Tremont hates him." I turn the vial over in my hands. "Um, I need to tell you guys something."

"What? Are you okay, Lillia?" Mary asks. "Please don't worry. Everything is going to be okay."

"It's not that," I say, and then bite down on my lip. I know I don't have to tell them about Alex. It's not like it makes any difference at this point. But I want to be honest with them. Like

Mary said, there can't be any secrets between us. They have a right to know. "I talked to Alex. And it looks like everything with my sister was a big misunderstanding."

Mary's eyes get big. "Wait. Seriously?"

"But I saw them in his car," Kat says.

"Fine, but did you see him kissing my sister? Like, actually see them doing anything?"

Kat sucks in a breath. "No. I guess not."

"Alex swears they never hooked up, and I believe him. Maybe it's stupid, but I do." I lower my eyes. "I'm really sorry."

Kat waves off my apology. "We can't dwell on the past. Now it's our time, mine and Mary's."

Mary adds, "And it's not like anything *that bad* happened to Alex. It was only a couple stupid jokes." She turns to me. "You're still in, right, Lillia?"

I squeeze the vial of liquid ecstasy tight in my hand. It's true. We really only screwed with Alex a bit. It was nothing like what we've got planned for Reeve and Rennie. There's no doubt in my mind that those two deserve everything that's coming to them. "Definitely."

"All right, beotches," Kat says, running her hands through

her hair. "I guess this is it. The grand finale." She turns to Mary. "You ready?"

Mary nods. "I can't wait."

She doesn't seem scared at all. Just excited. Same for Kat. I'm still scared, but I'm excited, too.

I feel closer to Kat and Mary than to any of my other friends. The three of us, we are a circle. We're bound to each other now. I can feel it. I feel power, too. All the talking, the hard work, the pranks we've pulled, have brought us to right here, right now.

I open the front door, and Mary bounds happily down the steps. She goes and gets her bike from underneath one of the bushes.

Kat lingers for a second. "One thing," she says to me. "When you put the E in Reeve's drink . . . get it done as quickly as you can and don't make a big deal about it. Hand him a drink and go dance."

I nod. "Okay."

Kat's face suddenly changes. Her mouth gets tight, and I see her looking over my shoulder. I turn around, and there's Nadia, in her nightshirt, holding a glass of water.

"What are you doing up?" I put my hands behind my back and turn to Kat, hoping she'll have some kind of excuse. But she's already gone. I look back at Nadia, my heart thudding in my chest.

"What was Kat DeBrassio doing here?" Nadia asks me, confused. She sticks her head out the door and looks down the driveway.

"She . . . she was hooking up with Alex this summer," I say, squeezing the vial in the palm of my hand. "And she heard some weird rumor about you two having a sleepover one night. She came here to threaten you."

Nadia's face turns pale. "But we never—"

"I know. Don't worry. I set her straight. I told her you would never do that. I just hope she believed me."

Nadia shuffles back from the open door. "Lillia! What should I do?"

I close it fast, for drama. "Don't say a word to anyone about her being here. Don't give her a reason to come looking for you. I can protect you at school and at home, but I'm not with you 24/7. So just steer clear of her." I give her a stern look. "'Kay?"

She nods. In a small voice she says, "Thanks for sticking up for me."

"You're my sister," I say, averting my eyes. "Of course I'm going to stick up for you."

Impulsively Nadia runs up to me and gives me a tight hug and then scampers up the stairs. I lock the front door and let out a sigh of relief. Then I follow her up.

My homecoming dress is hanging on the back of my bedroom door. I set out my shoes and the clutch I'm borrowing from my mom. That's where I put the vial of liquid ecstasy. In the little satin pocket where a lipstick is supposed to go.

Then I turn off my light and climb into bed. I hope it doesn't take me long to fall asleep. Tomorrow's a big day.

CHAPTER THIRTY-THREE

MARY

I'VE GOT DRESSES AND DRESSES PILED UP ON MY BED. Every single one I brought with me to Jar Island. I've tried on six, but none of them are right for tonight. I put on number seven, a lacy white dress with a crinoline skirt, but it looks babyish, like an oversize christening gown. I want to look beautiful tonight. Beautiful enough to have been homecoming queen myself, if I wasn't the new girl, if I'd never had to move away.

As I sort through the pile, I wonder if maybe Aunt Bette

has something I could borrow, or if it's not too late to go to that fancy boutique on Third Street in White Haven. The dresses there cost, like, three hundred dollars, but I'm pretty sure my mom would agree that it's worth the expense. Looking good, I mean. Not just good. Tonight I have to look perfect. Even though Ashlin is the one who's going to be crowned homecoming queen, tonight is *my* night.

Then I find it, right at the bottom of the pile. A dress I don't even remember buying. It's a one-shoulder, long and floaty and shell pink. Layers and layers of chiffon. I check the tag. It's from that fancy boutique.

And then I realize—Aunt Bette. I told her I was going to the dance. She must have gotten it for me as a surprise, hid it in my closet for me to find. I could cry!

I throw the white christening dress off and put this one on. It's not a dress I would have ever picked out for myself. And as I slip it over my shoulders, I hope I can pull it off. It's so stylish and unique, and definitely the most expensive piece of clothing I own. You can tell just by touching it, how nice the fabric is. It feels like spun cotton candy on my skin.

I walk slowly over to the mirror and have a look. I almost don't recognize myself. It's so nice. More than nice. Perfect.

Exactly how I want to look when Reeve meets his downfall tonight.

I run out of my room to go find Aunt Bette, to thank her and to show her how perfectly the dress fits me. She's not in her bedroom, and she's not downstairs, so I try her art studio. I haven't been up there yet since I've been back. It's her private workspace, and she's been keeping the door closed, the way she used to when she didn't want to be disturbed. Today her door is open, but just a crack. Maybe it's unintentional. Maybe it just blew open or something.

I'm not sure if I should leave my hair down, or maybe wear it to the side? Aunt Bette would know. Anyway, I'm dying to thank her, give her a big hug.

"Aunt Bette?" I call out, running up the stairs.

The attic walls are lined with paintings. Stacks and stacks of studies. Sometimes Aunt Bette will paint the same scene fifty times before she gets it right.

The roof is pitched, and I have to walk down the center if I don't want to bump my head. Aunt Bette's easel is set open at the end of the room. She likes to paint with the window at her back. Next to the easel is the table where she sets out her paints and brushes. The tiny puddles of paint glisten, still wet, fresh.

I see her legs, hear the sound of her brush dotting the canvas.

"Aunt Bette!"

She leans past the canvas and looks at me. I do a spin for her. "Mary, you look beautiful."

"Thank you. I love this dress."

Aunt Bette nods and smiles. "I'm so glad you're happy now."

"I am," I say. "I really am."

I go back down to my room and brush my hair. Then I open my jewelry box, take out my daisy pendant necklace, and put it on.

For my twelfth birthday party I invited my whole class to Jar Island, to my house. That's how it was at Montessori. Everyone invited everyone. All the other years, I had the party on the mainland, because that's where the other kids in my class lived. We'd have it at a bowling alley or the laser tag place, or a pizza parlor. But this year it had to be at my house, because of the theme.

I got the idea when I went to the card shop on Main Street to pick out invitations with my mom. I saw cards that were shaped like circus tents, with red and yellow stripes, and you had to peel back the flaps of the tent to see the party info.

I could already picture it. A carnival theme party, with a ring toss and a basketball free throw and fun foods like cotton candy and popcorn and maybe even funnel cakes. Our backyard was huge, so there'd be plenty of room. For a second I worried that a carnival theme was maybe too babyish for seventh grade, but then I reasoned that the boys would be excited about the games. They'd like showing off how many shots they could make in the free throw, and the girls would like the prizes. We ordered those on the Internet—stuffed animals and fruity lip balms for the girls, and baseball caps for the boys.

My dad cut holes in a piece of plywood, and then Aunt Bette and I painted an elephant and a giraffe and a monkey around them so people could stick their heads inside and take photos. We rented an old-time popcorn machine and a cotton candy spinner. Dad was going to grill hot dogs, and Mom would make her potato salad.

Even though everyone hated me now, if I threw a great party, it could change their minds about me.

I was sitting on the curb, staring down the street, waiting for my mom's car to come back from the ferry with all the mainland kids she was picking up. They were supposed to come in on the three o'clock. But it was after four, which meant three boats had stopped at Jar Island already.

I had this terrible feeling in my stomach. No one was coming to my party. Not even Anne. I thought of my mom waiting at the docks, holding a sign we'd painted together. It said CIRCUS THIS WAY. All I knew was that I couldn't be in the backyard with Aunt Bette and Dad anymore. They kept fiddling with the decorations and the games we'd already set up, to have something to do. And they offered a couple times for me to open the presents they'd bought me, as if that would make me feel better.

At around four thirty Reeve's mom drove down our street. As soon as I saw him, I jumped up. I'd been casually bringing up my party to him for weeks, telling him about the kinds of games I planned to have, the prizes, the chocolate cake we were ordering from Milky Morning. I came up with the basketball free throw idea just for him, because I knew how much he liked basketball. I asked Dad to buy a hoop. He mounted it to the garage.

His mom parked the car. I could tell they were arguing. Eventually Reeve got out. He slammed the door really hard.

"Hey," he said, sullenly. "Sorry I'm late. My mom had to drop my brothers off at a game first."

"It's okay!" I grabbed his hand and pulled him toward the

house. I knew he didn't want to be there. I knew his mom probably forced him, but I was so happy he came.

Aunt Bette and my dad were standing under the basketball hoop drinking coffee. As soon as they saw me and Reeve walking up the driveway, they sprang into action. Aunt Bette hit play on the stereo, and circus music filled the air. Dad grabbed the game tickets and tore off a fat strip for Reeve.

"So no one showed, huh?" Reeve wanted to know.

I didn't answer. Instead I took Reeve up to the food table. "Are you hungry? We have hot dogs, cotton candy, popcorn. You can have whatever you want."

Reeve sighed. "I guess I'll have a hot dog."

I fixed him one. "Do you like ketchup or mustard?" I asked him.

"Ketchup."

At about that time my mom came back. Alone. She was frowning, but when she saw Reeve, she brightened. "Reeve, I'm so glad you could make it," she said.

"Umm, you know. I think I heard on the radio just now that it's raining on the mainland. I bet everyone at school thought the party was canceled," he said. His cheeks were burning up.

I looked at him gratefully. "That's got to be it, Mom." And

then my eyes went to the box in his hand. I'd noticed it the second he'd come out of his mom's car. A small white box tied with pink ribbon. It had to be for me.

"Here," he said, shoving it toward me. "Happy Birthday."

I started opening it right in front of him. I couldn't wait. He watched me, peering over my shoulder instead of eating his hot dog.

He'd bought me a necklace, an enamel daisy with a yellow center and white petals. It was the most beautiful thing I'd ever seen. I almost couldn't get it on, because my hands were shaking so bad. Mom had to help me with the clasp.

He looked nervous. "Is it okay?"

"I love it," I told him.

Despite everything that happened after, he was good to me that day. On that day, when I needed him the most, Reeve was my friend.

The necklace is shiny, not a bit of tarnish, even after all these years. As sad as it is, wearing it again makes me happy. As happy as I was when Reeve gave it to me on my twelfth birthday, once upon a time.

JENNY HAN AND SIOBHAN VIVIAN

RENNIE AND I ARE GETTING READY FOR THE DANCE AT my house. It's our tradition. My mom always lets us take over her and my dad's bedroom. When she helped design our house, she made sure to give herself a huge master bathroom and an attached dressing area with a three-way mirror. She also had the electrician set up a bunch of different lighting settings— daytime, office, night—so we can make sure our hair and makeup look perfect.

My mom has tons and tons of amazing clothes, Chanel

and Dior and vintage Halston. Floor-length off-the-shoulder gowns, silky blouses that tie at the neck, tweed suits. Definitely not anything I'd ever wear to school, but my mom says she's putting a padlock on the door once I turn twenty.

It's stuffy in the room, with the blow-dryers and the curling irons heating up, so I go open the sliding glass door to the balcony. My mom and Ms. Holtz are on the patio below, having a glass of white wine, watching the sky turn pink as the sun sets over the water. Ms. Holtz lights up a cigarette. We don't have any ashtrays, so my mom takes a tea light out of a glass candle holder she had sent from Italy, and lets Ms. Holtz use that. Ms. Holtz and my mom are definitely friendly, but I wouldn't call them friends, exactly.

"Lillia!" Nadia calls out from the bathroom. "Can you please, please, please do my eyes?"

Nadia's nervous because she has a date. A sophomore named James Melnic asked her. He's short, but he seems nice enough. I asked Alex because he knows him from football, and he said he's a good guy. I'm still going to keep my eye on them.

I tell Nadia to sit up on the counter. Then I do her eyes like mine with black eyeliner, but I make the line a bit thinner, since she's only a freshman. I also use some lilac shadow on her, because her dress is a light, almost silvery purple. It looks like it's made up of one piece of ribbon, wrapped tight around her like a bandage.

"What about lipstick?" Nadia says as I give her a bit of blush.

"Just do gloss," I tell her. Nadia pouts. "Lipstick will be too much," I say, annoyed

She looks at my face. "What about the one *you're* wearing?"

I bought a pale pink one, special for my dress. "Too much," I repeat.

"Lil's right, Nadia," Rennie calls out from the dressing room. "You don't want to look like a hooker."

"Fine," Nadia sighs, not entirely convinced, and she disappears into her bedroom.

I take a last look at my hair. I swept the front part across my forehead and twisted it into a low side bun. A few pieces feel loose, so I tuck in a couple more hair pins and spray everything down with hair spray. A touch of that pink lipstick, pink cheek, and black eyeliner. It's a pale girly look, to compliment the starkness of my black dress, and to match the heels I bought in the palest shade of pink. I've been wearing them around the house in thick socks ever since I got them, in the hopes that I'll break them in.

Rennie is fretting in front of the three-way mirror. She looks great in her sequined dress, which she paired with a sparkly cuff bracelet that my mom lent her, and a bright red lip. Her hair isn't done, though. Rennie keeps piling it on top of her head, and then letting it go, so it falls around her shoulders.

"Ren, we'd better get going," I say. Everyone is meeting at Ashlin's house for pictures.

"Shit," she says. "I can't decide if I should do up or down." She's nervous and blotchy. She lifts her arms up and fans her armpits. "Help me, Lil. Which do you think Reeve will like best?"

"Come here."

Rennie flops into one of my mom's stuffed chairs. I stand behind her and curl the ends of her hair with the big barrel curling iron. I want to ask her about Reeve, what she did or didn't do with him after I left Ash's, but I don't. I just pin back the sides. "Pretty."

Rennie gets up and looks at herself in the mirror. I'm standing behind her, looking too. I think it looks great with the dress, that there's a touch of softness to counteract her sparkle and glitz. For a second I'm afraid she doesn't like what I've done. But then I realize she's not even looking at herself. She's looking at me, my reflection behind her.

"Lil?" she says, spinning around to face me.

"What?" I say nervously.

Rennie leans forward and hugs me tightly. Then she peels herself away, looks me in the face, and says, "I feel like my whole life would have been different if we hadn't become friends." Her eyes glitter with tears.

"Ren," I say, and then I can barely swallow, knowing what's going to happen to her tonight. I tell myself Rennie will be a better person after this is over. It'll be like how things went with Alex. We'll all come out better on the other side.

The doorbell rings. Nadia screams for me to come downstairs. Rennie and I grab our shoes and our clutch purses and go see what's up. Nadia's taking a white box from the hands of a delivery man while Mom signs his clipboard.

"Hmm," Mom says, and then turns and gives a secret smile to Ms. Holtz. "What could that be?"

Ms. Holtz smiles back, but it doesn't quite reach her eyes.

I open the card in the tiny white envelope. *For my two girls— have fun tonight. Love, Daddy.*

Nadia tears open the box. I swear she's an animal when it comes to presents. "Daddy sent us corsages!" Nadia screams, sliding hers onto her wrist. It's a purple orchid, and it goes perfectly with her dress.

Rennie looks over my shoulder as I take mine out of the box and put it onto my wrist. Mine is a pale pink orchid. "That's so pretty, Lil," she says in a small voice. I can tell she's jealous.

When I turn around, I see Nadia opening up my clutch. I lunge at her and scream, "Don't go into my bag!"

Nadia's mouth drops open. I literally rip it out of her hands and say, "I said, NO LIPSTICK!" My hands are shaking.

Nadia recoils. "Sorr-ee."

Rennie gives me a funny look. "Ease up, Lil."

My mom takes a picture of Nadia and me with our corsages on, and e-mails them to my dad. Then Nadia's date comes to take her to her friend's house. He brings her a corsage too, so now she's wearing a corsage on each wrist. Of course Mom makes them pose on the stairs together. Nadia threads her arm through her date's and smiles. In her heels they are the same height.

After they leave, Ms. Holtz and my mom drive us over to Ashlin's in my mom's car. The limo we rented is already there, parked out front.

PJ, Reeve, and Alex are standing together awkwardly, passing around PJ's water bottle with vodka inside. They all have suits on. I think Reeve's is the same one he wore to junior formal. I can tell because it's charcoal gray, and because the jacket is tight across his shoulders. PJ has on these weird plastic sunglasses he swears are cool, despite the fact that he bought them for $5.99 at Beachcombers. Alex is the only one who actually looks comfortable in his suit. It's nice, a black jacket, his tie is gray, and his shoes are freshly shined. Alex goes to a lot of dress-up functions with his family. I know that because his mom's always trying to invite my mom along.

Reeve's mom is pinning Rennie's corsage on. It's a hot pink rose with baby's breath. Rennie freaked out when Reeve gave it to her. She jumped up and gave him a kiss on the cheek. It's not like he went to the florist shop and was, like, *This rose will match my date's shoes,* or whatever. I'm sure his mom picked it out.

Ashlin looks beautiful in her dress. It's short with an empire waist and a swingy skirt of rows of cream-colored silk, and it makes her look really tan. Her hair is twisted and pinned up, a few pieces in tiny braids, and her heels are strappy pale gold.

She's going to make a great homecoming queen. I just hope Reeve doesn't totally ruin the moment for her. Kat said a couple big drops of the E would do the trick, but maybe I'll just do one. I don't want him to throw up on her or something.

Ashlin's mom directs us to the front steps of the house. As

we line up, I find myself next to Reeve. He looks at me for a quick second and then walks away and stands on the opposite side of the group, slinging his arm over Rennie. Everyone else shifts over to make room for them.

We take a few pictures like that. Then Rennie calls out, "Couples!"

I walk off the stairs, and she and Reeve cuddle together, his arms around her waist. She throws her head back, laughing at something he whispered into her ear.

Mrs. Lind jumps out with her camera and says, "Lillia! Go stand next to Alex."

I turn, and Alex blushes. "We're not going together, Mom," he says.

Mrs. Lind lifts her camera up to her face. "I know, but the two of you look so cute together. Don't they, Grace?"

My mom nods approvingly. "Send me a copy of that one, Celeste."

"Of course," she says, gesturing for us to stand next to each other.

Alex comes up next to me, and we smile for the camera.

"A little closer," Mrs. Lind urges. "Put your arm around her, Alex."

Alex sighs and puts his arm around me, saying, "Come on, Mom. We have to leave soon." He put on cologne. He doesn't usually wear cologne. It smells nice, though, like lavender and woods.

Mrs. Lind starts snapping away. My smile feels like it's cracking. I wish we were already at the dance, so my part was done.

CHAPTER THIRTY-FIVE

I'M STANDING OFF TO THE SIDE, NEAR WHERE THE TABLES and chairs are set up, watching as Lillia ladles punch into two cups over by the drink station. She reaches into her black clutch, touches up her lipstick, and oh so casually tips the vial into one of the cups. It's so smooth and fast that if I hadn't been watching her like a hawk, I wouldn't have seen it.

Lillia walks back over to her table, pretending to look for Rennie, who is in the bathroom. "Where's your girl?" she asks

Reeve, who is sitting alone. "She asked me to get her some punch."

Reeve looks taken aback. "Rennie's not my girl."

"Well, that's not what she thinks. You really shouldn't lead people on like that."

"You're one to talk." I can tell Reeve's checking Lillia out by the way he keeps looking away and then quickly looking back. "Rennie's my bro. That's all."

"Alex and PJ are your bros. Do you make out with them, too?" She's still holding on to both of the cups, her clutch tucked underneath her arm. The plan was for Lillia to just offer him the punch. I don't know why she's still talking to him.

"We were playing spin the bottle!"

"I wasn't talking about spin the bottle. Or that night at Bow Tie. I was talking about last night."

"Why do you care so much?" he asks with a smirk.

"She's my best friend," Lillia says automatically.

I wish she would look over at me so I could signal to her to wrap this up already. This exchange is going on so long, I'm starting to wonder—is she going to chicken out? I hate to admit it, but maybe part of me would be relieved. Just the tiniest bit.

I've known Reeve as long as anybody else. Everyone on Jar Island knows how bad he wants a football scholarship. How bad he wants off this island. As much as I do, even.

I find myself holding my breath as I wait to see what Lillia will do. Across the room I see Mary come in through the doors. She looks beautiful in a long pink dress, her blond hair down in waves.

I guess Lillia sees Mary at the same time I do, because she finally holds out the cup to Reeve and says, "Cheers. Good luck with homecoming king."

Reeve looks surprised, maybe even pleased. He takes the cup, taps it against hers, and then he downs it in one swallow. Smacking his lips, he says, "Good luck to you, too, Cho."

I turn, hoping that Mary saw that. She winks at me.

Lillia doesn't answer him. She just takes another sip of her drink, looking nervous.

Now that that's done, I head out of the gym and toward the girls bathroom to pee. I've already had, like, three cups of punch.

I walk in, and there's Rennie, standing in front of the mirror wearing this ridiculous silver sequined dress that barely covers her butt. She gazes at herself in the mirror, pursing her lips and making her eyes wide. I know that mirror face so well. I've seen her do it a thousand times. For, like, two seconds nostalgia washes over me, and we're back in my room, mixing up lip glosses for the perfect red and trying to figure out how to pluck our eyebrows.

Her eyes flicker over at me in the mirror, and the moment is over. "Oh, wow," she says. "I can't believe you came. Alone."

"Well, it is our senior year," I say. That's it, nothing more.

She gives me a weird look before walking out. I guess because she was expecting another fight? One of my bitchy comebacks, perhaps? Don't worry, Rennie. It's coming. The bitch slap to end all bitch slaps.

I'm pouring myself more punch, because damn, it's seriously good, when I feel a hand on my shoulder. I turn around, thinking it's Mary. But it's not. It's Alex, dressed up in a black suit. I have to admit, he looks hot.

"Hey," I say.

Alex makes a mock surprised face. "You remember me? Alex Lind? The guy you haven't spoken to since school started."

I can't hold back a smile. "I've been busy."

He lets out a laugh. "I'm kinda surprised you're here tonight."

Mockingly I say, "How could I miss *homecoming*? It's the biggest night of our lives." I say it mockingly, but I'm actually feeling real feelings. Because I've missed Alex. More than I want to admit. And it feels really good to be talking to him again, like old times.

Alex smiles. "You look nice, Kat."

"Yeah, I know," I say, smiling at him to soften it up. I'm wearing a tight black dress made out of stretchy material, and short black boots, plus a ton of eye makeup. When my dad saw me leaving the house, he was all, "Katherine, are you going to a *biker bar*?" As if there are any real biker bars on Jar Island.

"What about me?" Alex asks. He says it jokingly, but I can tell he actually cares what I think. "How do I look?"

"You look okay," I tell him. When the smile on his face falters, I say, "You look good."

His face gets serious. "Kat, I just want you to know, no hard feelings."

Huh?

He rubs the back of his neck. "I had a lot of fun with you this summer—and that night on the boat. But I get it. You weren't into it. Probably wasn't meant to be anyway, right?"

"Right." I'm dazed. The only reason I didn't keep after Alex was because I thought he liked Nadia. My pride—I just couldn't take it. Now that I know it wasn't the case, that he and Nadia were never a *thing*, maybe something could happen with us.

Alex heads back over to his table, where Lillia and the rest of his friends are. I feel a pang in my stomach. I tell myself it's because I'm hungry.

Mary comes over. She doesn't look me in the eye; she just stares at the food.

"Have a Dorito, Mary," I say in a low voice. "Or a cupcake."

Her head snaps up. "I'm too nervous to eat." I see her looking around the room for Reeve. "Shouldn't he be feeling it soon?"

I examine her, her thin wrists, the way her clavicle sticks out under her dress. It makes sense now, the fact that she never eats. This too must be Reeve's fault. Eff him and his football scholarship. "Don't worry," I say, covering my mouth up with a chip so no one sees us talking. "It should be any minute now. All we have to do is sit back and watch."

Mary nods and tries to smile. "I'm going to miss our secret midnight meetings."

"Are you kidding? I keep falling asleep during first period. I can't have that bringing down my GPA any more than it already has." Not if I want to go to Oberlin next fall.

"I just hope we can figure out a way to still be friends." Mary blinks rapidly. "You guys are all I have here."

I hesitate. I don't know how to answer her, because I don't know myself. Yeah, Lillia and I are cool right now, but I'm not about to suddenly start wearing that friendship necklace tomorrow morning. But Mary's looking at me with pleading eyes, and I don't want to disappoint her, so I say, "Mary, don't worry about that stuff tonight. Let's just enjoy the show, okay? This is what you've been waiting for." I have to talk a bit louder than I want, because of the clapping. I stand on my toes and look out to the dance floor. A circle is forming. I grin at Mary. "Follow me."

I lead her to the center of the gym, right on the periphery of the crowd that has gathered around Reeve. Everyone's clapping and giving him the floor. He's flushed and sweating through his shirt; he's unbuttoned the top buttons and loosened his tie. He is dancing his ass off, bopping around like an idiot. I can't tell if it's the ecstasy or if it's just Reeve being Reeve.

Mary and I exchange a look.

I know for sure that it's the E when Reeve starts to break-dance. He can't break-dance for shit. I start to laugh. I laugh even harder when I see Rennie trying to get close to him, dancing sexy, but it doesn't work because Reeve's moves are too wild and jerky. Once, he almost punches her in the face. Rennie grabs him by the tie and pulls him closer to her, and then he takes the tie off and wraps it around his temple. It dangles as he dances away from her and grabs Mrs. Dumfee, who teaches chemistry and is about a hundred years old. She tries to protest, but he puts her arms around his neck and jumps up and down. She actually goes along with it, the old hag. Probably the most action she's seen in, like, thirty years.

The DJ starts throwing props out into the crowd, feather boas and beach balls, cheesy stuff like that. Reeve runs up to the DJ table and grabs a pair of maracas and starts galloping around the dance floor like a prize pony, shaking the maracas above his head. I swear, he's shaking them so hard, I half expect them to split and drop seeds all over the floor.

Reeve's friends, Alex and PJ and those guys, are doubled over, cracking up. But when I glance over at Mary, she looks upset.

"He's making such a fool of himself," she says sadly.

I'm not sure why, but I feel like something's slipping away.

"When is someone going to catch on? Maybe you should go get Senor Tremont."

But then the music cuts off and the lights come on. Coach

Christy is onstage in a red dress. It's weird to see her dressed up. She usually wears gym shorts and a visor. Into the microphone she says, "Will Jar Island's homecoming court please come to the stage?"

They file up onstage behind her. Rennie's hanging on to Reeve like she can barely stand in her five-inch stripper heels. And from the way she's smiling her cat-that-ate-the-canary smile, I know she thinks she has it in the bag. She takes the tie off Reeve's head, puts it back around his neck, and straightens it. Of course Rennie wants the two of them to look picture perfect when they win.

I stand up straighter. This is *my* moment. I'd better enjoy it.

Coach Christy introduces everyone onstage, and then she opens up the cream-colored envelope in her hand with a flourish. "Jar Island's homecoming king is . . . Reeve Tabatsky!"

Everyone screams and claps and stomps their feet like this is some big surprise. Coach Christy puts the crown on his head, and he is hamming it up, dancing around and moving his hands as if he's holding glow sticks at a rave. He hugs Coach Christy with so much force that he lifts her into the air. She disentangles herself from him, smoothing down her dress and looking somewhat freaked out. She quickly says, "And your homecoming queen is . . . Lillia Cho!"

Oh, damn.

I don't want to look at Mary, not after I told her it was cool, that I'd made sure Ashlin had enough votes to win. Honestly, I didn't even think to count Lillia's votes. I did see a bunch in there for her, but she'd said that she wasn't going to be a factor, so I didn't worry about it. Damn.

Maybe things will be okay. Rennie lost, and Reeve's as high as a kite. This can still work.

Onstage, Rennie's mouth is hanging open. She's not even mad; she's just confused. Like, there must be some mistake. And poor Lillia is looking out into the crowd like a dazed baby deer as Coach Christy puts the tiara on her head.

Reeve sprints over to her, grabs her, and practically throws her into the air.

"Shit," I say.

CHAPTER THIRTY - SIX

LILLIA

It wasn't supposed to be me. This isn't the way it was supposed to go down.

Ashlin is clapping. She doesn't look disappointed, probably because she never ever thought she'd actually win. Rennie's standing next to her, with this empty look on her face, this sad, empty look. Nadia rushes up to the edge of the stage, and she jumps up and down cheering for me and screaming my name. I reach up and touch the tiara on my head with a shaky hand.

Out of nowhere Reeve grabs me and lifts me into the air and

spins me around like we're ice-skaters. I shove him away from me and scream at him to put me down, but everyone is clapping and shouting so loudly, I don't think he even hears me.

The rest of homecoming court comes down from the stage, Rennie last, and I'm left alone up here with Reeve. I search for Kat or Mary in the crowd, to try to find out what in the world is going on right now, but then someone dims the lights and the music starts. A slow song.

Reeve pulls me tight to him. I try to push him away, to create some space between us, but he just holds on tighter. I look up at him, and his pupils are completely dilated and he's sweating. He says, "I voted for you."

I think I heard him wrong, because he doesn't sound like himself. His voice is far away and dreamy.

"Why are you so mean to me, Cho?"

"I'm not," I say.

He reaches out and touches my hair, and I jerk my head away from his hand. "Your hair is so soft. Like, really, really soft. Shit. I don't think I'm allowed to say that."

Reeve spins me around so I'm facing the crowd again, and I spot Alex watching us from down below. His jaw is set, his eyes fixed on us.

Reeve keeps swaying me round and round in a circle, faster and faster. I finally see Mary, standing in the crowd. She's biting her lip, her arms wrapped around herself.

"My heart's beating so fast," Reeve says, breathing hard. The lightness is gone from his voice, replaced by something lower and more labored, even though he's smiling.

His heart *is* beating fast, so fast I can almost hear it. Feel it through his suit jacket.

I draw back. Reeve's eyes are watery and unfocused. He's scaring me. I don't think he even knows where he is, much less who he's with. He's holding me so tightly, it's hard to breathe. I feel light-headed. I'm going to faint, for real this time.

"You're blurry," Reeve mumbles, touching my face blindly.

"Reeve," I say. "Stop."

"Before . . . you asked about me and Ren. Now I want to ask you something. What about you and Lindy? What are you guys?"

"We're friends," I tell him and force a swallow. "That's it."

I expect him to say something cruel, the way he usually does when it comes to me and Alex. But it's different this time. This time he lifts my chin, his fingers trembling. And he kisses me. His mouth is open and wet and warm. I try to push him away, but his hand is on the back of my neck pressing me toward him.

All I can think about is Rennie.

She's going to kill me.

With all my might I push Reeve off me. He staggers backward a few steps, totally off balance, and I'm afraid he might fall over the edge. The DJ lowers the volume of the song, and everyone down on the gym floor goes silent. Reeve shakes his head, as if he's trying to get a hold of himself. He starts walking toward me again, but his arms and legs don't seem to be listening to his brain. "Oh, no," he moans. He turns and gazes into the crowd, like he's looking for somebody, and inches his way to the edge of the stage. "Sorry," he says, shielding his eyes from the spotlight. "I'm sorry, Alex."

Suddenly Reeve's whole body tenses up. The color drains from his face. He whispers something.

"Big Easy."

CHAPTER THIRTY-SEVEN

MARY

BIG EASY. BIG EASY. BIG EASY. IT DOESN'T MATTER how pretty I look tonight. You can put lipstick on a pig, but it'll still be a pig. I'm Big Easy.

I'll be her forever.

I'm still in my homecoming dress, I can see it on me, but it feels different. Like soaking wet jeans and a dirty, gravel-covered T-shirt. I rub my hands together, rub my arms. They look normal, my arms, but the skin feels tight and stretched, as if, inside, I'm ballooning to the weight I was when I was twelve.

Suddenly everything electrical in the gymnasium rushes toward me, as if a match were set against hundreds of little rivers of gasoline. If you touched me, I would burn you alive. The hum of sizzling currents drowns out the whispers. The lights overhead, the extensions cords running to the DJ booth, the heartbeats of the people standing around me; it all comes at me. I am magnetic. With trembling hands I push my hair out of my face. Each strand is a live wire.

He's staring at me, stunned, disbelieving. Disgusted. I shut my eyes, but it's too bright. There's nothing but burning white inside me. It has nowhere to go but out.

When I open my eyes, there is the most terrible spark.

CHAPTER THIRTY-EIGHT

LILLIA

EVERY SINGLE LIGHT IN THE WHOLE GYM POPS AT THE same time, and everything goes dark for a second. Then tiny bits of glass start to fall from the ceiling; yellow sparks fly like indoor fireworks. The DJ speakers screech out squeals of feedback interference. Everyone's screaming and running for cover. The entire place is short-circuiting.

"Lillia!"

It's Alex, pushing his way through the crowd to the edge of the stage. He's trying to get to me.

I'm almost to the stairs when I remember Reeve. He's standing at the edge of the stage, looking out. His whole body is shaking.

I run back to him.

"Come on! We have to get out of here!" I grab the lapels of his suit jacket in my fists and try to pull him away from the edge. But even though I'm right in front of his face, he doesn't see me. He's somewhere else. I can tell, because his eyes are dead. Unfocused. He jerks free of my grip.

And then I realize. He's having a seizure.

He shakes harder and harder, so violently I can't hold on to him. "Stop!" I scream, falling to my knees.

Reeve plunges off the stage and onto the floor in a twisted heap. His body is in a pile on the ground, his leg bent gruesomely beneath him. He's not moving at all. Not even blinking.

Someone screams, louder than any other voice, any other sound. So loud, it's the only thing I hear.

CHAPTER THIRTY-NINE

AT FIRST I CAN'T EVEN TELL WHAT IT IS. THE NOISE. IT'S so loud and shrill, I have to cover my ears. Even then I can still hear it. So loud it's like it's permanently trapped in my ears.

Then I realize. It's Mary. Our quiet, shy Mary is screaming so hard that it hurts to hear it. I spin in a circle, trying to find her. But it's too dark. And there are so many people.

It's pandemonium. Other girls are shrieking, and guys are yelling, and teachers are begging us to stay calm and head for the nearest exit. I'm breathing hard, trying to push my way through the crowd, throwing elbows to get to the door, bits of glass crunching under my boots. The whole gym smells like burning, and sparks are raining down from the broken lightbulbs.

I turn around before I reach the door, and see Lillia, kneeling at the edge of the stage, looking down to the floor. "Call 911!" she's screaming over and over.

Finally I make it outside and suck in a huge breath of air. It feels sharp and cool. The kids who got out before me are hugging each other and making cell phone calls. The sound of an ambulance siren is getting closer and closer.

That's when I notice the tingle on my forehead, right at my hairline. I touch it gently and feel a warm wetness. My fingertips are red. The flying shards of glass. It's not just Reeve. Other people could be hurt. Hurt badly.

Lillia seemed okay, but I still haven't seen Mary. A breath catches in my throat when I realize she might be stuck inside the gym.

Shit.

"Mary!" I shout, and try to run back inside. "Mary!"

Senor Tremont throws an arm out to try to stop me. "You can't go back in there, Kat."

"But my friend is inside!"

He turns away from me, directing traffic, telling kids to keep it moving away from the building. A few feet away Coach Christy is limping around, checking to see which students are hurt.

The ambulance arrives, flashing lights and sirens. The EMTs rush in, and a few minutes later they take Reeve out on a stretcher.

I don't see him moving.

Girls are crying, girls that barely even know him. But I know him. I know he's allergic to shellfish, I know he has a scar on his left shoulder from when his brothers pushed him out of their tree house. I know he cried for a week when his cat got run over. I know him, and I'm the one who did this to him. I put this whole thing in motion.

Rennie pushes her way past everybody. She's completely hysterical. She tries to climb into the ambulance with him, but the EMTs won't let her. She drops to the sidewalk in a heap, crying.

Reeve fell so hard.

I can't even let myself think it. I won't, because there's no way. We only gave him some E, not hard shit. It's a party drug, for God's sakes. So what the hell happened to him? What the hell happened in there?

I have no idea where Lillia and Mary are, or if I should wait for them. Then I see her. Lillia. Alex is leading her by the hand through the crowd. Their hands are linked tightly.

I blink.

Lillia lets go of Alex's hand when she spots Rennie on the ground. She runs over to her and helps her up. They throw their arms around each other, both crying. Alex is on the phone with somebody.

The ambulance takes off, sirens blaring again. Some people are huddled around in groups, but the football players are already mobilizing. They jump into their cars and lead a caravan out of the parking lot.

A limo speeds into the loop. Alex quickly talks to the driver, who's got his head out the window. Alex motions to the girls, and they run over. Ashlin's there too now, holding Nadia's hand. They climb inside, and the limo peels out.

I turn back toward the school and see Mary. She's stumbling out the doors, as white as a sheet. "Mary!" I scream. She turns her head, but she doesn't see me. "Mary!"

CHAPTER FORTY

MARY

EVERYTHING'S SPINNING. IT'S LIKE I'M ON A TOO FAST merry-go-round. There are too many people; there's too much noise. It's all static. I'm walking, moving without purpose or direction, just following the surge of the crowd. I feel like I'm in a trance. I have to stop and steady myself against a building.

And then Kat's in front of me, and suddenly everything stops moving.

I stare at the trickle of blood running down the side of her face. I've hurt her, too.

"Are you okay, Mary?"

I start to shake.

You can only chalk up things to coincidence so many times before you have to face the truth. It wasn't wind that day that made the lockers slam shut. It wasn't a misstep that made Rennie almost fall off the pyramid. And tonight, the lights popping, the surge of electricity.

It was me.

Urgently, Kat says, "Let's get out of here."

She reaches for my arm, but I back away. No. I am not leaving. I'm not going anywhere. Not before I know if Reeve is okay or not. Kat's losing her patience with me, I can tell. "Mary. We have to go. NOW!"

"This is my fault, Kat. I did this."

"Shut up, Mary. It was an accident. Reeve must have had an allergic reaction to something."

I press my lips together and fight back the tears. "You're bleeding. I hurt you."

She shakes her head incredulously. "Are you serious? Mary, that was a *power surge*. Or something. Whatever. Please. I'm begging you. Let's just get out of here, okay? We need to lay low and get in touch with Lillia."

"I never wanted to hurt him." As soon as the words come, so do my tears. I cry like my heart is breaking, because it is. "Is he dead?" I ask, my voice breaking. "Is he?" When Kat doesn't answer, I fall to my knees, put my head in my hands.

Reeve might die tonight.

It makes me want to die too.

CHAPTER FORTY-ONE

THE HOSPITAL WAITING ROOM IS SO CROWDED, I THINK everyone who came to homecoming must be here. The boys are mostly on the floor or leaning against the walls, and the girls are sitting on the chairs and couches. I'm on a couch sandwiched between Rennie and Alex. Rennie's head is on Ash's shoulder, and she's finally stopped crying. I want to cry, but I can't. I don't have the right. I am responsible for this. I am the one who put that ecstasy in his drink.

When Reeve's parents got here, I couldn't even look at them.

Ash whispered to me, "Mr. Tabatsky is crying." I just kept my head down and stared at the floor. Mrs. Tabatsky had on house slippers. Rennie jumped up and gave her some tissues from her purse, and they hugged each other for a long time.

Next to me Alex says in a low voice, "He's going to be fine."

It's not comforting. Because Alex can't know that. Nobody can know that. They say he's in stable condition, but they're running tests on his brain and heart to find out what caused the seizure. He definitely broke his leg. They don't know yet if the fall caused permanent damage to his spine. Reeve. Reeve the quarterback. Reeve, who loves to dance and goof off and swim, not being able to walk anymore? It's inconceivable.

I'm praying with all my might that the doctors don't do a drug test. I know that was the point of tonight, to get Reeve kicked off the team. But what if someone does an investigation? What if they figure it out somehow, that Kat, Mary, and I were behind everything? What's going to happen to us then? I wish I was there with them.

When Alex gets up to go get the Tabatskys some coffee, Rennie sits up straight. "Lil, what was Reeve saying to you up there? On stage?"

"When?" I ask, not meeting her eyes.

"Right before he kissed you," she says flatly.

I feel my cheeks heat up. "Nothing. I don't know. He wasn't making any sense."

"From where I was standing, it looked like you kissed him back."

"No, I didn't! He practically attacked me!" I lower my voice. "He didn't know what he was doing, Ren. He must have had a lot more to drink than the rest of us."

Rennie nods. "He definitely didn't seem like he was in his right mind." She chews on her fingernail. "But you know how I feel about him."

"I swear, Rennie. I didn't kiss him back. I don't know what else you want me to say."

Rennie bites her lip and nods. A few tears fall down her cheeks. She wipes them away, then goes to sit near Reeve's brothers. I get up and go to the soda machine. I want to turn my phone on and make sure Kat and Mary are okay, but using a cell phone at the hospital is against the rules. I guess I'll have to wait until I can slip away.

What on earth are we going to do now?

CHAPTER FORTY-TWO

KAT

WE'RE SITTING OUT ON THE DOCK BY MY BOAT. MARY is quiet again. She hasn't said a word since I finally managed to get her into my car. She just cries every few minutes. I sit next to her and pick broken glass out from the sole of my boot.

Around midnight I get a text. It's Lillia. *Where are you?*

I text back that we're at my boat and for her to get over here ASAP. I have no idea what to do with Mary. Is she having a breakdown? Should I take her to a hospital or something? She's not hurt or cut anywhere, but the look in her eyes, it scares me.

Twenty minutes later Lillia comes running down the dock. She's breathless. I stand up. "How is he?"

Lillia bursts into tears. "He's in the ICU." She sits down and hugs her knees. Her hair is falling out of its bun. "How did everything get so messed up?"

I look away. "It was my fault. I thought we took out enough votes."

Mary wipes her nose on her arm.

Tonelessly she says, "I gave the drugs to Reeve. I'm the one who took homecoming away from Rennie. I'm right at the center of everything."

"Don't worry," I interject. "No one's going to suspect you of anything."

Lillia's staring out at the water. "I don't even know what to think right now. Reeve might be freaking paralyzed, you guys."

Mary makes a small noise.

"He's not paralyzed," I say, as confident as I can. "Trust me, Lil."

"You didn't see him. You don't know." She shakes her head, tears running down her cheeks. "I should go home. I'm sure my mom's waiting for me."

I almost say, *Wait. Shouldn't we get our stories straight first?* But then Mary finally speaks.

"This is all my fault," she says.

Lillia sighs and shakes her head again. Wiping her face, she says, "It wasn't your fault."

Mary's shivering, curled up in a ball. "It was," she says, looking up at me. "I know it was."

I fish my lighter out of my purse and light up. Inhaling deeply, I say, "It was all of us." I take another drag. I let the smoke seep through my body. "I just hope we get away with it."

ACKNOWLEDGMENTS

To the JAR ISLAND HIGH Class of 2012

PROM QUEEN: Zareen Jaffery

PROM KING: Justin Chanda

CLASS PRESIDENT: Carolyn Reidy

CLASS VICE PRESIDENT: Jon Anderson

VALEDICTORIAN: Anne Zafian

NATIONAL HONOR SOCIETY PRESIDENT: Julia Maguire

MOST OUTSPOKEN: Paul Crichton

GLEE CLUB: Lydia Finn, Nicole Russo

PEP SQUAD CAPTAIN: Chrissy Noh

PROM COMMITTEE CO-HEADS: Elke Villa, Michelle Fadlalla

EDITOR IN CHIEF, JAR ISLAND HIGH CHRONICLE:
Lucille Rettino

CLASS PHOTOGRAPHER: Anna Wolf

MOST ARTISTIC: Lucy Cummins

YEARBOOK COMMITTEE CHAIR: Venessa Carson

EDITOR OF THE LIT MAG: Katrina Groover

ACKNOWLEDGMENTS

FUTURE BUSINESS LEADERS OF AMERICA: Mary Marotta, Christina Pecorale, Jim Conlin, Mary Faria, Teresa Brumm

MOST SCHOOL SPIRIT: Emily van Beek

PRESIDENT OF THE MODEL UN CLUB: Molly Jaffa

DEBATE TEAM CAPTAIN: Jita Fumich

MOST LIKELY TO SUCCEED: Riley Griffin